7 Figure Publications Presents . . .

When What God Has
. . . Ain't Good Enough

by

Falicia Rose Blakely

Names, characters, places, and incidents either are the product of the author's imagination or are used fictitiously, and any resemblance to actual persons, living or dead, business establishments, events, references or locales are entirely coincidental.

Copyright © 2018 by Falicia Rose Blakely
All rights reserved.

7 Figure Publications
PO Box 9334
Augusta, GA 30916
http://7figurepublications.com

Printed in the United States of America. No part of this book may be reproduced in any form, stored in any retrieval system, or transmitted by any means, electronic, mechanical, photocopying, recording, or otherwise, without written permission from the author.

(Paperback)

ISBN-10: 0-9988984-6-5
ISBN-13: 978-0-9988984-6-9

Library of Congress Cataloging-In-Publication Data:
LCCN 2018935115

Editor, Linda Wilson

Cover design by Davida of Oddball Designs

Published March 2018

Dedication

*Almighty God, full of mercy and compassion to Your people!
Thank You for seeing fit for this to become a reality for me. Your
plans for my life are beyond me. I didn't think I would even see
twenty-one, but You predestined something different. Thank you for not
allowing me to die in my sins and putting some of the most amazing
people in my life! I am in love with you, Lord. You're the greatest!*

To my son because you give me reason to live.

*To those who have thought but never had the courage to say . . .
"Sometimes what God wants, doesn't seem good enough."
Remember 29:11. It's a good thing that what we think doesn't
dictate what God is willing to do.*

Acknowledgments

Afrika, I have to tell you thank you because you're the link to all this! I want to thank Ms. Sereniti Hall, author and publisher of *A Treacherous Hustle* (the real Falicia Blakely story), for giving me this opportunity to reach out to my sisters and brothers in the world by giving them all something to think about. Thank you for allowing me to be a part of the 7 Figure team, when so many told you not to fool up with inmates! Thank you for assisting me and pushing me NOT to procrastinate! For taking what was simply me trying to find peace in ending a relationship and transferring it into my first novel. Your presence in my son's and my life is a kiss from God. I love you!

Mrs. Linda Wilson, you are hands down the greatest editor in the ENTIRE United States! A woman filled with passion and creativity. Thorough and well-appreciated. Thank you for driving me crazy with all your corrections and suggestions. Lol! I consider it an honor to strive for the standard you have set for me. With you as a part of the team, it only gets better!

To my son, a mighty man of God! Thank you for loving and forgiving me. You would have been justified in holding a grudge toward me for subjecting you to a life without me, but you chose to accept me as the woman I am today and not the naïve, misguided young girl that I used to be, who lacked wise judgment. Thank you for not judging me and striving to be better than our entire family. You are the answers to my prayers! I'm so proud of you, and I love you with all that I am.

Momma, I love you! Don't worry about what the world thinks of you. You have redeemed yourself, and I wouldn't trade you for the world.

To the rest of my family—I love you. I appreciate those who are still present and manage to still ride this sentence with me. To those who are MIA, I miss you, but I understand life doesn't stop just because I'm not present. I just wish you would find time to come around.

Minister C. Greene, thank you for being a mother, friend, spiritual advisor and corrector. You have been everything I needed and some.

One day we'll be together again! Travis, Kim, and Shalonda, we are still siblings . . . I miss y'all!

Danielle Beurney, I love you! I bless God for your life. I'm the woman I am today because you chose to be brutally honest with me, no matter what. Thank you for taking the time to correct me with wisdom, instead of criticizing me. Hoping for a couple of forevers!

Tiawanna Kidd, you are the bestest friend anyone could have. No distance or time can hinder what we share. Thank you for always being the one still standing when the smoke clears.

Raquel Phillips, I LOVE YOU! You have been my rock in some of the hardest times during the last fifteen years of my life.

Cam and Bre, thank you for rewriting my entire draft. I'm working on my penmanship! Lol!

To Amiariya, four years old going on twenty. Thank you for telling me all I need to do is look into the mirror and say, "Self, I love you!" I haven't been the same since.

Mrs. Cassandra Beedles, thanks for never taking 'no' for an answer and making When Love Kills: The Falicia Blakely Story happen. I'm blessed to know you. Together we are reaching the world.

Lance Gross, thank you for taking the time to concern yourself with my thoughts.

To everyone that has embraced me, forgiven me, supported the purpose; God spared my life and joined me in this fight to take back our youth—I love and appreciate you. Your compassion has assisted in my healing. God gave me you, so I know I'm never alone. Especially you Bunkie, Jennifer Derrberry, don't forget to live on purpose.

Finally, Sheldon Lee Sutton, thank you for showing me what it's like to be with a man who lives according to God's heart. I apologize I didn't want to be the woman you dreamed of. I hope by now you have found a woman who can love you like you deserve. You inspired this story. Enjoy!

. . . And from such people turn away! For of this sort are those who creep into households and make captives of gullible women loaded down with sins, led away by various lusts.

2 Timothy 3:5-6 (NKJV)

CHAPTER 1

Jacksonville, Florida

Thursday (8:30 p.m.)

Aching and abused, Mya Jenkins staggered from her circular king-size bed and into the master suite bathroom. The Italian white marbled flooring cooled her bare feet. She leaned against the wall in utter shock. "Sss," she hissed with a wince as the chilled wall tiles pressed against her exposed back. Her upper and mid-back burned like an open wound. Anguished, she slid down into a sitting position. *He dragged me across the carpet like a toy. My God! I can't believe he just . . .* Mya parted her lips slightly and gently rubbed her right jaw. "Ow," she whispered once she opened her bruised mouth wider. The left side of her face felt dislocated. Heavy footsteps echoed just outside the door. *He's in the hallway!* "He's coming!" Mya fumbled with the doorknob, turning the lock until she heard it click. No sooner than the door was locked, Sway stood on the opposite side banging on it.

"Open this door, Mya!" he demanded.

"Please God, make him stop! Don't let him hit me again," she prayed from her heart. A light trail of blood stained the doorknob and her

1

gown. She reached for the elaborate purple face cloth on the rack, but was blindsided by uncontrollable tears. Slowly, she stood and started toward the mirror, but her knees buckled after glimpsing her face and neck covered in blood.

There was no time to think. Sway was having a fit!

Bangbangbang! Bangbangbang!

It sounded as if he was hammering something against the door. Mya scanned the bathroom for any object she could use to protect herself. Something . . . anything! Shears in the sink drawer! The thought popped in her mind like a flipped light switch. She crawled the short distance to the sink, pulling the drawer open, and searching frantically. Thank you Jesus! She grabbed them.

The extravagant space had become her favorite room in the house. Usually, the bright, cheery area served as her refuge after a long day, or after an argument with Sway, and even for some of their most romantic encounters. Never had she anticipated this same room would be her escape from the sudden, violent wrath of her man.

Bam!

Mya turned around in terror as Sway kicked the door in. His six-foot physique dominated the entire threshold. She stared into the eyes of the man she had grown to love almost two years ago. She barely recognized him; his hazel eyes were so cold, it was as if his heart were numb. Chills ran down her spine, and she securely held the shears with both hands behind her back. She couldn't break his menacing glare. She just couldn't! That same demonic look petrified her when he came in and yanked her out of bed just two days ago. Simply because she wasn't at the door to greet him with a kiss.

"Why do you have to be so selfish?" she had asked herself after he'd shaken her like unblended fruit at the bottom of a blender. "I never should have taken a nap." Her sincerest apology had smoothed things over, and Sway behaved as if the incident never happened. And so did she, but with some precaution. She assumed he had lost big money out there in the streets and for some reason, he decided to come home and make her the object of his anger. She also assumed this would never happen again.

Today, nevertheless, brought with it a similar nightmare but for a different reason. Since the previous evening, Mya had been up working, trying to make sure that her client's invitations, location for the art gallery, and reservations were secured. By 5:07 p.m., she was exhausted and had decided to only close her eyes for ten minutes that eventually turned into two hours. Dinner was not made. And now she feared for her well-being because of it and because of the monster standing before her.

"Mya Sincere Jenkins, you got one more time"—he extended his index finger to emphasize his threat—"to act like you don't hear me talking to you. Do it again and I'm gon' knock yo—"

The truth was, she hadn't heard a word he said once his fists began flying. She cut him off. "Sway, baby . . . why . . . why can't you understand that I love you. I don't want to fight." She couldn't help but whine, feeling defeated. He didn't say a word. His clenched jaw and fist spoke his intent. "Sway, look at me. Look at my face! What did I do to deserve this? What did I do to you?" Although she took her left hand off the shears to wipe away her tears, her right hand gripped the black-handle tight. She stood, waiting for his response. It never came; instead, he calmly walked over to the hot tub and started the water.

Mya remained motionless and silent as he took her favorite bubble bath and added it to the water. It wasn't long before the tub was full.

"Baby, come here." He extended his hand as he sat on the edge of the fancy tub. *Is he serious?* Mya didn't budge. "Mya Sincere Jenkins, come here." His voice was calm and loving. "I made this just for you."

"Sway, I don't want to fight," she stated as she finally released the shears.

"I know, baby." He extended his hands toward her. "I love you. Come here."

Just stay right where you are, she told herself, but her legs had a mind of their own.

3

Slowly, she made her way into his arms. She was so weak for him—his touch—the way he looked at her, as if no other woman could compare. Even now, with her face partially bloody. He helped her out of her red-stained gown and into the tub. Then he attentively washed away the blood.

"You know what, baby?" He didn't give her a chance to say anything. "I just want to hold you tonight. Is that okay?"

Mya wasn't sure if she wanted to answer, but for the sake of peace she nodded in agreement. Although movement brought her great discomfort, she dressed in pajamas and made her way over to the bed and fell asleep effortlessly.

The agonizing soreness in her back woke her from her sleep. She glanced over at the clock. *Seventeen minutes after ten. I can't believe he did this to me.* Sway's bare body stretched possessively across her. Tears filled her eyes, but even that natural reaction seemed too painful. A few seconds passed as she wrestled with the idea of whether it would be in her best interest to get up. Gently, she inched herself from beneath him, praying he would remain asleep. It wasn't until her feet touched the floor, and she attempted to stand that she realized her head was banging just as hard as her back. She began tiptoeing to the bathroom that only hours ago had served as a safe-haven. Quietly, she closed what was left of the door and reluctantly faced herself in the mirror.

Oh my God! I look a hot mess! She stared in disbelief at the discoloration of her rich, mahogany skin. Gingerly, she shuffled through her micro-braids, realizing an entire patch had been snatched from the back of her head. *Oh, my God!* Mya inhaled deeply, greatly relieved that her nephew Judah was over to his friend's house. She could only imagine how he would react seeing her this way. She grabbed the hand towel off the rack to muffle her scream, but her bruised, swollen lips almost forced her to drop it.

Mya leaned against the sink's counter for support, trying to make sense of the entire situation. *I have never been bruised . . . ever . . . in my entire life!* she thought. She had no strength to fight her tears, nor the squeals that escaped her lips. Feeling ugly and alone, she bawled uncontrollably. *Maybe had I just been up when he came home . . . or maybe I shouldn't have tried to get out of his grip. That's what this is all about. I mean, Sway has never done me like this before. He might have grabbed me by my arm during an altercation, but he has never put his hands . . .*

Mya knew she should've woke him up and demanded he get out of her house, or even called the police on his behind. But then again, she thought she had brought all this on herself. "I just can't deal with this right now." Mya reached for the medicine cabinet and took a couple aspirin. Grabbing a ponytail holder, she carefully pulled the rest of her braids back. She daubed Neosporin on the cut that split her lip, and then cleaned her face. Mya cut the light off before opening the bathroom door. In hopes of not disturbing Sway.

Wearily she turned the knob, not sure what awaited her. The darkness of the room matched the night sky. She tiptoed out, purposing to go downstairs to get something frozen to put on her back. As she headed toward the door, she noticed the bed was empty. The sight brought her feet to a halt.

"So, you gon' leave?" Sway was standing so close behind her, she could feel his breath in her hair.

"Jesus!" Mya screamed. "You scared me!" She turned to face him.

"Are you going to leave me!" he repeated very sternly.

"Baby, no . . . why would you ask me something like that?"

He didn't reply.

"I'm just going down to the kitchen for a second. I'll be right back."

Sway didn't budge. Mya gradually took steps backward in the direction of the door. "Baby, lie down. I'm coming right back." She was leery of turning her back to him.

"Mya, baby, please don't leave me. A brother is just stressing right now. I really don't know how to be without you," Sway pleaded as he walked toward her to close in the space between them.

"I'm not leaving. I'm just going downstairs," she spoke, barely over a whisper and inched away from his reach.

5

"What? You don't want me to touch you anymore?" His critical eyes danced over her curvy frame.

"Baby, what are you talking about? I am just going—"

"Mya, don't play with me!" he interrupted as he punched his fist.

What is wrong with this man tonight? My God! "Sway, I'm not going to fight with you all night."

"Why you keep walking away from me then!" His voice boomed against the silent house.

"Baby, my head and my back are aching. I am only trying to get something for my back. Please, calm down. Please."

"Your head and your back, huh?" In an instant, his expression changed. "Well, let me make you feel better. I got just what you need." He flashed her a mischievous grin.

Usually this expression aroused her, but the stinging in her back was unwilling to let up. "Baby, I . . . I don't know if I'm up for it; it has been a long evening."

Sway's faced turned cold again as he walked over to the bed. "You got a couple of seconds to get over here and see about me!" he threatened as he sat on the bed. Suddenly, he stretched his body across the bed as if posing for a Calvin Klein underwear photo shoot. "I'm trying to be nice."

Nice? He's gotta be out of his freaking mind! Mya hoped for this nightmare to end. She made her way to the bed; he grabbed her by the neck and forced her on the mattress. Sadly enough, she discovered another type of pain. One that excelled the agony of her head and back—her heart. Her most inward place was being ripped and wounded, as Sway handled her like everything except his fiancée.

Despite the condition he'd already put her body in, he yanked, pulled, and snatched her into submission. Mya cried without sound as the man she loved took what he wanted. Through silent tears, she hoped for better days. Yet she didn't pray and ask God for His help. What she failed to realize, was that her tears were already having a conversation with a God she knew nothing about. He was examining them.

Anxiety in the heart of man causes depression, but a good word makes it glad.

Proverbs 12:25 (NKJV)

CHAPTER 2

Friday (10:58 a.m.)

Is he gone? Mya lay as still as she could. There was no way she was going to get up before Sway. Neither did she have any intentions of fixing him breakfast like she normally did. Mya shut her eyes when he leaned over to kiss her cheek. *I really can't believe he is acting like yesterday never happened, but I won't be the first to mention it.* It wasn't long after that, she heard the shower running. Relief coursed through her mind and body, knowing that he'd be leaving. The abuse made her feel foreign in her own bedroom. Sure Mya entertained the idea of rushing over to her dresser, getting her car keys and dipping out, but she wouldn't be surprised if Sway was just standing in the bathroom watching her. So she'd rather just lie here.

Not long after the shower stopped, Sway was out and shuffling around the room. His spicy, sweet, floral cologne scented the air. The swishing sound told Mya that he was brushing his waves. She didn't even have to look at him to know he was checking himself out in the mirror. *Pretty boy!* Seconds later, she could hear him picking up keys, and then descending the stairs. Mya jumped up to look out of the window to see which vehicle he was leaving in. It was his own, but when she made her way into the kitchen to check for her keys they were gone.

"Bastard! Why would he take my keys but leave in his truck?" she asked aloud, as if someone was present to answer. *I'm not staying in this house all day! There's more than one way to skin a cat.* Mya headed back upstairs to her bedroom.

She looked around the room. It looked like the scene from a homicide with her blood on the sheets and a few drops on the plush pearl carpet. Along with those couple of micro-braids and the lamp Sway threw against the bathroom door.

"I need to pray," Mya confessed, but she just couldn't bring herself to do it. Why would God listen to someone like me? Forgetting that God had responded to her cry the night before when she begged him to make Sway stop shaking her and not put his hands on her again. Someone so selfish! Especially when I brought all this on myself. Mya looked around, playing the entire incident in her mind over and over again. She felt so alone, so confused. "If you were here, Big Momma, this would never have happened," she spoke aloud to the picture of her mother hanging on the wall. Big Momma was the only parent she had ever known. Her father had died of a heart attack while fighting in the Gulf War when she was just a toddler. All she knew of him was the stories her mother shared with her.

Another void had filled her heart and it wasn't due to death. Just pure neglect. Mya missed her best friend Janelle like crazy too, but distanced herself from her once Sway entered the picture. Janelle would probably dog her out if she knew Mya was letting Sway hurt her.

The sun was bright outside, but darkness filled her spirit. So did a huge tidal wave of anxiety. "What am I supposed to do now? What am I supposed to do?" Mya screamed at the top of her lungs, and then sank to the floor where she balled up, crying to whoever was listening. Deep down inside she hoped the Lord heard her cries.

All the blood on the bathroom walls and carpet, along with everything that had been knocked over came as a welcomed distraction.

Mya mentally prepared herself to clean and pick up the pieces and face whatever the day would bring. It was by the grace of God that once she put some ice on her mouth and then lipstick, and made use of her MAC concealer and foundation, there were no signs of an altercation just by merely looking at her—well, that's with her clothes on. Fresh bruises marked her body like ink blots. Her eyes were a little puffy from crying, but that was nothing a pair of designer shades couldn't hide. By the time she finished cleaning, she decided to call the closest car rental service for the weekend.

She settled for an outfit she'd purchased from the Louis Vuitton fall collection. A pair of white skinny jeans, a turquoise knitted short-sleeve sweater with a white tank underneath and a pair of turquoise spiked ankle boots. She was determine not to think about how she had seen a side of her man that she hoped to never face again. Nonetheless, it wasn't long before she was overwhelmed and unable to control her tears. One thing she did do was purpose in her mind not to call him, nor apologize for being asleep. His response was extreme and couldn't justify him. But . . . then again, maybe he just had a lot on his mind.

"I know that he loves me; he gives me the world," Mya said, not realizing she had spoken aloud. She deciding on curling her braids so they would still look full. She gave herself a half smile and proceeded to get ready for Judah's football game.

"God, please let these folks hurry up. I need to get out of this house," she prayed. Sadly though, she felt convicted for only acknowledging God when she wanted Him to do something. Mya began to reflect. How did I get to this point in my life? When Big Momma passed away three years ago, she had grown to know God as her source of life, her strength, and backbone. He had become the beginning, the in between, and the ending of her every day. She hadn't mustered up the courage to join anyone's church, but she was attending here and there. However, she made time for God's word. Whether in front of the television, on CD, or on the Internet, she gave God His time. As a matter of fact, all was well with her soul up until that moment she slipped up and slept with Sway. Well, it wasn't a slipup. She sat around a little too long thinking about him touching her in places she had never been touched. Once Sway left the following morning after it happened, Mya could feel God's disappointment. She believed in her heart that God forgave her, but what was the point in asking Him to keep forgiving her if she had no intentions of stopping? Sway definitely wasn't trying to hear anything about her saving herself for marriage, especially when he felt she was the one he would spend the rest of his life with. Now, she didn't know what to expect with him. After the way he'd been acting lately, she thought he'd just might take it! And he had.

Ring! Ring!

Her ringing cell phone snatched her from her thoughts. She didn't even realize she had cut the lights off upstairs and had made her way into the living room, and was standing by the front door. Nor did it occur to her that the entire afternoon had passed. I have got to get myself together.

"Hello?"

"Hello, Ms. Jenkins. This is King Lee. I'm calling to inform you that I am outside your home with your rental."

"Wonderful! I'll be right out. Thank you." She grabbed her matching handbag, set the alarm, and exited her home. She decided against putting on her shades, being that the sun was practically setting. That just might look suspicious, she reasoned.

As she approached the champagne-colored Chevy Malibu with soft tinted windows, a very handsome brother exited the vehicle. His locks were neatly pulled back into a ponytail. His almond-shaped eyes, like two little pools of love, seemed to penetrate her soul. His stare was gentle, and his smile, genuine. The darkening sky radiated the glow he wore. His presence touched her.

"Ms. Jenkins." He extended his hand for what she thought was a handshake. To her surprise, the brother raised her hand to his lips and kissed the back of her hand. The gesture was considered gentlemanly once upon a time, but inappropriate for today's standards. Mya, however, wasn't offended at all. She appreciated the deed and thought of it as chivalrous. She didn't mean to stare, but he looked extremely good in his suit, which appeared to be tailor made. His skin was perfect, not too dark and creamy looking. The only thing about him that wasn't to her exact liking was his height. He was a little shorter than her.

"Ms. Jenkins?" He smiled again. Mya had to clear her mind and focus on what was at hand. He even smelled good.

"You need to see my identification, right?" she asked, trying to stay a couple steps ahead of the handsome man.

"Yes, ma'am."

She handed it to him. "Thirty-one?" he asked as he looked at her ID. He made eye contact with her briefly, and then gave it back. "You don't look a day over twenty-one, if you ask me."

Yeah right, she thought. When she didn't respond, he said, "All right, then. I hope you have a wonderful night."

"Thank you. I'm sure I will. I'm headed to a football game."

He smiled. "Are you a fan, or you're going to show some support?"

"Both!" She caught herself smiling for the first time in almost twenty-four hours.

"Wow!" His facial expression turned serious. Mya became a little uncomfortable and self-aware, wondering if by chance he saw her swollen eyes, or any scratches she may have overlooked. It was time to go. She walked around him and got into the driver's seat without saying a word.

"Ms. Jenkins, I didn't mean to make you uncomfortable. It's just that when you smiled, I thought to myself, a smile that beautiful should be shared with the world." For that split second Mya forgot all about the pressing concerns of her life.

"Are you serious!" She was stunned. Why would anyone say something like that about me?

"As a matter of fact, I am." Mya sat there embarrassed, realizing she had asked that question aloud.

"Ms. Jenkins, I know this may sound unrealistic to you, being that

13

you just met me, but you are the most beautiful woman I have ever laid eyes on. I know with everything in me that you will make the perfect wife. I can recognize a good woman when I see one."

Mya wanted to believe him, but subconsciously her mind flashed back to the horrifying events of last night, and she dismissed his remarks. "Mr. Lee, you seem—" He interrupted her.

"Please, call me King. That's my first name."

"Okay . . . King, you seem like a very nice and pleasant man, and I appreciate the compliments, but everything isn't always what it appears to be."

"You're exactly right. We don't have to become what we go through. At times our hearts can be very misleading. We can go through trials, learn the lesson from them, and become better than our circumstances."

She had to fight the urge to ask him why he was saying all of this to her. Even though it made sense, Mya still had a hard time applying it to herself. It was definitely time for her to go. The notion that he somehow knew how she was feeling struck her after he shut the door before she even reached for it. Mya was dumbfounded. Sway had never closed the car door for her.

"It was nice meeting you." Mya started the engine and took one last look at this mysterious, good-looking, milk chocolate, suave brother. He was clean, with matching cuff links and all. They made eye contact one last time. Maybe she was looking too much into his facial expression, or could it really be that his eyes were filled with concern, or even empathy? Somehow she managed to excuse herself.

"Good night." Strangely enough, she couldn't understand why her heart was getting heavy at the thought of leaving him. Mya put the car in drive and slowly pulled off.

"Ms. Jenkins," he called after her. Mya stopped. He approached the window. "Let it go."

She was sincerely confused. "Let what go?"

"He doesn't have the slightest idea how to love a woman of your caliber. Don't allow anyone to drag you. Let it go."

14

There was nothing she could say. Really, what more could anyone say? Mya didn't know how to let go of Sway. He was the only man she had been with. The only man she had ever loved.

King used his finger to turn her head toward him. Looking her in the eyes he said, "I'll be seeing you around, Ms. Jenkins." Then he headed back to the company truck parked across the street, where a heavyset male occupied the driver's seat.

"King!" she called after him. He stopped in his tracks and turned to look back at her. "Call me Mya." He smiled, and her heart changed its pace. Mya waved and drove off into the sunset, feeling relieved for some reason. A sense of hope came over her, as if God was with her. She only hoped reality matched her current emotion. She also hoped her nephew Judah didn't see her broken master bathroom door.

A hot-tempered man stirs up dissension, but a patient man calms a quarrel.

Proverbs 15:18 (KJV)

CHAPTER 3

Friday (5:00 p.m.)

"Hey, Ju dawg, you gon' share the ball tonight or what?" Shon asked as he, Judah, and Alfred headed to the locker room. It was a home game tonight, and everybody would be there to see Jackson verses Raines. Judah had been the best wide receiver in the district since his freshman year, and now he was a senior.

"I hope not! I got four big ones on this game. I know you gon' bring it home for the team," Alfred stated, rubbing his hands together as if he could already feel the money in his hands.

"Four big ones, huh?" Judah looked as if he shared the same feeling. "Too bad you'll only be getting two." Alfred knew what time it was. "Dawg, you ain't pimping me. I got to get my cut for making sure we win. Besides, it's time for another pair of One's."

"Whatever, dawg!" Alfred brushed it off.

"Al, you already know. Gon' up the dough anyway," Shon stated, giving Judah some dap.

"I'm just saying though, you don't need my cheese. Mya is going to make sure you straight. Dude, you got shoes you only wore once, anyways."

"What does that have to do with you trying to hustle me?" Judah looked at his friend, waiting for a response. He didn't reply. "My point exactly! But I already told you, you can have a pair of them shoes."

"Speaking of Mya, is she coming tonight? Maybe if you let a brother get the ball, she'll see me handling business and let me show her how the Brooks' brother do it!"

"I feel ya', dawg, straight up!" Shon gave Alfred some dap.

"Naw, what you need to be is trying to feel me!" Judah got very defensive. "I know we cool, but I promise you'll feel like my worst enemy if you touch my folk. I'll let you see how this Jenkins man get down," he retorted as he invaded Alfred's space.

"Man, why you always threatening a brother? I can't help that she just happens to be the hottest, dark-skinned . . ." Judah glared at Shon, begging him to finish his statement. He was itching to rip! Shon just threw his hands in the air. Judah left them standing there as he rounded the corner to go to his locker and put on his gear. He needed to keep his mind on the game and nothing else.

"How about you use that energy on the field?" Alfred yelled after him.

Judah knew his remark needed no reply. They knew like everyone in his school and the recruiters who had taken notice of him, that he was a beast on the field! His skills weren't the only thing in his favor. He was good looking, tall, and kept a muscular physique. His pearly white smile and dark brown skin tone stole everyone's attention. His respectful manner was welcomed by all of the school staff. Although his friends were few, many adored him for his kind acts, such as buying strangers food. In Judah's eyes, no one was beneath him. Judging from his appearance, life was good. He rocked the latest trends, freshest sneakers, and a couple pieces of flashy jewelry, and always a crisp lining with his well-maintained locs. Judah was living the ideal life of a black teenage boy, but what his peers didn't see was his heart aching for his biological parents. Both of whom he didn't know. His mother went missing when he was just months old. To date, there were only myths about her disappearance. Even his father's whereabouts were still a mystery. Judah didn't understand why he had this cross to bear. Why him? What had he done so wrong that neither his mother nor father thought enough of him to stick around? And why did God take his grandmother away? To a certain degree these unanswered questions made it hard for him to see in himself what everybody else saw in him.

Big Momma was the reason he had dedicated much of his life to becoming the best student athlete. That woman believed he could switch the sun into night and the moon into day. But she was gone now. As much as he wanted to say the heck with this football stuff, he knew Big Momma wouldn't stand for it, and his aunt Mya would not understand. So he pressed forward, determined not to be another black statistic for the sake of the only family he had left. It was clear the One everybody referred to as a good God, was in control of all things; the One who was supposed to love him, had given a deaf ear to his prayers and overlooked his needs. As far as Judah was concerned, God hadn't done anything for him but cause pain. His Big Momma and aunt made sure his needs were met, and he was willing to devote the rest of his life to making sure his aunt wanted for nothing. Forget God . . .

He would protect her, provide for her, and put no one before her, even if it was the death of him. And anybody who got in the way of that would be dealt with; she was all he had. The day Big Momma died was the day he stopped believing he would ever see his parents dead or alive.

All hope for the unseen went out the door.

. . . For love is as strong as death, jealousy as cruel as the grave . . .

Songs of Solomon 8:6 (NKJV)

CHAPTER 4

Friday (8:35 p.m.)

By halftime, the game was all the way live! Now it was the fourth quarter and Jackson High School and Raines High School were tied at 23-23. Mya saw how focused Judah appeared. She couldn't believe her little baby—well, her almost-grown nephew ran a sixty-yard touchdown. His talent never ceased to amaze her. Judah was only months away from being eighteen, but already had a lifetime of pain. The day he almost didn't make it would forever remain in her memory. She would never forget the expression on his two-year-old face when she walked up to her sister's car in front of their home where Big Momma had been raising them, and realized he was in the car alone and strapped down in his car seat. His cry had become a little over a whisper from being so hoarse.

"Oh my God!" Mya had yanked at the car door handle, but it was locked. "Big Momma! Big Momma!" Mya screamed for her mother the whole time. Judah was dripping with sweat, overheated, and in distress. "Momma, he's stuck inside!" she yelled.

21

"What in the heck was that girl thinking?" Big Momma asked in exhaustion as she descended the front porch in a hurry. She raced over to the vehicle and peeked inside. "My God! I just never know with Honesty anymore." With a calmness that only she could put on, Big Momma glanced around, looking for something to break the window.

"For God's sake! Big Momma, it's the middle of July and ninety-five degrees out here. That baby can die of heatstroke. Honesty knows better." By now Judah's face was covered in fresh tears. "Don't worry, JuJu, auntie is going to get you. Auntie is coming," Mya said, attempting to comfort him through the window. She looked around for something to pry the door open with. Nothing.

"Go get one of them big bricks over there," Big Momma said, pointing to the manicured lawn two houses down. "Hurry."

Desperate, Mya raced to the lawn and grabbed up a heavy red brick. She dashed back to the car and was getting ready to smash it through the window by Judah.

"No, Mya! Use it on the front driver's side. Right there," Big Momma said. "We don't want him to get hit with any glass."

Twice, Mya brought the brick against the window hard and the glass shattered. She reached her arm around to unlock the back door and crawled over the backseat to get her nephew out. He was frightened, sweaty, and wet. "It's okay, it's okay. Nobody is coming to hurt you. I promise." She ran into Big Momma's arms where she and Judah both found comfort. That day changed all their lives. It was the last day Judah had seen his mother, Mya had seen her sister, and Big Momma, her eldest daughter. That was sixteen years ago.

"Touch down!" the announcer suddenly shouted. The bleachers went wild! Judah had just scored the last play that would send the Vikings home defeated. After the field goal had been made and the clock ran out, Judah looked up toward Mya who was beaming with pride. She blew him a kiss, but he motioned her to come to him. She took her time coming out of the bleachers, giving his teammates and fans time to congratulate him.

Apparently, she was taking too long because Judah ran up to her and swung her in the air. He probably could have assumed she was scared, but she was trying not to let him see her face. She winced because her body was still in so much pain that it literally took her breath away. Mainly her back and neck.

"Hey, Aunt Mya. You okay?" he asked after he put her down.

"Yeah, yeah." She perked up. "Just can't believe how easy you picked me up." Mya tried her best to look normal, avoiding eye contact as she straightened up her clothes. However, she wasn't surprised at how direct Judah was.

"Why your eyes look so puffy?" She had to think of something and quick.

"Boy, you're always worrying about me. I'm fine." She wrapped one arm around him and rested her head beneath his chin.

"Aunt Mya." He wasn't letting up.

"Judah . . . Baby, I just been thinking about Big Momma. That's all! I miss her so much, ya know?"

"Yeah, I do too." She could feel the tension releasing in his posture. "But you know what? You always got me!" He wrapped his arms around her to emphasize his point.

"I know, and I wouldn't trade you for the world." I mean that." Mya looked up to make eye contact. Her eyes misting.

"Aww, Aunt Mya, you don't have to cry." Judah tilted his head, giving her a look of pity, as if he could feel her pain. He didn't know those tears were mere relief that her secret wasn't out. There would be no room to guess what Judah would do, or try to do to Sway if he found out about the abuse.

"Ms. Jenkins," said the male voice that had recently become familiar.

"Coach Riley," she responded, taking her attention off her nephew. One of Judah's friends called him over so he told Mya to wait for him, and he'd be right back.

"I'm glad I have this chance to speak to you alone. If it's possible, one evening or one day over lunch I would like to talk with you."

"To me?" she asked.

"Yes you." Coach Riley laughed briefly. He could see by the crease in Mya's brows that she wanted to know why.

"About what?" Mya didn't have the slightest clue what was so funny. "Your sister."

"My sister?" Mya was all ears now. This brother had said a mouthful in less than one minute. Her heart raced with anxiety.

"So you knew my sister, Coach Riley?"

"I did know Honesty," he said soberly. "Very well."

"Well, don't you think that is something you should've mentioned way back when you expressed your desire to help guide Judah in the right direction and be of any assistance to him? Shouldn't you have stated your familiarity with his mother . . . Coach Riley?" Mya felt herself getting worked up, like it just might be some BS going on. But before he had a chance to answer, Judah returned. Suddenly, Mya relaxed.

"Coach, you better not be over here hitting on my folks." It sounded as if he was joking, but his piercing eyes told the real story.

"Nah, nothing like that." Coach Riley held up both hands, indicating he didn't want any problems. "But I do need you to give her my number so we can further discuss this stuff about these recruiters and scholarships."

Mya hated lying to Judah, but decided to go along with Coach Riley so she could find out more about her sister.

"I'll think about it." Judah meant every word. "You ready, Auntie?" He grabbed her hand and proudly strutted away toward the locker room.

Mya looked back in time to see Coach Riley mouth "call me." Then he turned and headed in the opposite direction.

Judah released her hand once they were off the field and made a promise to be right back. Mya turned to go in the opposite direction, but stopped to watch Coach Riley walk with a pronounced bop in his step. *Why is he so happy all of a sudden?* She smiled curiously, and forced herself to turn around before she kept staring too long.

The closer she got to the concession stand, her stomach reminded her that she hadn't eaten all day. A bag of chips would have to do until they decided where they were going to celebrate. Most of the crowd had dispersed, and there were very few people left at the stadium.

Mya finished her chips, and Judah was still nowhere in sight. She started toward the restroom, but a cold chill ran down her back. The night air was cool, but this felt more like a piece of ice. She stopped in her tracks. "What in the world?" She wasn't sure why she felt this way, but one thing was for sure, she wasn't about to go a step further out of view. Mya turned on her heels and rushed back to the front of the concession stand, trying not to look so spooked. She felt as if she was being watched, but when she looked over her shoulder, there was no one. The individuals who had been working inside the concession stand began exiting. "There is no way I am going to stand out here alone," she said as she texted Judah to come on. By the time the last person was out of the stand and locking the door, Mya decided to trail behind. Her stomach churned, as if cautioning her. This is crazy! What is it? She kept looking behind her, but she didn't see anyone.

"Maybe once I get to my car I'll feel better," she told herself.

The exit gate was about three feet away, but there was no light to guide the path. Her nerves were shot as well. "What is wrong with me?" Something about walking in the dark area alone wouldn't settle, so she turned around, and as soon as she did she spotted Judah. She felt relieved.

"Sway, what's up, dude?" Judah called past her.

"Sway?" Mya was shocked to hear his name. She turned, and there he was, standing right behind her. Oh my God! she thought. He must have been watching her, waiting for her out of sight. His stare was empty. He reached out and wrapped his arms around her; his touch was cold. Her back was hot. Throbbing.

"What's up, Ju?" Sway's expression changed as Judah came further into view. "I see you put a hurting on these county boys!" He gave him some dap while still embracing Mya like he always did.

25

"I didn't know you were here." Judah smiled in approval.

"Neither did I," Mya said.

"Come on now, you know it's going to take a lot of money for me to miss out on my boy. Besides, a woman that looks this good doesn't need to be out here alone; somebody . . . just might . . . try to snatch her up."

Sway leaned down and spoke directly into Mya's ear. She half smiled, trying to look normal. While Judah was talking with Sway, she also knew he was watching her. His words sent fresh chills down her back.

"Aunt Mya, you cold?"

"Just a little, whenever the wind blows."

"Where y'all headed?"

"Don't know yet," Mya answered Sway before Judah had a chance to.

"Dude, you're not coming?"

"I wish I could, but I got to handle some business before it's too late. You know your aunt don't like a brother coming in too late." He smiled and kissed Mya on the neck.

"You want us to bring you back something to eat?" Judah was doing all the talking.

"Well, I was hoping my baby would whip me up something. There ain't nothing like her cooking," Sway said while affectionately holding Mya. Rocking her from side to side.

"Baby, is that all right with you?" he asked.

"Of course," Mya answered as he turned her to make eye contact with him.

"Mya, I love you. I really do," Sway said. Mya's eyes searched his eyes for answers. He looked like the man she loved. "You have to believe me." He pulled her close and kissed her forehead.

"I love you too." With that, he released her, wrapping one arm around Judah's neck, playfully putting him in a headlock. Judah broke contact.

"I'll see y'all later then," Sway said, strutting away toward his car.

Who just ducks off in the darkness of the night, watching someone . . . waiting to pounce . . . like I'm prey or something. This isn't animal life in the wild. What type of person would do that?

She knew the answer, but refused to speak it.

And it shall come to pass in the last days, saith God, I will pour out of my spirit upon all flesh: and your sons and your daughters shall prophesy, and your young men shall see visions . . .

Acts 2:17 (KJV)

CHAPTER 5

Saturday (8:20 a.m.)

"Mmmm, Aunt Mya, you got it smelling good up in here!" Judah sang as he approached his aunt as she stood over the expensive Fisher and Paykel stove. He kissed her on the cheek.

"Good morning, my joy!" Mya lit up at the familiar gesture.

"Good morning!" Judah responded, stealing a piece of bacon. Mya held up the spatula she was using and pointed it toward him, as a silent threat not to try that again. Judah held his hands up in defense and made himself comfortable at the marble island.

"What are you doing up so early?" Mya looked upon him lovingly.

"What! How do you expect a brother to sleep with all this?" He extended both his arms and gestured toward the food he would be enjoying momentarily.

"Child, you are a mess!" Mya laughed at his exaggeration, wondering what her home would be like when her baby went to college.

"Hey." Judah met her smile and winked. "I tried, but the aroma just got better and better." They both laughed.

"That's what I'm saying!" Sway entered the kitchen. "Baby, what are

29

you trying to do? Make a brother stay home all day? I almost pulled a muscle trying to get down them stairs."

"Okay! You feel me!" Judah gave Sway some dap.

"Good morning to you, too." Mya couldn't help but smile.

"Give a brother some of those lips." Sway pulled Mya into his embrace and kissed her. "Now that's how you start the day."

Mya looked into his hazel brown eyes. All she could see was adoration and love. It seemed as if they had gotten closer since the fight. Last night, however, seemed odd. Not only Sway's stalking behavior, but around 2:45 a.m., he hovered over her while she slept. She felt his presence near and wondered what he was doing, but she willed herself to keep her eyes closed until she fell back to sleep. Then he lay in bed beside her and gently shook her awake.

"Baby . . . Baby, wake up," Sway whispered into Mya's ear as he held her close from behind with his left arm. He stroked her hair with his right arm and tenderly kissed her neck.

"What is it, Jermal?" She stirred from her sleep just a little.

"Baby, I want you to know how much I love you . . . you're the only woman for me. Nothing in this world can make me stop loving you! I'm going to be here for a lifetime."

"Okay, baby. I love you too." She drifted back to sleep, but a few minutes later, Sway was nudging her awake again.

"Mya, I want you to know the amount of love I really have for you. I'm serious, baby. I don't think you understand. My life isn't worth living without you in it, baby. That's real talk right there. And did you see that I got a new door for the bathroom? I made sure they were in and out before Judah came home. I'm so sorry, baby. I am."

"Yes, I did. Thank you, baby. I love you so much, Jermal." He had pecked her lightly on the lips. This time she turned over, and he lay beside her and rested his head on the pillow. She fell back to sleep, thinking he would do the same. But he broke her sleep a third time. Maybe he just needs to reassure me of his love and devotion. Or does he think I'm cheating on him?

The bacon sizzled, ending her thoughts of the previous night. "You two can really ruin a surprise. I wanted to bring it to you in bed." She pouted a little.

"Baby, I'm sorry. It's just . . . I tried . . ." He stumbled for the words to say. ". . . maybe you should have cooked outside."

"That's what I'm saying, because it's lit up in here!" Judah helped him stress his point. "Too bad I missed out on the breakfast in bed though. I would've felt like a king."

Every now and then Mya overly spoiled Judah and fused the present with the past. She felt it was her responsibility to make up for her sister, Honesty abandoning him inside of a sweltering deathtrap on four wheels. Although Judah was now a happy, healthy, thriving teen.

"Speaking of outside! Excuse me for a second." Mya grabbed a plate, brushed past Sway, and slid the patio glass door back. She stepped outside and went to the grill. Once she returned, Sway had gotten comfortable next to Judah.

"Steaks too!" Both of their eyes grew wider as Judah openly expressed his appreciation.

"So baby, what all did you fix?"

"Cheese omelet stuffed with bacon, ham, sausage links, cheddar and provolone cheese, home fries for Ju and hash browns for you with fried ham chunks on top just the way you like. Grilled steaks and some fresh-squeezed orange juice." Looking at them both smiling like they were auditioning for the Kool-Aid commercial made her glad she decided to cook.

It took no time fixing their plates. Subconsciously, she placed Judah's plate down in front of him first. In her heart, her nephew always came first. No questions asked. He was her baby. She didn't see the displeasure on Sway's face, because she was in the clouds. The two men she loved were happy, or so she thought.

"Is something wrong, Sway? Your jaw twitched, and your neck muscles flexing while you looking crazy at Aunt Mya. You mad 'cause she gave me my plate first?" Judah asked.

"Nah, man. Nah," Sway answered. The tripped out thing was, his subtle ticks were gone just as fast as Judah first spotted them.

"Last night, Aunt Mya was looking kind of spooked when I caught up with her after the game. She even made a remark about not knowing you were there. I just want to make sure everything straight with y'all."

"Understood," Sway replied with a slight nod.

Judah rested his back against the barstool and waited for his aunt to join them. Not another word was spoken until they joined hands as Mya blessed their breakfast. For the first five minutes all you could hear was moans of pleasures and the clicking of their forks against the plates.

"Aunt Maya, I might have to go to college somewhere around here. Can't nobody cook to my liking, like you." Judah was the first to speak.

"Boy, it's not all that! Besides, you know it's been my dream for you to go to college, and then get drafted." She reached across the table and rested her hand on his.

"How did I forget?" Judah snapped his flip the bird finger and thumb together. "Speaking of your dream, I thought about something. The other night when I stayed over Shon's crib, I had this dream, and it took me a minute to even get back to sleep. I started to just get up and come home, but Shon's mom would have flipped if I left in the middle of the night like that."

"Baby, what type of dream did you have that you felt the need to come home?" Mya sincerely asked as she pulled the tender meat from its bone."

"It was crazy! You had on this white flowing dress and you were just running. Like in circles, as if you were running from someone, and then all of a sudden, someone just knocked you off your feet. You were struggling to get up. I couldn't see who the dude was, but he was just hitting you. At times you fought back, and then at times you didn't. You were really freaked out. You managed to get out of his reach, but he chased you. Next thing I know, you started screaming, 'Sway, please stop! Please stop!' That's when I woke up."

She was so grateful to be chewing because she wasn't prepared to respond. Mya couldn't help but admit within herself that Judah's dream happened on the same night that Sway flipped out on her. It amazed her at how close she and her nephew were.

"Well, a dream like that would have taken me aback as well," Mya said.

Sway remained quiet, finishing up his meal. Judah took notice.

"I vowed in my heart right then, that if I ever got a whiff of anyone putting their hands on you, I promised on Big Momma's grave that I was gon' ki—"

"Ju, calm down. Baby, it was just a dream," Mya said, noticing Judah had his eyes fixed on Sway.

"For whoever sake, they better hope so!" Judah said, obviously threatening Sway.

"Was it a dream, or did you just make it up?" Sway finally asked sarcastically.

Judah wasted no time meeting his tone. "It was a dream, but if I find out different, somebody will never have a chance to dream again." He stared Sway directly in his eyes to let him know there was no fear or intimidation inside of him. He loved him, but Mya was his world. He had to draw the line.

"I know that's right." Sway started laughing. "If anyone puts their hands on my baby, he'll take his last breath."

"Ju, I feel you, dude." Sway smiled. "Mya is like the best of both worlds, and she always got a brother's back."

"Judah, baby. You don't have to worry about me." Mya's voiced snapped him back from that place of rage where he didn't mind going.

"Aunt Mya, it's not even about worrying, it's about respect! You are all that I have left. You already been through a lot. We've been through so much together, and you're still strong. Ain't nobody going to handle you like anything less."

"Did I tell you I was thinking about going to church tomorrow?" Mya figured that changing the subject was the best escape. "I want you to come with me, Ju."

"Aunt Mya, what would I look like going to church?" Judah responded. Sway burst out laughing.

"Okay!" He reached over and gave Judah some dap.

Mya cut her eyes from Judah to Sway, a little annoyed with them making a joke out of what she said, but relieved that they appeared to still be cool. "You look good going with me. Can't you see something is missing in our lives?"

"Actually, I can't. Besides, God ain't never did nothing for me."

"Judah Jenkins, don't you dare talk like that. Every time you take a breath, God is doing something for you because he gave you the very air you breathe."

"He hasn't. All he's ever done was take from me. It seemed like he answered my prayers by inflicting me with pain." Mya didn't know what to say. "Nah, Aunt Mya, I'm straight. I'd rather not go." Judah thanked her for his breakfast and headed back to his room.

"Now that's disrespectful," Sway complained. "But that's your baby," he mocked, then muttered something about wishing Judah would step to him.

"What did you just say?" Mya asked.

"You don't even want to know." Sway forced his empty plate toward her chest. She blinked.

"But I do," she heard herself say, surprising her own self as she took the plate to the sink.

"You really don't. Believe me, you don't," he threatened, accentuating his words with a slight nod, then bucking his eyes.

For reasons beyond her own understanding, she couldn't let up. "Say what you feel, Sway. Be a man and answer me," she nearly whispered so Judah couldn't hear her.

"Be a man!" Sway jumped down from the barstool and ran up in her face. "So now I'm not a man?" he questioned as he wrapped his hands around her throat.

"Now just because that lil coward disrespected you and you didn't do nothin' 'bout it doesn't mean either one of y'all gon' disrespect me."

34

"Aaarrrrgghhh . . ." Maya eked out, clawing at his hands, trying to free herself.

"So you better tell that lil punk to stop trying me! And you better watch your mouth when addressing me as well." With that, he released her. She fell to the floor coughing and gasping for air. Sway stood there long enough to glare at her before he walked out of the kitchen. Standing to her feet, Mya knew she had to do something and do it quickly. She could tell that chaos and pure hell were on the verge of breaking out within her household.

You know how I am insulted, shamed and disgraced; before you stand all my foes. Insults have broken my heart to the point that I could die. I hoped that someone would show compassion, but nobody did; and that there would be comforters, but I found none.

Psalm 69:19-20 (CJB)

CHAPTER 6

Sunday . . .

Mya sat in her rental car, overwhelmed, tears just flowing. She couldn't believe how cold Sway had been with her this morning because she wanted to go to church. He suddenly had to use the toilet, which lasted twenty minutes. After she fed him breakfast and was ready to take a shower, he suddenly had a headache. Then unexpectedly, he made plans for them to go over to his adoptive mother's house, Ms. Sheryl, a lady who wasn't much older than Sway, took him under her wing and taught him the do's and don'ts of the street life. How to hustle and obtain respect in the streets. Normally, they only visited her on holidays, birthdays, or after a close family member's funeral.

When all else failed, Sway criticized Mya's suit. "Baby? That's the suit you're wearing today?" he had asked, face all scrunched up.

"Yes, it is. I love it," she responded with excitement. "So, you're going with me next week then, right?"

Sway mumbled something, so she switched up the dialogue. "The car rental is due back on Monday at noon. You still have my car keys."

He returned her car keys right away because he knew she'd be asking him to drive to church with her come next Sunday or drop her off.

"And you know what? The Lord doesn't care what I wear; all he's concerned about is what's going on, on the inside and how my actions show my intentions. Sway, that's why you need to come with me."

"I'm good, Mya. You go ahead." Defeated, he cut the lights out and got back into bed, pretending to be asleep.

Mya now sat in front of A New and Living Way Fellowship Church, and she just couldn't pull herself out of her emotional funk to go inside. Three times she had cut the engine off, and then cut it back on. There were only a few people still pulling up and going inside. "Lord, why is this so hard for me? It's not like I have never been to church before." She rested her head on the steering wheel. She hadn't even made it inside, and she already felt awful for the way she had been living. Mya was a mess. Life was too confusing right now. One day she meant the world to Sway, and then the next she felt like anything but that. *Judah knows something is going on between Sway and me.* Yet Sway refused to admit he needed the Lord, and now she was too jacked up mentally and emotionally to simply get out of the car and go face the Lord. Sadly she sat there drowning in her pity. "Lord, if you're still listening to me, please help me." No sooner than the words left her mouth, there was a knock at the window.

"Is anybody in there?"

Mya sat straight up, startled. She wasn't expecting anyone. The male tried looking through the tinted window. Then he peered through the windshield. "Ma'am, are you okay?"

"I'm fine. Everything's fine," Mya responded, having difficulty seeing through her tears. She caught a glimpse of her face. *I look so pitiful!*

"Ms. Jenkins . . . I mean, Mya, is that you?"

She didn't even bother answering. She was too busy looking for something to wipe her face with. To her disappointment, this wasn't her car. She couldn't find anything.

"Mya, are you okay?" This firm voice rang familiar to her.

"Oh my God! He can't see me like this." She panicked and started the car, preparing to drive off, but he pulled on the driver's side of her door, and it opened.

"Mya, are you okay?" She froze and looked up into those precious, small, dark brown pools of love again. "Are you gonna run me over?" he teased. "Please, put the car in park."

"I'm sorry, I'm sorry." Mya realize just how stupid she must have looked. "There is just so much going on." Fresh tears wet her cheeks. He half squatted and pulled out a handkerchief and began wiping her face. "I know I must look awfully pitiful sitting here like this."

"I don't perceive it in that manner at all. And to me you look conflicted, maybe a bit scared, yet very strong. And let's not forget very beautiful."

Slowly, Mya received the navy and maroon handkerchief he had just wiped her face with. "King, you are just saying that, trying to make me feel better."

"Come on now. Give me a little more credit. I'm standing in the parking lot of the Lord's house, and you think I'm going to lie?" His smile made her smile.

"Wow! There it is again," he said, referring to her smile. King looked this beautiful woman in her eyes. He could feel the heaviness of her heart. In his spirit he began to pray for her.

Mya, unaware of his deed of love, began to sob quietly. She wanted to go inside the church and get what she had come for, but she didn't quite have the strength to get out of the car.

"Mya, may I pray with you?" King asked.

"If . . . if you . . . you want to," she responded in between sobs.

He took her left hand and placed it in between both his hands. They both bowed their heads. "Most gracious, loving father . . ." He spoke with confidence and authority. "Thank you for allowing me to forget the first lady's gift in my car so I could come out here and see Mya parked next to me. You alone order our steps. I bless your name for this day. Now Father, I'm asking you to look upon your precious, beloved daughter, my sister, with grace and mercy. Father, hear her heart, lift every burden, destroy every yoke. Break soul ties, Father. Those she's connected to that are not in line with your will for her life, a part of your plan—separate. Give this beautiful woman back her integrity, and restore her in her rightful place in you. I know that you are able. Open her eyes that she may see that you love her and recognize the one you have ordained to love her through. In closing, I ask you to give her strength right now to exit this car and go into your house to receive all that she needs from you this day, in Jesus name. Amen."

"Amen. Oh, thank you so much." Mya extended her arms for a hug. "King, you are so thoughtful."

"I simply thanked the Lord."

"I can't recall the last time someone prayed for me."

"I pray for you every single day."

"What! I mean, are you sure?" *He prays for me?* King took her by surprise.

"Yes, I'm sure." They both shared a laugh.

"I'm just saying . . . you know . . . you don't even know me. Why would you take the time to pray for me?"

"The thing is, I do know you. I recognized you at first sight." He knew she wouldn't fully comprehend what he was saying. "There are some people that come into your life that you know God ordained you to before the foundations of the earth was laid. It's like something in your spirit confirms in the natural what you've been carrying in your spirit all the while."

"I kinda understand." She nodded.

"I'll say this. I have been praying for you ever since I was sixteen years old, when my heart got broken for the first time. God gave me a vision of you. I couldn't see the details, but I saw you. When I met you the other night, I knew I would see you again. Therefore, I'm not even surprised God brought you here today."

What does that even mean? Mya thought, but just decided to keep listening. Some things didn't make sense. She formed several questions in her mind, but then there was something he said that had to be true. She recalled how she felt leaving him and just being in his presence. Even now something was awakening in her by just listening to him. When he held her hand to pray, it was as comforting as resting in his bosom. It was weird, but she kind of understood. She could listen to him for hours.

He reached for the handkerchief, wiped her nose, then stood to his feet and extended his hand. Without protest, she got out of her car. She locked her door while he held her Bible and the gift he originally came outside for. Together they headed for the church.

"This is my first time here," she whispered, as if someone was listening to them. Amazed at how her fear turned into excitement.

"I know. This has been my church since I was a boy." They were about to mount the first step when he reached for her hand. She'd stopped because he did.

"What's the matter?" She surprised herself at how genuinely concerned he was. "Is everything all right?" She searched his face and physique for any sign of pain or injury.

"I just wanted you to know that you look extremely beautiful and that color against your skin seems to help the sun shine brighter." Mya beamed. She was so happy she decided to wear the soft pink linen Calvin Klein skirt and jacket. She didn't even realize she was smiling so hard until she felt a little pull in her jaw muscles. "Wow, I haven't felt this good in years," she admitted.

"Every day you should feel like the queen that you already are, and nothing less," King replied, looking her straight in the eyes. There was nothing Mya could say. He took her hand and led the way. Mya took a deep breath and stepped into the first day of her renewed life as a prodigal daughter.

It amazed her that in the midst of such a beautiful experience, thoughts of Honesty flooded her mind. *Is she alive and well somewhere, held against her will?* All this talk from Coach Riley instigated her inquiring mind. His need to talk about her, forced her sister Honesty into her mind. One thing was for sure, if God saved her, he could surely sustain her sister. Possibly bring her home, that is, if she was still alive.

I don't understand my own behavior—I don't do what I want to do; instead, I do the very thing I hate! Now if I am doing what I don't want to do, I am agreeing that the Torah is good. But now it is no longer "the real me" doing it, but the sin housed inside me. For I know that there is nothing good housed inside me—that is, inside my old nature. I can want what is good, but I can't do it! For I don't do the good I want; instead, the evil that I don't want is what I do!

Romans 7:15-19 (CJB)

CHAPTER 7

Tuesday (1:49 p.m.)

The last four weeks had been bittersweet for Mya. She had been attending church and Bible study as much as her schedule allowed. She found herself wanting to seek the Lord as soon as her eyes opened. Her smile found its way onto her lips much more than it had been in months. There was a lot of buzz going around about some college recruiters planning to come see her nephew dominate the field.

Things between her and Sway were fine, considering the circumstances. Sway hadn't really acted a fool about her spending so much time at church, well . . . not yet anyway. Mya found herself feeling guilty for shacking up with him. So she would stay up till the wee hours of the night in her office painting, or planning an event as an excuse to keep from giving herself to him. Nonetheless, at times he was relentless. Sway knew he was her weakness, and he made it his business to touch those places that responded to him. Mya desperately tried not to give in, and she tried to think of others, or what she needed to do, or what she had read in the Bible that day, but just like the sun setting and the night sky that covers the earth, the gratification of his touch and the pleasure from the contact created the illusion of being wanted so badly it took over every reason why she needed to say no. Once again, when Sway finally left her alone, she found herself repenting with tears for the same thing that initiated her downfall. If somehow they could readjust their living arrangements, it would be easier.

Mya sat in silence, using her paint brush to display the torment she felt within. With the stroke of her brush, she captured in detail the face of a woman with two sides. One half of the face was bright, cheerful, and passionate. Inspired by the love God has for her, even knowing her shortcomings. The opposite side of her face displayed agony, perplexity, shame, tears of remorse, a visage yet drained by the weight of sin. She poured herself into the masterpiece. So indulged that she didn't notice the phone nor the doorbell ringing, and neither did she hear Sway calling her name. She was in her office, door shut, crying out to God for help with her stability through her art. Each stroke of the black brush's metal picks expressing what she didn't have the courage nor words to express.

"I'm just saying, Mya. What's up?" Sway yelled from the opposite side of her office door.

Mya thought he might have come back for lunch. She had fried some fish for him to put it on top of a chef's salad.

"Your lunch is in the kitchen, baby," she yelled back. The salad was in the refrigerator with a sticky note telling him the fish was in the warmer, and next to the to-go plate was a thermos filled with homemade lemonade and two slices of strawberry cream cheese pie.

"You not gon' come and sit with me for lunch?" Sway questioned, sounding more like a demand than a question.

Mya barely answered. "I should be done by the time you get in this evening." It wasn't that she was being cold; she simply was spending time with the only one who couldn't hurt her heart.

Without Sway entering the office, Mya felt his temper beginning to rage. Call it intuition, or the vibes his spirit gave off, but in any case, she intercepted them.

"What I look like talking to my woman through a closed door? What you doing in there, girl? Hiding something or somebody? You disrespecting me, Mya? Huh?" he reasoned. With no warning, he turned the doorknob and slung it open.

Bam!

The back of the door slammed into a small shelf that held a variety of art supplies. The noise caught Mya by surprise.

"What in the world?" she said, looking past her picture to see a deranged looking Sway standing in the doorway huffing and puffing. The idea of her art supplies spilling on the door and maybe even possibly getting paint on her plush gray carpet that lay on the other side of the room struck a nerve. She sprinted off her stool and hurried toward the back of the door. "Boy, what in the world . . ." She almost cursed. "Sway, what is your problem?"

"Who you calling a boy?" He hovered over her, flexing his hand as if preparing himself for a brawl. Eyes dancing and glazed over like someone under the influence of drugs. Mya didn't even notice, occupied with cleaning up the mess.

"Whoever it was that slung the door open to my office and knocked around my stuff!" Mya yelled, unexpectedly.

"Who you got up in here?" Sway started looking around.

"What? You know good and well ain't nobody in here!" She straightened her shelf back up. "Look at what you did! Just look!" She rushed past him to grab a towel to clean up the powder-pink paint that spilled from its container. Sway didn't seem phased; what she was saying was the last thing on his mind!

"Who you hiding up in here?" He got busy tossing chairs and shoving small furniture around, in one of his crazed rages. He went into the different storage closets, peeking his head inside looking for this mystery lover of Mya's.

"Sway, what is it that you want? I fixed you lunch. I just don't understand. All I'm doing is working. Boy, what else do you want from me?" Mya snapped.

"Call me boy one more time and watch what happens."

"This right here is so unnecessary." She wiped away more of the spilled paint. Then made her way to the other side of the room where some of the paint dotted the carpet.

"Why didn't you answer the phone? What were you doing that you couldn't answer the phone?"

"Are you serious, Sway? Is this *really* about the *phone*? I was working. Boy, I didn't even hear—"

As she was bent down, tending to the carpet, Sway backhanded her. *Whop!*

"I told you to watch your mouth!" he shouted. Mya flipped over like a stunt double, holding her face, trying to find a secure place to get on her feet. "And you better check your tone, too," he said as he stepped toward her.

She inched away, stunned by the blow. "Now, I'm going to ask you again. What were you doing that was so important that you couldn't stop and make time for me!" His tone increased with every word.

Make time for you? "It . . . it . . . it wasn't like that, Sway. You know I wouldn't do you like that," Mya whined, trying to stay clear of him as she got to her feet. With each step he took forward, she stepped back.

"Ever since you started going to that church you act like you don't want me no more. What? Am I not good enough for you now?" He punched himself in the chest, adding emphasis to his remark. "Is that what it is, Mya?"

"Sway, you know me better than that. Please stop—" She held her hands up in front of her.

"Shut up!" Sway cut her off. "Am I wrong for wanting to make love to my fiancée? Is it my fault that I think about you all day and can't wait to get home to hold you and to see you? Huh, Mya? What is it going to take to get some of your time?" Sway's eyes welled up with tears. He looked vulnerable instead of angry. "Mya, just because I don't go to church with you right now doesn't mean I won't go eventually." A tear rolled down his cheek. "Mya, I love you too. You always say that God loves you. Well, I love you too. I need you!"

Mya couldn't hold back her tears any longer. Seeing Sway cry was too much for her. Like a mother running to rescue her child, she caught Sway just as his knees hit the floor. He wrapped his arms around her waist, pressing his face against her belly and cried. Mya had no idea that her distance affected him like this. What was she thinking? This man couldn't help how much he loved her. For years she had been the closest thing to a mother that he'd had.

"Baby, don't cry. I'm here. I love you." She comforted him, stroking the back of his neck and shoulders. "Sway, look at me." Mya asked him three times to look at her, but he wouldn't. Instead he squeezed her tighter. "Jermal Swayze Edwards, if you love me, look at me." With tears still in his eyes, Sway slowly loosened his embrace and looked up at her. Mya squatted down to eye level with him, holding his face in her hands. She kissed him, then wiped away the trail of tears.

"Baby, I love you. You are still the amazing, confident, and very good looking man I fell for two years ago. Yes, I'm changing some, but it's for the better. But I promise you, I'm not trying to abandon you. I'm just trying to put everything in its proper perspective. That's all. Sway, you know I love you. You are the only man I have been with."

While wiping away his tears, a smile slowly spread across his face as he comprehended her words. He affectionately caressed the back of Mya's head as he kissed her. She closed her eyes to inhale the man that made her romantically intoxicated. He parted her lips with his. She was beginning to drift to that place where desire reigned when King's face flashed before her eyes. Her body tensed. Subconsciously she held her breath and immediately opened her eyes. *Oh Jesus! What just happened?* she thought.

"What's up?" Sway questioned, obviously aware of the change in her disposition.

Mya was almost spooked out. Why would she be thinking of King at a time like this? She was nearly speechless. "Uh nothing, baby. The weirdest thing just happened to me." Mya tried not to let it show. She reached for the back of Sway's neck to pull him near as she leaned back against the carpet. Hoping he wouldn't ask her to explain. He leaned down to kiss her; she waited for his next move. When it didn't come right away, she opened her eyes. Sway immediately wrapped his hand around her throat, pinning her to the floor.

"Let me just make sure we got an understanding. This"—he pressed his body against hers—"is mine." Beneath his grip, Mya gasped for air. "Can't nobody love you like I can, and won't nobody tell me when I can or can't have you. You my woman! You hear me?" Sway demanded, releasing his grip.

Instantly she began choking, gasping for air, but again he grabbed her by the neck and as she sat up, he slammed her into the floor. Dazed, Mya stared into his crazed eyes. *Where did my baby go that fast? Only minutes earlier he was so sweet, so loving.*

"One more thing. You got a few seconds to get upstairs and put on something sexy and set my lunch before me. Time is money." With that, he released her and brushed himself off. Mya held her neck with both hands as if to magically stop the discomfort. Light-headed, she reached for a nearby table for support to get up. She waited for her head to stop spinning. Fearful of what he might do next, she hurried to her feet. He stood there without helping her. Slowly, she walked by him as she headed down the hall, and then the stairway. Looking at him with contempt in her eyes. "Who you looking at like that?"

Bam!

Sway punched her in the back of her head. "Mya, your best bet is to get up them stairs and fix yourself up and meet me in the kitchen."

Mya peeled herself off the wall that had kept her from hitting the floor. Please strengthen me, Father. In Jesus name, she prayed. Assuming silence was best, she rushed upstairs, not wanting him to see her cry, more so than heed to his command to change from her worn pair of overalls and T-shirt into something shorter and revealing.

She hoped that she'd wiped away her last tear. *I'll find a way to fix all of this.* She sprayed on a little perfume, staring at herself in the mirror. The ash-blue, satin spaghetti strap designer dress stopped inches above her knees complimenting her long legs and ideal shape. Mya decided

50

against putting on heels, just in case he still wanted to fight. A pair of flat silver sandals would have to suffice. As she pulled her hair out of the bun and brushed it down, she quoted the scripture she carried in her heart since she was a child. "I can do all things through Christ which strengthens me."

"Mya, hurry up!" Sway yelled just as she entered the kitchen. His instant straight face told Mya he felt a bit stupid. "Now *that's* what I'm talking about." He nodded, expressing his approval of her appearance. "What must a brother go through just to see his future wife and get his lunch set in front of him? Now, baby, come here." Sway sat back in his chair and affectionately grabbed Mya by the waist as she placed his silverware on the plate. Mya's body tensed as he pulled her into his lap.

"You smell good, girl."

Exactly who is this man I think I love? Mya looked into his eyes for the truth. "You know it's your fault I am the way I am," Sway said in between the kisses he placed on her shoulders.

"What do you mean it's my fault?" Mya sincerely inquired.

"Come on now, Mya. You already know how you make a brother feel. I'm the only man you've been with, your first. You've never made me feel like I had to be second to anyone or anything."

"And I have never started being that way toward you. I still make sure everything is how you like it."

"Now you on some other . . ."

"Sway, you have to understand I'm only one person. I can't make everyone happy at the same time."

"No! What *you* need to understand is I'm the only one you need to be concerned about making happy." Mya sensed Sway's attitude adjusting. So she decided to hold her peace, rather than state that her nephew was her first priority. To avoid another altercation, Mya gracefully set her attention on his food and began deboning his fish, then sliced it on top of his salad. It was obvious that he had gotten his point across.

He did most of the talking as he ate. Mya did her best to remain

51

attentive to the conversation, but for some odd reason, something kept telling her she needed to stand her ground. She hoped he didn't take notice of her constant adjusting in her chair, or the chills she suddenly got, or her difficulty with maintaining eye contact. Mya just could not settle down or relax. Sway probably would grave her if he knew just how relieved she was when he finished and was ready to head back to work, back to his hustle.

"I should be in around eight-thirty or nine," Sway stated after he kissed her. "You need to be here."

"But I have Bible study."

"I want some spaghetti for dinner." He proceeded out the door without looking back. "I love you."

Mya stood watching him descend the front porch and head for his Land Rover, wondering what her next action would bring. He backed out of the driveway and headed down the street. She even watched a couple of leaves whisk in the wind and a few birds soaring in the sky. *What would I have to give in order to be as free and as careless as one of them?* After releasing a deep sigh, she closed the door and headed back to her painting. Maybe I can call the church and find out if they are recording tonight's message, she thought.

With everything going on in her personal life, she had forgotten about contacting Coach Riley. He was the key to getting information on her missing sister.

How blessed is the man who does not walk in the counsel of the wicked, nor stand in the path of sinners . . . But his delight is in the law of the Lord, and in His law he meditates day and night.

Psalm 1:1-2 (NAS)

CHAPTER 8

Tuesday (6:23 p.m.)

Am I a darn slave? I should just go on to Bible study. I need to be there anyway. Why do I feel like I need Sway's permission? Mya's heart ached with longing. Her desire to attend Bible study was great. Likewise, she desperately needed to keep peace between her and Sway. "Oh Lord, my God, what am I going to do?" Mya rested her head in her hands as she sat on her bed and reflected on the message she heard only days ago at Sunday morning service.

"In order to get what God has for you, you have to put some things aside, make sacrifices, put forth an effort to be in right standing with God. There will be situations that arise that will prove your love for God. God is looking for people that will stand up for God no matter what may come or what may go . . ." Bishop Greene had preached.

On that Sunday, Mya was one of the first people on the altar for prayer, petitioning God for this type of zeal and conviction for Him. In an instant, Mya knew exactly what she needed to do. Quietly, yet swiftly, she began her preparation for dinner. Spaghetti, tossed salad, and garlic bread would take no time.

Praise and worship was already in full effect by the time Mya found a place to park. She wasn't sure what all would be awaiting her once she got home. She just believed somehow God would make it all better. She grabbed her Bible off the passenger seat, locked the door, and hurried in. As always, she was greeted by some of the most loving people she had known.

"So glad you could make it," the deaconess who had prayed the Salvation prayer with her, stated.

"So am I," she responded as they embraced.

Mya walked through the double doors that led to the sanctuary, planning to sit in the back, so no one would take notice of her arriving late, but her plan was short-lived because an usher came and escorted her to the fifth row from the front. Some smiled and waved, a few extended their arms for a hug while a few continued to worship, never breaking their concentration from God. She was relieved no one made her feel ashamed for being late. Briefly, she looked around hoping to see King, even though she knew he worked on Tuesdays. Not wanting to draw attention to herself, she kind of just blended in, joining the congregation. She wasn't comfortable with raising her hands yet. Her conscience reminded her of her willful sinning. To her, the extending of the hands was a form of surrendering, and as long as Sway was shacking up in her house, she hadn't lain down her will before God. So, Mya just clapped, or folded her hands in the praying position.

After some time, Bishop approached the pew, and the congregation began to settle. There were a few who had really been moved by the flow of God through the choir and praise team. Mya admired them, yearning to feel what they felt. To be touched by the Messiah. She sat still, looking down at her hands as she fumbled with her fingers, until Bishop decided to speak. He greeted the church and gave a few words of exhortation, reminding the church that God loves us. That he wasn't concerned about our shortcomings as much as we are. Mya sat there attentively, but couldn't ignore what she was feeling. She glanced around but saw no one meeting her gaze.

By the time service was over she felt liberated, knowing that God sees man's desire to withstand sin and He acknowledges that. Plus He gives us the desire to change, therefore, he shall finish what he started.

"Sister Jenkins, are you okay, sweetie?" the deaconess asked, breaking Mya's thoughts.

"Uh, yes, ma'am," Mya replied as she realized she was still sitting in her seat after the service had been dismissed. "I was just thinking about something Bishop said." Mya stood to her feet, brushing her blouse and cuffing her Bible.

"I'd love to know what that was, if you don't mind sharing," she said with a kind smile. "I don't mind being edified in the Word."

"Um, sure. No problem." Mya was caught off guard, but didn't mind elaborating. "Bishop made the remark that some people don't have the desire to change because they don't feel that there's anything wrong with them. They cast blame on their parents, other people, or the mishaps that happen in their lives, and as a result, the mirror is never reflected on self, but toward someone else. The blamer always points out others as being the ones with the problem."

"Amen to that, Sister Jenkins. Learning to be responsible for our own actions is the first step to getting closer to God. I used to blame my mistakes on other people too. Adam tried to blame Eve and even God for his own disobedience in the Garden of Eden. That gets me every time I read it."

"What do you mean? Eve ate the fruit and gave it to Adam. It was her fault."

"Yes, but that old devil named Satan gave her the fruit of lies. The Bible says Eve was deceived. It never says that Adam was. So rather than stopping sin in its tracks by rebuking Eve and the devil, as well as repenting and telling God his wrong, he told God that the woman that God had made just for him gave him the fruit and he did eat it."

"Ooooh, like Adam was saying it was all God and Eve's fault and he didn't have anything to do with it. I get it."

"Right. Exactly." The deaconess smiled and nodded yes. "God had already gave Adam instructions not to eat from the tree of the knowledge of good and evil."

"He pointed the finger somewhere else instead of at himself for his part." *The same way Sway blamed me for his own actions when he hit me.* Yes, Sway had shared his tumultuous upbringing with Mya and the memory of his words struck her hard. Had that made him into the person he had become? He hadn't been abusive and mean spirited until recently. Something had definitely changed. His childhood was nothing nice.

My mama put me in the system at seven. She gave me up because she was selfish. Chose her job over me. I remember her telling me that I deserved to be loved, but she didn't have what I needed. She was supposed to come back and get me once she got herself established. Do you know that while I was hoping for her to show up and take me back with her that I spent ten years in and out of foster homes? I got beaten, sometimes over beaten, and in one home I had to eat my meals to a timer. When it went off I had to be finished. Otherwise, they threw whatever was left into the garbage. They didn't want me at all. They just wanted the checks that came in my name.

By age eighteen, Sway decided that it was him against the world. Everybody had a motive, and his was simply surviving. The streets didn't have love for anyone, and that was a feeling he grew accustomed to. To him, he had finally escaped the curse of being forced to deal with people who were just outright messed up mentally, and treacherous, no doubt. He discerned who he was: a hustler. And up until he met Mya, he honestly believed a woman's only purpose was to serve him as a momentary satisfaction.

The deaconess's voice broke Mya's train of thought. "Well, it was nice talking to you, Sister Jenkins. I hope to see you here again," the attractive woman said with a kind smile.

"It's Mya. Me too."

"All right then, Sister Mya. Goodnight." The deaconess began to walk away.

Mya started to exit the row when she looked to her right and spotted King, who was speaking with someone, but staring directly at her. Without realizing it, she began smiling.

"Oh, honey, by the way," the deaconess came back to address Mya. "Oh, look at you," she teased, looking in the direction of Mya's gaze.

"What?" Mya questioned, taking her attention off King.

"'What!' Baby girl, *you* just lit up like a Christmas tree."

"Did I?" Mya was a little surprised by her own behavior.

"Yes, ma'am! You did." They both laughed. "Minister Lee is a good young man. Devoted and consistent. I've watched God do a work in him over the years."

Minister? Mya thought. *I don't want to marry no preacher. Marry? Where did that come from? I'm not even with this man. I already have a man.* Mya shook off the internal conversation she was having.

"I came back to give you this." The deaconess extended a piece of paper with a number on it. It was signed Lisa Price. "Call me whenever you want. No matter what time it is. Okay."

"Okay!" Mya hugged her again. Thanking God in her heart to finally know her name. She was too embarrassed to ask her.

By the time King was making his way toward her, she decided to meet him. "Well, hello, beautiful." King was the first to speak as he took her hand and kissed the back of it.

"Good evening. I didn't expect to see you tonight." Mya beamed.

"Were you looking for me?"

"What? What kind of question is that?"

"A simple one. Were you looking for me?" King stared directly into her eyes. Mya briefly looked him over. She was very pleased with his attire. The gray dress pants, white button-down shirt, and white, gray, and smoke-gray tie set his belt and shoes off. White diamond cufflinks matched his necklace. His dreads looked freshly maintained. This brother was an eyeful.

"Well, I kind of hoped to see you," she finally admitted.

King smiled. "Good, because I've been praying for you, and I wanted to see how you're doing." Mya stood there trying to ignore how her heart raced.

"Let me get that." King took her Bible, and they headed for the door. "Do you have some spare time? Can we go get something to eat, or stop by Starbucks or something?"

Mya wanted to scream *yes*. She was beginning to enjoy being around him, but she didn't want to give King the wrong impression. "King, I would love to, but I'm involved with someone."

"I already knew that. He doesn't deserve you, but I feel like as your brother in the Lord we could get to know each other. Nonetheless, I respect your decision."

Mya couldn't ignore the disappointment in his eyes, even though his disposition and tone never changed. He walked her to her car, where he opened the door for her. "Do you mind if I sit with you for a second? That is, if you have time?" King asked.

"No, I don't mind," Mya said. It felt awkward having a male other than Judah and Sway sit inside her vehicle. Once he asked how she was doing, and she began to share how well Judah's football career appeared to be going, the discomfort subsided. She went from looking straight ahead, to avoiding eye contact, to sitting sideways in her driver's seat so that King could feel the magnitude of what she felt. Then she had to briefly explain who Judah was to her and how they ended up together. He bluntly inquired about her man and listened attentively. Mya chose her words carefully.

After about thirty minutes, Bishop and First lady were pulling out of the parking lot and stopped to have a few words with King. Mya decided she had better call it a night. So when he returned, she reluctantly told him goodnight and headed home. She thought it best to call her nephew to see if he was at home. Believing Sway would be mindful of his actions with him in the house. But before she had to pick up that burden again, she closed her eyes and inhaled King. She thought about his smile and his attentiveness to everything she said. She even thought about his touch, his hugs, and his hands brushing against her. He carried this piece of calm, or something with him. To the point where she felt as if life wasn't so chaotic when she was in his presence. One thing was for sure, she felt so comfortable around him, and she never wanted to part ways. Maybe one day they could share a meal. After all, he was her "brother in Christ."

A simple believes everything, but the prudent gives thought to his steps.

Proverbs 14:15 (ESV)

CHAPTER 9

Mya's residence (9:40 p.m.)

"Wow, Aunt Mya! That spaghetti was on point!" Judah greeted as soon as she walked through the door. "I murked it like two hours ago!"

"Boy, you're just greedy!" She smiled at him with adoration.

"I might be, but those sausages in it and that cheese on top! For real, me and Sway was like 'thank you Lord for this meal.'"

She smiled. Judah was saying it in a joking matter, but Mya was grateful to hear him refer to the Lord in a positive manner. Judah had forsaken any idea of God being good and loving toward his people once Big Momma died in the hospital. Because Big Momma lived the way she loved, she underwent surgery to donate her kidney to a young mother who was hospitalized and couldn't find a match. Big Momma had been her nurse and felt compelled to help her. The surgery was successful. However, Big Momma was infected with staph and never made it back home. Mya decided to sue the hospital that Big Momma had worked in for twelve years. They agreed to a private settlement, not wanting it to leak to the media, but many were affected by this misfortune. Judah stated several times that God allowed bad things to happen to good people. He found fault with God for allowing his

63

grandmother to die while trying to spare someone else's life. He said he didn't want to serve someone who permitted things of that nature. Mya perceived the situation differently. That her mother died the way she lived, always sacrificing herself for someone else. Plus, she wanted them to have all that they needed. God worked it out, and they didn't have to be concerned about money, ever! Likewise, God was also trying to show them that life is in his hands. You never knew when he would call you home, so you must be ready. And the only way they'd see Big Momma again was to get right with God.

"Auntie, what's up?"

"What do you mean?"

"You glowing, kind of like Big Momma always did."

"Hm?" Mya questioned sincerely. "I suppose it's the Lord." Her insides smiled just as bright as her outward appearance.

"It doesn't surprise me, you would say something like that."

"Really?"

"Yeah . . . still thinking that God cares what we're going through." Judah said, not knowing but fully convinced that God had more pressing concerns than the likes of his.

"Baby, you have to at least attempt to understand our days are already numbered, and God longs for us to know him as he is. He doesn't set out to do us harm; he allows—"

"I don't want to hear anymore!" he cut her off.

Mya sat there with her heart filling with heaviness for her nephew. *Lord, you have to do something,* she prayed.

"Aunt Mya, I'm trying. It's just too much right now."

"May I say one thing?" Judah nodded his permission.

"God knows why you feel the way you do, and he still loves you. He still keeps you, watches over you, provides for you, and still blesses you. No matter what you think of him. One thing is for sure: we can look back over our lives and see the hand of God on us. One thing about truth, it will speak for itself."

Judah sat say much more, but that was okay for Mya. He was

probably thinking about what she said. She leaned over to kiss him on the forehead, where he relaxed on the sofa, and whispered goodnight. She made her way to the kitchen, made herself a plate with the last of the spaghetti, rinsed the rest of the dishes off and put them in the dishwasher, where the men had placed the others.

She took a few bites and headed upstairs to her room. The door was pulled up, but not shut. She took a deep breath. "Father, please allow Sway and me not to get into a confrontation. Please be merciful to my prayer," she whispered. Slowly, she peeked in. The TV was the only light that lit up the room. Sway was stretched across the bed as if he had fallen asleep watching TV. His woodsy cologne filled the room. Mya noticed he hadn't left his clothes and shoes scattered across the floor like he normally did. She started to go back downstairs and finish talking to Judah, but decided to finish up here and take a shower. She could tell by his breathing that he was asleep. Slowly, she sat down with her plate in hand. Mya was down to her last bite by the time Sway detected her presence.

"Hey, baby." He lifted his head and stretched out his hand to make physical contact.

"Hi." Mya took her last bite and set the plate down.

"That spaghetti was good, wasn't it?" Sway smiled, still asleep.

"Yes. Thank you for saving me some," she teased.

"Oh, man, my fault. Well, our fault. You know how Ju and I are. We kind of assumed you had already took you some out."

"It's cool. There was just enough left for me," Mya joked with him, but with caution, wondering if he was about to trip.

"Come here." Sway pulled on Mya's thighs so he could rest his head on her.

"Wait a second. Let me take off my shoes."

"Nah, let me." He got up, walked around the bed, and kneeled down to unstrap her two-inch heeled sandals.

Her insides were flipping because she had no idea what to expect. She watched his bare muscular back that displayed several tattoos; his rich pecan complexion, and his head full of waves. His arms, his chest, even his smile, the brother was ripe eye candy. She would never forget when they first met. Mya was meeting a male client over lunch, about the location for an art gallery he was hosting, when Sway and another young man came inside and were seated across from her. It took Mya only a few seconds to check them both out. Mya was most impressed by his attire. He was extremely attractive, and the suit he wore appeared expensive, created by some high-end designer who required it be professionally tailored. But what really tripped her out was they had on the same colors, beige and off-white. Sway wasn't too obvious about checking her out, but made sure they made eye contact. Mya wasn't budging though; she was handling business, so she remained focused and professional.

After finishing the loaded baked potato, she excused herself to the ladies room. She knew her two-piece skirt suit was a killer, and being that she had no intentions on getting involved with anyone, she decided to hit the runway, knowing all eyes were on her. It took no time for her to freshen up, and she headed back to the table. However, Sway made it his business to almost bump into her in the hall.

"Oops, please forgive me, beautiful." Mya smiled to herself because he tried to act like it was an accident.

"Forgiven," Mya responded as she attempted to step around him.

"A woman that looks this good should be here with me," Sway said, feeling sure of himself.

Mya just smiled and proceeded to wrap up her business. By the time Sway came back to his seat, Mya was shaking the hand of her client, and promising not to disappoint him. The two of them had planned to leave together, but Sway intervened and asked Mya's client if he would mind if he had a few words with her.

"Well, why in the world would I?" was his response as he paid Mya respect and headed out the door. Mya was kind of taken aback by Sway's aggressiveness, but those brown eyes and long lashes were just too adorable.

"Don't you think you were just a little out of line?" Mya had questioned him about his approach.

"Maybe a little, but I couldn't risk the chance of you walking out of my life." Mya smiled a little.

"What is it that you would like to speak with me about?"

"You. What is your name? How old are you? Where are you from? What's your mother's name? Where have you been all these years, and can I get your number?"

This time she really laughed! "Are you serious?"

He laughed as well. "Actually, I am, but you don't have to answer everything now. Maybe you can, tomorrow night over dinner." Mya couldn't help but smile. The brother was fine, and she was just a little curious.

"I'll tell you what. Saturday night, I'm putting together an event, and maybe if you show, I'll think about your invitation to dinner." She stood her ground.

"Sounds good to me." Mya wrote down the address to the place and politely excused herself.

Seconds later, Sway was behind her.

"Excuse me." Mya stopped walking and turned around. "What is your name? At least give a brother your name."

"Mya . . . My name is Mya. By the way, you look very nice in that suit." With that, she headed to her car, got in and left.

Sway's movement halted her reminiscing. He looked up at Mya, who was rubbing her hand across the top of his head.

"What are you smiling about?" he questioned.

"Just thinking about the day I met you."

"Oh, how you were shutting a brother down!"

"No, I wasn't." Mya laughed, beginning to relax.

"I hear you. You made me jump over all types of hurdles just to get your number."

"Sway, you know you need to stop exaggerating."

"So you saying you didn't, huh?"

"That's exactly what I'm saying." They both laughed together. Mya hadn't realized how good it felt to laugh with him until they stopped.

"What's the matter? Why are you looking like that?" Sway asked, noticing the change in her expression.

"Just thinking about something Big Momma used to tell me."

"What, baby?" Sway inquired as he began rubbing her feet.

"I really don't know how to say it . . . I don't want you to take it the wrong way."

"Baby, I love you. Just say it."

"Well, let me ask you this." Mya didn't want to ruin such a pleasant moment. "Was there someone that you dated before me that you felt was the one you could spend your life with?" Sway tilted his head, as if considering what she was saying.

"When I was with Yasmeen I thought she had a lot of qualities that showed she had the potential to become a good wife, but you are the only woman I've ever felt like I wanted to spend the rest of my life with."

Mya beamed as she bent over and kissed Sway. "Okay. I guess I can ride with that." She smiled. "Big Momma used to say that whenever you prayed to God for particular things, be aware because Satan would always send the counterfeit first."

"What you mean?" Sway released her left foot and picked up the right one.

"Like . . . some people ask God about their careers. They might get a promotion at this big company. So they take it, thinking it was what God wanted. But when a position in the ministry is presented, they turn it down. They already assumed the big company promotion was God's answer, when in fact, it wasn't. Because the big company could have been under investigation because the owner may have been squandering money." Sway kept a straight face, but his chest rose and fell as he took a deep breath.

"Or, or, or a woman praying for God to send her a husband and some man comes along declaring all this love. She knows he has some hang ups, but because she professes to love God, she overlooks his mishaps, thinking God sent him for her to help. And all the while, God's hand was nowhere near that relationship." The second she stopped talking, she realized how her remarks pointed to her relationship with Sway.

"But I'm not saying that in relation to you. I was just making a point about not waiting on God and settling for a counterfeit." Sway stopped rubbing her feet. Mya closed her eyes, wishing she hadn't opened her mouth.

"So, do you feel like I'm not your real husband—the one God called you to be with?" He looked so confused.

"No . . . I didn't say that." Mya leaned in and kissed his forehead.

"Well, I mean, keeping it real—I do take you through a lot. And I got a lot of stuff I'm trying to change about myself."

"I know, baby, and we gone be all right."

"Mya, you ain't got to sit here and act like everything is all right. I know I ain't perfect." She wished she felt comfortable enough to just say that sometimes she wondered if he was God sent, but deep down in her heart she couldn't. Instead, she just stared at him briefly, mulling over the question until she forced it to stop looping in her head.

"Jermal, I miss you." Mya cuffed his face in her hand momentarily, then released it. Sway began rubbing up and down her thighs.

"I miss you too." Mya knew that look in his eyes. That sensual look where he desired her in every sense.

She grabbed his hands to make him stop. "No, baby. I miss *you*." She slowly pointed at his heart. "We used to never fuss. We used to talk about everything. Now I don't even know how to take you. What is going on with my baby?" She began to cry. "What are you feeling? Sway, you must tell me, so we can work through this together. I don't understand you anymore. Please, baby, just tell me what's the matter," Mya pleaded with tears as Sway remained kneeled before her. Several times his lips moved as if to say something, but no words ever departed from his lips.

"Baby, this is me. Surely, you can talk to me." Again Mya attempted to get him to open up. Sway reached up to wipe away her tears.

"Mya, I . . . I . . . I'm sorry." He choked through his words, releasing a fresh dam of tears. He buried his face in her lap and wept loudly. "I'm sorry, Mya. I'm so sorry . . . I . . . I treated you so bad. I'm sorry."

Mya sat there holding her twenty-nine-year-old baby, praying for him, crying with him as he held on for what felt like dear life. *I'm all he has,* she kept telling herself. *Without me and Jesus, he doesn't have anyone.* The longer she held him, the more she was convinced that she possessed the power to change him.

"Come on, baby. Let's just lie down." Mya slid back, offering him her side of the bed. He complied and tucked her pillow beneath his head, pulling her as close to him as possible. Where she remained until he fell asleep.

She quickly showered and slipped into a silk, oversized button down pajama top. Mya slipped the covers back on Sway's side and got in bed, relieved that he was still asleep. She hoped to fall asleep as soon as her head hit the pillow, but she couldn't get comfortable. Turning over onto her stomach, she folded her arms beneath the pillow, but when cold steel met her skin, dread took over her senses. Slowly, she eased upright, and with caution, Mya lifted the pillow. Fear immediately dominated her being as she discovered the nine-millimeter gun that Sway kept just inches from where she lay.

How long has he been sleeping with this? What is he doing with this in my house? Had he been the man she first fell for, she would have assumed he just wanted to protect them. But this dude asleep beside her now . . . Everything in her made her reconsider his intentions for bringing the gun into her home. She eased off the bed, dumped the pillow out of its case and onto the floor. Wrapping the pistol in the case, she then headed down to the hall and into her guest room closet to hide it until the morning.

There was no way she could get any sleep knowing that he had hidden a murder weapon in their bed.

Wherefore, put away lying, speak every man truth with his neighbour; for we are members one of another. Be angry, and sin not: let not the sun go down upon your wrath.

Ephesians 4:25-26 (KJV)

CHAPTER 10

Monday (10:17 a.m.)

Ring, ring, ring.

"Yeah," Sway answered his cell phone.

"Hey, baby!"

"What's up?"

"Baby, I just got off the phone with Coach Riley. He wants to meet for lunch, so we can discuss Judah and these scholarships."

"Oh yeah?"

"Yes. I'm calling to ask if you want to join us? It would be nice to have you present."

"On the real, baby, I would, but I think I'm going to pass this time."

"Baby," Mya whined a little, hoping he would accept the invitation. The last couple of weeks had been like heaven on earth. Sway had been acting like his old self, nor did he mention his pistol that she had thrown over the Matthew's Bridge. Surprisingly, they had been doing everything together. Well, except going to church. Even though he did listen as she read the Bible aloud from the scriptures the church had assigned to all the members.

"I know it, beautiful. I would stop the moon for you if I could, but

73

you know how I am about this money. I had planned to surprise you, but guess what I've been thinking about?"

"What?"

"I've been thinking about going to church with you."

"Oh my God! Sway, baby, don't play with me. Are you serious?"

"Yeah, I've been thinking about it. I mean, when I look at you, there is definitely a change in you."

"Oh, baby. I'm so proud of you!"

"I'm not saying it's a definite, but I think I want to."

"You have no idea how good that makes me feel. I love you."

"I love you too."

Mya hung up feeling so relieved and excited about what God was doing in Sway's heart. *One day my baby will be sold out, serving God.* The thought was so encouraging. She felt as if her prayers were being answered.

She arrived at the restaurant feeling as if she could conquer any giant. Coach Riley was already seated inside. He stood to greet her with a hug like he always did.

"Mya Jenkins, your mother has to be smiling down on you," Coach Riley said. "You really have turned out to be quite a lovely young woman."

"Well, thank you, but I give all the glory to God. He has truly blessed me." He stood to pull her chair out.

"Thanks for coming," he stated as he returned to his seat once she was settled. They took a few minutes to discuss how God had been revealing himself in their lives. Exchanging the messages that had been preached at each one's church the previous Sunday. Coach Riley spoke of how important reading the *Bible* is as well as the coming kingdom of God. After Mya discussed repentance and baptism, she glanced at her menu, trying to decide on what she wanted to eat.

"Mya, I've been trying to figure out how I would tell you this, but I can't find a perfect way to do it." Coach Riley looked a little disturbed.

"What is it? Just say it," Mya encouraged, her brows lowering.

"I have reason to believe that Judah is my son."

A moment of silence passed before Mya spoke.

"Coach Riley, if this is some type of sick game you're trying to play because of my baby's chance of going pro, I serve you notice—God is not mocked." Mya could feel her defense rising.

"Mya, this is not a game to me. I am genuinely trying to be a part of my son's life."

"Well, if you are his father, where have you been all these years? Why didn't you step up and be a man a long time ago? Besides, Honesty said Ju's father moved to another state once he found out she was pregnant, claiming he wasn't ready for a child."

He raised one hand, as if asking to speak. "I didn't skip town as an attempt to flee my responsibility. I went off to college to prepare a way for our child. Shortly after, I heard Honesty was missing, and the supposed father was behind it all. I was in college; I wasn't trying to go to jail for something I had nothing to do with."

"So you leave my nephew without either parent? Did you not think for one second he would need someone? Why didn't you man up, Riley?"

"Hold up . . . It was Honesty who told me not to step to Big Momma and tell her she was carrying my child, for fear I would end up in jail."

"I mean, you had every right to. My sister was fourteen. You were what? Eighteen, nineteen?"

"Nineteen."

"You've got a bunch of nerve to come around now. Did you ever wonder if he had a roof over his head, clothes on his back?"

"Sure I did."

"Well, how about a peace of mind? You play a big part in my nephew's life. My baby was feeling like he wasn't good enough to be loved by his father. That he was born only to be subjected to pain." Mya's right foot tapped the floor rapidly as she tried to keep her composure, but she couldn't stop thinking of the many nights Judah would come crawl in bed with her, crying about feeling alone, or the days he went on field trips and the other kids had one or both parents while he had his aunt or grandmother.

"Mya, Judah is the reason I left Michigan and moved south. I took the coaching position for him. For two years I've been active in my son's life."

"Oh, let me break out the violin! You act like you've done us a favor. For two years you've been deceiving my baby. Acting like you grew up with his mom, when in fact, you knocked her up and got cold feet— leaving her to bear the responsibility alone. I'm sorry! I don't have any sympathy for you. In fact, I need God to deal with me because I don't know how I feel about you right now." She crossed her arms.

"I'm not looking for your sympathy. I'm looking for your assistance in building a relationship with my son."

"With *my* son." Mya took out a twenty dollar bill and placed it next to the untouched turkey sandwich and potato wedges. "Wouldn't it be nice if you would man up and tell him yourself?" She slid out her seat and stood to her feet. "But let me bid you a small warning. Right now is a very vital time in my baby's life. You need to put yourself in his shoes, and think about what your desperate desire to be his father would do at a time like this." With that, she exited the restaurant.

A friend shows his friendship at all times—it is for
adversity that [such] a brother is born.

Proverbs 17:17 (CJB)

CHAPTER 11

Same day (11:50 a.m.)

Mya exited the interstate, turned onto Edgewood Avenue and pulled into a Raceway gas station to fill up her tank. She had abandoned her lunch with Coach Riley well over an hour ago. At this point she didn't have a destination; she just got behind the wheel and drove. A couple times she circled the block and considered going back inside the restaurant and kicking him between his legs, just on the strength of him trying to pull this "I'm the father" mess after all these years!

"How could I have been so stupid? I should have figured it out! All that time he was spending with Judah," she spoke aloud as she opened her door and walked up to the pump. After she swiped her debit card, she picked the nozzle up and placed it in her gas tank. The tears were building in her throat, but she didn't want to cry. She wanted to feel the anger that also was forming in her chest, and for reasons beyond her understanding, she wanted Coach Eric Riley to suffer. Men like him were the reason dudes turned out like Sway. Putting their hands on women. Instead of their fathers taking the time to demonstrate how to treat a woman, govern a healthy household, and become a man worth respecting, they run off. Leaving the male child to sort through his feelings and figure out life on his own, sometimes unwilling to disclose to his mother what he feels because she is not a man. So why try? Unfortunately for some, the closest thing they see as an example of a man is the streets or what the television displays. Resulting in a woman being anything but respected. Why would he value the life of another, if the value of his existence wasn't instilled in him? But by the grace of God, Judah knew better. Big Momma was determine he wouldn't be another statistic.

She glanced over at the pump and noticed that the digits weren't moving. She released the handle and squeezed it again. Nothing.

"What in the world?" she asked aloud, looking around to see if anyone else wore the same look of confusion. There was only one other patron who had just pulled up and he was getting out his SUV and headed toward the store.

"How you doing?" the Rick Ross lookalike smiled and greeted her.

"I've been better," Mya confessed as she reattached the nozzle to the pump.

"Can you spare a moment so that I may introduce myself?" the dude asked, standing only a few inches away from her. He wore jeans, a white Tee, and a pair of LeBron James with a lot of flashy jewelry.

"I don't mean to be rude, but no I can't," Mya stated, then got inside her vehicle and pulled up to the pump in front of her. The dude stood in the same place watching her, looking surprised, as if she had changed her mind about pulling off without entertaining him. She avoided eye contact as she got back out of the car and repeated the same method.

"Let me help you with that." He approached her.

"No, thank you. I got it," she replied as politely as she could.

"Nah, I don't mind. It's a pleasure," he said, taking the nozzle from her hand. Mya did her best not to roll her eyes. As she shut the driver's side door and put some space between the two, she leaned against her car and watched to see if the digits would change on this pump.

"My name is Charles," the guy stated as if she had asked. "And yours?" He stared at her with a goofy grin, waiting on her to reply.

"Mya," she finally spoke.

"That's a beautiful name! You're beautiful. A woman as beautiful as you shouldn't be pumping no gas. If I was your man, I would make sure this tank was full every night before my head hit the pillow." He really didn't know how bad Mya wanted him to shut up. She wasn't in the mood for some sweet talking.

"Nothing is coming out," Mya stated.

"What? I'm not sure I understand." Charles looked confused.

"The gas pump . . . It's empty or something. Nothing is coming out, just like the first one I used." She pointed to the meter. He squeezed and released the nozzle a few times.

"That doesn't make any sense." Charles was the first to admit. He pulled the nozzle out of her tank and pointed it toward the ground. Charles stepped back to keep any gas from spilling on him as he gently squeezed it. They looked at each other, dumbfounded when nothing came out.

"Let me see something," Charles said as he put the nozzle back into the tank, pulled out a credit card, and continued his mission. "Squeeze it now," he instructed Mya after a few seconds. Nothing.

"What is the world coming to?" Mya wasn't shy about displaying her frustration. "What type of gas station doesn't have gas?"

"I'm going to step in here for a minute to speak to the cashier. I'll be right back." Before she could say a word, Charles was walking in the entrance.

"I was just going to say thank you, but I'll try somewhere else," Mya stated aloud as if he was standing there listening.

A few minutes later, she was up the street at a Circle K. She could see someone putting the nozzle back on the pump.

"Thank you, Lord!" She rejoiced as she pulled into the available spot. She exited and went to stand in line to pay for her gas.

"Twenty-five dollars on pump three," she addressed the young black man with glasses who stood at the register.

"Will that be all for you today, ma'am?" he replied politely.

"Yes, thank you." She handed him her cash. He made the transaction.

"Have a good day and thank you for choosing Circle K," he said.

"No, thank you! And you have a wonderful day." Mya turned on her heels and couldn't help but release some of her frustration. That young man's aura was peaceful. Pleasant even. She walked up to the pump and placed the nozzle in the tank again, but when she squeezed nothing came out.

"Nah . . . You have got to be kidding me!" She squeezed a few more times. "Ain't no way!" She spoke aloud as she looked around at the other pumps. "God, is this some type of sick joke you're playing on me?" She closed her eyes and took a deep breath. "This day really does have a way of getting worse." She tried the nozzle again. Nothing. She left the nozzle in the tank.

"Stay calm, Mya Sincere," she coached herself as she walked back into the gas station. She walked up to the counter, overlooking the person who was standing there and the individual that was behind him.

"Could you please push whatever button back there so I can get my gas?" She tried not to show just how unstable she was feeling.

"Ma'am, I did already," he replied politely.

"Well, do it again; it's not working." She stormed out the store and walked back to her car. She gripped the nozzle, and it still did nothing!

"I'm really about over this mess! I will never attempt to get gas on this side of town again!" Mya felt as if she was turning into a mad woman as she slammed the nozzle back on the pump and stomped back inside. Everyone in line was already staring at her.

"Excuse me." She looked at the man who was trying to pay for his items. She was anything but calm. "Just give me my money back!"

"Ma'am, please get in line, and I'll be able to assist you in a second," the cashier requested. Suddenly, his professionalism was now getting beneath her skin. She folded her arms across her chest, stood there for a moment as if she was considering challenging him. Then, without saying a word, she went and stood in the back of the line.

About two minutes passed before she approached the counter.

"How may I assist you, ma'am?" the young man asked.

"Something is wrong with your gas pump; I want my money back."

"Are you sure that you are squeezing the handle correctly?"

Her temperature was boiling. "Do I look slow? Do I look like I would have a problem completing such a small task?" She glared at him, itching for him to give her a reason to come across the counter. "Just give me my money back, and I'll be on my way." The attendant didn't respond at first. He just stared at her, and then after a few seconds of awkward silence, he opened his register and handed her a twenty and five dollar bills. Mya stormed out.

"Today really isn't my day!" she confessed as she pulled out into traffic. She was over it and quickly switched lanes as if someone was chasing her; she couldn't wait to get off this side of town and longed to be in the shelter of her own home. God, I really don't understand what your intentions are for me as I consider the day's events. I am going to go home, get on my knees with my face on the floor and release the dam that's threatening to break forth any second. A single tear trickled down her cheek.

"I cannot do this, not in the middle of traffic," Mya tried to coach herself as she stopped at a red light. She looked around just to see if the person in the car next to her could see that she was upset, but when she looked to her left, she spotted King pumping gas at a Chevron gas station.

"Is that King?" she asked. "But what would he being doing on this side of town?" She squinted to get a better look. Nah, that's not him. When the light changed, she proceeded to the interstate, but suddenly felt compelled to turn around. She flipped on her blinker and got into the turning lane. Looking around, she made a quick U-turn. As she approached the gas station, King's physique came into view.

"It's really him!" she exclaimed as she pulled in on the pump opposite him. Mya exited her car and swiped her debit card to pay for gas, avoiding eye contact, acting as if she didn't know King was present.

"Mya?" King called her name in disbelief. She looked around the pump suspiciously once her transaction cleared. "What a wonderful surprise!" King declared.

"Hey!" Mya sang. "What are you doing on this side of town?" She pretended to be just as surprised.

"I just left pastor's house. What about you?"

"You don't want to know! You'd be surprise to hear what kind of day I've had." A lump formed in her throat.

He put his nozzle back on the latch, closed his gas tank, and walked over to where she stood.

"Let me get that for you." He opened her gas tank and started pumping her gas. She stood there holding her breath.

"Is that thing really working?" she asked in disbelief as she watched the meter tick. King burst out laughing. "You wouldn't believe that I've been to two different stations just trying to get some freaking gas, and all of sudden you do it and . . ." Tears poured down her face.

"Whoa, whoa, whoa, what's the matter?" King locked the pump and pulled Mya into his arms. "I tried another station as well and couldn't get any gas either."

"You did?" Mya asked, looking into his eyes, dabbing at her face to catch her tears.

"Yeah, but I got a feeling there's more to them tears than the frustration of not getting any gas." King respectfully patted her back.

"It's just too much . . . I don't know what I'm going to do . . . I just don't know," Mya confessed through sobs.

"Do me a favor.'" King lifted her head and made her look into his eyes. "Get in your car, then pull over there by the pay phone. I'll be there in a second so we can talk. Okay? Can you do that for me?" Mya nodded and did accordingly.

By the time he pulled his car next to hers and sat in the passenger seat, Mya was slumped over the steering wheel crying uncontrollably. *How was she going to tell Judah that the same man he had grown to trust and look up to for the last two years was his father? And if she didn't tell him, surely he* would feel betrayed by her. Either way, he would be affected. Either way, he would be hurt. The weight of it all was far too heavy for her to bear. She kept praying, asking God to help her; she couldn't deny the urge to go back and slap Coach Riley. She had too many emotions all at once. If only God would speak to her; promise her it'll be all right.

King closed the door and pulled her limp body into his embrace. Mya began to pour out her heart about the entire situation with Judah, Coach Riley, and Honesty. King was very solemn, wiping away her tears.

"Should I tell him myself? Or should I let him tell Ju first?" Mya asked King.

"I think you need to take this to the Lord in prayer. Then allow him to direct you as to how and if you should bring this to Judah's attention." For a minute, Mya sat there silently.

"King, would you pray with me?" she asked.

"Yes," he answered without hesitation. "Father, in your word you said that all things work together for good to them that love God. I believe Sister Mya loves you with all her heart, soul, and might. I ask that you give Sister Mya wisdom and knowledge in handling this situation according to your will. In Jesus name I pray."

"Amen," they both said simultaneously. Even after they had said Amen, Mya didn't move out of his embrace; her head remained rested against his chest. To her, his heartbeat was so soothing. She leaned up slightly to make eye contact with him. "How is it that you always manage to be there when I need someone the most?"

"It is the grace of God. God has a way of orchestrating things."

"Thank you." Mya stared into King's eyes. "Thank you." One tear streamed down her cheek. He wiped it away. For some reason, Mya couldn't break her stare. It was as if he was searching her soul.

"What do you see?" she genuinely asked. "What do you see when you look at me?"

"I see the most beautiful, sweet-spirited woman. One so full of love and strength. A woman who deserves to be loved every second of the day. One whom God shall use to save souls. I see a wife and mother of children of integrity. I see the essence of my existence." Mya leaned in to close the gap between her and King, then gently began kissing him. It was as if she was drawn to him by a force stronger than her own. He had never felt a set of lips as perfect as hers felt against his. For that moment she had no concerns. No one existed but the two of them. By the time she realized she was kissing this man in a way that she had never kissed Sway, they were pulling apart. Mya refused to make eye contact, ashamed of her actions.

"Shhh, don't do that." King was the first to speak. "Don't feel ashamed." Mya wondered how he knew she felt that way. "King, I apol—"

"Don't apologize," he cut her off. "Because I won't. I could spend the rest of my life experiencing that feeling. But that's just my flesh talking. I apologize."

Mya tried to hide the smile that covered her face. She'd never felt such peace as she was experiencing right now in this man's arms.

"How about you join me for lunch?" King extended the invitation as he opened the car door before he got out. It was apparent his question caught her off guard by the way her head snapped around to face him, but once she discovered he was staring directly at her, she immediately turned her head.

"So that's a no?" King further inquired.

"No, I didn't say that," she blurted out, meeting his stare. She couldn't look at him for long. Something about the way he looked at her made her hands clammy and her armpits wet. There seemed to be some form of admiration for her in his eyes. *But how can that be, being that he barely knows me?* she reasoned.

"Then what are you saying?" He watched her as she nervously tapped her thumbs together. Mya wore a grin she kept reminding herself to stop doing. He loved to see her smile. It made the day seem so much brighter. He also loved the way her hair danced along her long beautiful neck.

"I don't see what's wrong with two people having lunch together.

I'm not asking you out on a date," he clarified, sensing her internal struggle.

"You're right," she finally agreed. "I would love to have lunch with you. What would be a good day?" She pulled out her phone so she could mark it as a reminder.

"How about now?" King stated. "Follow me," he instructed her. He got out of her car and inside his before she had time to even reply.

Thirty minutes later, she pulled into a Long Horn steak house parking lot, right behind him. She swiftly finger-combed her hair and touched up her lipstick before he approached her car. Without hesitation, he opened her car door and extended his hand to assist her in getting out.

Sway never did such a thing. Mya made a mental note as she hit her car alarm button, then dropped her keys in her handbag.

They were escorted to a table toward the back of the room, next to the window. The dim light and tinted windows were a contrast to the bright, shining sun outside. The wooden chairs, tables, and walls made the room seem more rustic, as if they were in a cabin. Jazz music played softly. Mya sat across from King waiting to order, trying not to stare into his eyes. This lunch arrangement was beginning to feel like an evening out with one of the most handsome men in the city! In the state! She gladly welcomed the distraction of their server, who set two waters on the table and proceeded to take their order.

"So tell me a little about yourself," she said as soon as the server left the table. She had been curious long enough!

"What is it that you would like to know?" King responded, promptly setting his glass of ice water down and directing all his attention on her.

"Who are you? . . . How did you become so close to the Lord? Like, how did you get to a place of being so sensitive to His voice? Where were you born? Do you have kids? Are you involved . . . you know?" She sighed as if it took her a lot of nerve to get those questions out. He chuckled, apparently aware of her apprehension.

He leaned forward and rested his elbows on the table as he stared into her eyes. To her he had the most beautiful smile. Mya tried not to squirm beneath his stare, so she just reached for her glass of water.

"I grew up in East Point, Atlanta. Raised in a single parent home. My father did his best by me . . . My mother lost her life having me."

"I'm so sorry," Mya sincerely confessed.

"It's all good. She chose my life over her own. Everyone says I resemble her a lot."

"What do you think?"

"I can see why they say that." He grinned a little. Her heart raced. "I'll have to show you some pictures of her one day, and you can tell me what you think."

"I would like that." She returned his smile.

"So one day during my last year in high school, I was walking up the street headed home from track practice. My homie Will stayed around the corner, and we both ran track, so I would catch a ride to his house and walk the short distance home. This particular evening we had stayed at the school a little longer because we had regionals coming up, and it was dark outside. Well, I didn't think much of this smoky gray Ford Taurus that passed me until I was walking up my driveway, and it pulled up behind me. I looked back but kept walking, thinking my dad was having company.

"'What you doing, boy?' I heard a Caucasian male ask me. I looked back and noticed he was walking up my driveway.

'I'm going home.' I stopped and turned around, still holding my book bag on my shoulder. 'What it look like?' I answered defensively. Then I turned back, walking from my driveway to my front door.

'This ain't none of your house, boy. You best get from around here,' he threatened.

"It pissed me off immediately, because I knew I wasn't doing anything. I started to reach for my phone in my pocket, but I figured he would think I was trying to reach for something else. Instead, I started yelling for my father and tried to speed up. Dude came up behind me and put me in a chokehold. I supposed he assumed because I was a teenager that he would just manhandle me. I made a few attempts to get him to release me, and when that didn't work . . ." King stopped talking and looked away for the first time.

Mya didn't understand why, but she felt connected to this man. She could feel the remorse building in his chest. She extended her hands across the table and took his hands into hers. The warmth of her touch got his attention. They locked eyes. Her heart melted as he took in a deep breath of air and exhaled as tears filled his eyes. He pulled his hands away and coughed, pushing his emotions back. Mya, however, allowed a few tears to fall from her eyes. She didn't know why, but she began to pray for his strength and healing. Still she wondered, *Why did he choose to share that? And what had he done?*

Train up a child in the way he should go: and when he is old, he will not depart from it.

Proverbs 22:6 (KJV)

CHAPTER 12

Winn Dixie (2:57 p.m.)

I can't believe I kissed that man, and what's worse—I enjoyed it!

At the entrance, Mya pulled into the grocery store parking lot, still surprised by her behavior, even feeling a little ashamed. *Sway practically had to force me to kiss him. Hmph! I didn't think I was the kissing type!*

"Mya, you should be ashamed of yourself!" she spoke to her reflection in the mirror, unable to wipe that silly grin off her face. She checked to see if she had any trail of dried tears, or if a strand of hair was out of place. "I will never allow that to happen again. Sway wouldn't stand a chance if I found out he had done something like that," she said, as if to convince herself. *Lord, I just feel like a different woman when I'm with King.* There was no room for denial; she felt beautiful and happy. Even though her life was surrounded by chaos, she found herself floating on clouds of bliss where only King alone managed to take her. It was like wind beneath her feet, and he was the force that lifted her.

She gathered her mini-handbag, cell phone, and car keys and exited her car, making sure her burgundy sweater dress was not raised in the back. Her cell phone started ringing as soon as she locked the door.

"Hey, auntie's favorite baby," Mya answered.

"What's up? Where are you?" Judah asked.

"About to step inside the grocery store. Where do you need me to be?"

"Right where you are. I was just calling because you were on my mind. I was in class earlier, and I just felt frantic—like I really needed to talk to you. I can't explain it; it was like maybe you were upset or not feeling well."

Mya immediately began thinking about Coach Riley. Her stomach started turning. "Well, actually I had met someone for lunch, and they kind of took me by surprise."

"Really?"

"Yeah."

"Who was it?"

Mya wasn't sure how she should answer. She didn't want to lie, especially not to Judah. She grew up believing that when you told one lie, you always had to tell another one to cover that one up. So the truth always worked out better. But this was a very sensitive situation.

"You know, Ju, just to be honest with you. I really don't want to get into that right now. Maybe later tonight we can talk about it. How does that sound?"

"It was that bad, huh?"

"I suppose it's safe to say that."

"Well, just tell me this. Was it Sway? Because I promise he got one time to—"

"Judah," she interrupted him. "Baby, chill with all that. It was not him. Baby, violence is not the answer to everything. You have to learn to allow God to avenge you."

"It may not be your answer, but it has always gotten my point across. Don't nobody put fear in my heart. I don't have time to waste, waiting for somebody to do what I can do."

"Lord, have mercy. Child, when will you understand that some battles aren't worth trying to fight? You have too much to jeopardize, to be getting caught up in some nonsense."

"I'm just saying—"

"I'm grown, Judah. I can carry my own weight."

"That may be true, but I despise cowards who try to break a strong black woman down, so he'll feel better about himself. Who chooses to hit women, thinking he can keep her through fear instead of stepping up and being the man she deserves. They make my skin crawl, and I put this on Big Momma's dead body. If I get a whiff that, that dude is coming incorrect, I'm going to set him straight."

Mya was at a loss for words. Here, her nephew was only seventeen years old, and he could see what she still lacked. Her nephew's theory made so much sense to her. Was Sway really trying to break her, or was the drama a desperate attempt to keep her?

"Very well then. Thank God I don't have to worry about any of that." She hoped Judah was buying into her response. He had no idea how badly she wanted to change the subject. "So what would you like for dinner?" Mya grabbed a shopping cart and headed toward the produce section.

"Anything I want, or something simple?"

"What kind of question is that? My baby gets whatever he wants."

"That's what's up!" She could hear the gratitude in his voice. "For real, Aunt Mya, a brother want some meatloaf."

"You got it."

"Ohh, can you make it with that thick tomato paste you bake over the top?"

"The paste that I put bacon all over as well?"

"Yes! Just like that. I love when you fix it that way. Straight up!"

"You got it. Anything for you!"

"Man . . . Aunt Mya, I love you. I don't know what I would do without you."

"If I could change anything about our life, it would only be to spare you of this pain you've had to go through. I don't know what sick individual is the cause for your mother being absent in our lives all these years, but I want you to know she loved you! She told me giving birth to you was her greatest accomplishment. Y'all were inseparable! I know she didn't just abandon you, she loved you more than life itself. And I'm convinced she would be so proud of the young man you have become."

"You think so, Aunt Mya?" Judah sincerely questioned.

"I know so . . . and I want you to know, no matter what, I am proud of you and you will always be my baby."

Mya pulled into the garage, hoping someone would be home to help her bring in the groceries, but by the time she got everything in, she found herself grateful she was alone. The Holy Spirit was pressing her to pray. However, she anticipated getting dinner started first. She knew better than to miss out on God's invitation to being in His presence. Besides, she needed his guidance concerning Coach Riley and Judah. She looked around the kitchen after putting away everything that needed to be refrigerated. "Lord, you'll just have to help me make up for lost time." She hurried into her office and turned on some soft music, took off her two-inch booties, and postured herself before the Lord.

"Oh, mighty God, my father who understands me. I have need of Thee," Mya confessed as she lay on the floor, before the Lord. Thoughts of Judah's possible confusion and pain flooded her mind.

"Lord, I don't know what to do . . . what to believe, and if I should even tell Ju? How can somebody be so selfish to allow months . . . years to go by without even saying a word? Who holds a secret as such? Why didn't he think about what Ju felt, not knowing either one of his parents?" She continued to unburden herself, unable to keep a handle on the rage building inside. She wanted Coach Riley to hurt like she had to witness Judah hurting. Maybe she should be the one to make sure Coach Riley knew that kind of pain.

Of course, thoughts of her chemistry with King came to mind, but she didn't have the courage to address that to God. But at some point, a conversation would have to happen.

Love is patient and kind, not jealous, not boastful, not proud, rude or selfish, not easily angered, and it keeps no record of wrongs.

1 Corinthians 13:4-5 (CJB)

CHAPTER 13

Mya's residence (5:45 p.m.)

"Oh! It smells good in here." Mya heard Sway say as he walked in the front door. He snatched her from her thoughts of King's touch.

"Wow, somebody is home early."

"As good as you look, and the way you put it down in the kitchen, I can't believe that you're surprised." Sway hovered over her from behind, placing soft kisses on her cheek. His athletic physique was like icing on the cake. She loved when he stood over her like that. It made her feel protected. A boyfriend was the only male figure she'd ever had in her life. Her memories of her dad were few and far between. But one that remained in the forefront of her mind when relating to him is: he left her mom to raise two girls alone.

"Baby, you had this dress on all day?" Sway stepped back to get a full view.

"Yeah, you don't like it?" she questioned, suddenly feeling self-conscious. "I know I usually would've freshened up and changed, but baby, I had a really hectic afternoon," she explained as fast as she could.

"Nah, baby, it's cool. It's just that you look"—he licked his lips, closing in the space between them—"like something to eat." He held her by the small of her back.

"Sway, don't start acting out." She patted his chest playfully. "I got you some scalloped potatoes, meatloaf, fried cabbage, dinner rolls with that sweet butter you love and some peach cobbler for dinner." She extended her neck to peck him on the lips, and then attempted to break his embrace, not wanting to give opportunity for him to get aroused.

"Where you going so fast?" He tightened his embrace.

"To check on your food in the oven."

"It can wait. I just want to hold you for a second. When was the last time that I told you, you were beautiful, and that you are good to me? I can't believe just how much you love me. There is no other woman for me. You make coming home something I look forward to. Mya, I love you. You are all I got, and to me that's the world."

Mya stood there in his embrace, listening to him profess his love for her. His eyes appeared sincere, his voice calm and genuine, and the stroke of his hand across her back, reassuring. Was this the man she had fallen in love with? Had he finally realized she loved him? So many questions raced through her mind. How was it just days ago that she longed to hear him say what he just did, but today she found herself wondering of what value it all meant to her. It was obvious he was waiting for her to respond.

"You know what? Your love is like ecstasy. Sometimes, I feel so high I don't want to come down. Then without warning, I feel like a wreck. Wondering if somehow I've overdosed because I can't get enough of you." Sway's eyebrows narrowed. He tilted his head slightly to the right, trying to decide how to interpret her response. Mya couldn't believe she actually had the nerve to tell Sway how she felt, especially to his face. Her truths came rushing out like a mighty river. "I suppose sometimes I'm hurt, but I remain by your side through thick or thin, because I do truly love you." Mya took Sway's hand into hers and placed it on her heart. "My love for you motivates me to love you like you've never been loved before." She cuffed his face in her hands and gently stroked him. "Every day, I strive to love you in such a way that you have no need to question where you stand in my heart."

"Mya, I want to be the man you deserve," Sway genuinely admitted.

"Baby, we first have to know who we are and what's God's purpose for our lives, and then we can shine to our capacity. God is always willing and able to show himself to you. All you have to do is ask."

When Sway didn't respond, she knew he was contemplating her remark. So she rested her head on his chest and held him, wanting to comfort him. He wrapped his arms around her, holding her securely as he whispered, "I thank God for you." Mya couldn't help but smile.

"Ay yo, Aunt Mya! You got it smelling good up in here!" Judah said as he headed toward the kitchen, pulling Sway from his serene embrace with Mya.

She practically jumped out of his arms. "You and this boy are so greedy!" Mya didn't realize she was the only one laughing. "Hey, Auntie's baby." She couldn't deny her excitement. "Boy, I really missed you today."

"Boy? Now you know you're looking at a grown man." Judah wrapped Mya in his arms. "Yeah, I know you see them muscles." He released her from his embrace and flexed his arms.

"Yeah, you're working with a lil something, but you gon' have to work out a lil more to catch up with my baby." Mya smiled, looking from Judah to Sway. Mya might have been blindsided, but Judah was definitely aware that his presence wasn't as welcomed as his aunt would have liked; Sway glared at him as if he had just spilled a drink on his fresh white Armani suit or bumped him repeatedly in the club. If looks could kill, Judah would be laid out on the floor. Judah kept his eyes locked on Sway.

"What's up, Sway?" Judah openly challenged him.

"Oh, I got to check on the food in the oven." Mya rushed to the oven, still oblivious to the building tension between Sway and Judah.

Sway never answered Judah. Instead he walked over to Mya at the stove and kissed the back of her head. "I'm gonna go freshen up. I'll be back." He left the two of them in the kitchen.

"Ju, you know we have to go get you a new pair of cleats. Next Friday is your big day. How do you feel?" Mya asked as she placed her final touches on the meatloaf, intending to join Judah, sitting at the kitchen island. When she didn't get a response, she turned to face him.

"Ju, did you hear what I said?"

He nodded yes.

"So why didn't you answer? What's the matter?" Mya's mind immediately went back to her conversation with Coach Riley. She couldn't help but wonder if he had spoken with Judah. She suddenly felt herself getting hot. The thing that troubled her most was that she couldn't interpret Judah's expression. She turned the oven down, put the meatloaf back in, glazed the peach cobbler with butter, and hurried next to her nephew. He wasted no time opening up once she sat next to him.

"Aunt Mya, I'm not feeling your boy."

Mya reached for his hand and took it in hers. "Baby, what do you mean?"

"Dude obviously got a problem with you setting your attention on me. He's jealous of me, or jealous of our relationship."

"Ju, baby. Don't say that. Sway adores you."

"Sway *used* to adore me. When was the last time he and I hung out? When you came in from Bible Study that night, where was he? Come on now, Auntie, open your eyes. Pay attention to him when I'm present. You know me better than anyone else. I'm not going to lie."

Mya sat there thinking about the likelihood of it all. It shouldn't have been a surprise to her that Sway was acting different with Judah, since he had also been acting different toward her. But things were getting back to normal, or were they? She looked into Judah's eyes, hoping to discover an answer. She knew he would have never mentioned it, unless he knew without a doubt that something was wrong.

"Judah, I know you wouldn't lie to me. It's just . . . he's been going through a lot. And I'm sure he didn't mean—"

"Aunt Mya." Judah cut her off. "Don't make excuses for him. Sway and I are cool. He was there for me when I needed him back in the day, but I'm a man, and I won't be disrespected, nor will I sit back and let him disrespect you."

"Judah, I'm saying . . ."

"*That's* the problem." He wouldn't let her get a word in. "You're doing too much talking and not enough observing. Something ain't right witcha' man, and you need to get down to the bottom of it." Judah words hit in the pit of her stomach like a ton of bricks. His remarks seemed to be more of a warning than an opinion.

"I'll tell you what. I'll put forth more effort to be aware, but let's get one thing straight, dear. I love him, Judah. You know I do. But I won't allow anyone to come between us." She held his face with one hand, and she gripped his hand with the other. "I love you. I'll lay down my life for you. Do you hear me, Judah?" Mya wasn't sure just how profound that remark was, with all she might have to face, but she had no intentions on taking it back. Judah was the only family she had left, and nothing or no one was worth that.

"Not only do I hear you, but I feel you. I'll get rid of any problem that you have. I'll do what you don't have the heart to do."

Cold chills ran down Mya's back. "Judah, don't talk like that." Mya studied her nephew's face. His words troubled her. She knew immediately she'd better start some serious interceding, or things could—no would—turn for the worst. She searched for the words to say, but before she found them, the cordless phone at the end of the counter began to ring.

"I'll get it," Mya said as she sprinted across the room. *I'll do what you don't have the heart to do.* Judah's words replayed in her mind. She knew Judah well enough to know there was a strong chance he had a purpose and possibly a plan behind his statement, and only God alone could fix the situation.

101

Mya felt as if her ears were about to blow smoke when the caller identified himself as Coach Riley.

"Right now is not a good time." It was nearly time for dinner. She spoke barely above a whisper, looking over her shoulder at Judah, who was seemingly aware of the change in her disposition.

"Mya, I was hoping you would allow me to join you all for dinner so we could speak with my son. I'm not too far from your house now."

"Your son?"—Mya had to catch herself. "Are you serious!" It was taking everything within her not to go off on him, but what was even worse, she recalled vowing to God only hours ago to remain open-minded and to walk in love. However, dealing with the present situation, that was the last thing she felt like doing. She took a deep breath and wanted to cry. The burden of not being able to curse him out, or simply hang up the phone in his face was more than she hoped it would be.

"Who is that?" Judah asked, observing her trying to stay still. She turned her focus away from Judah, hoping to buy enough time to get off the phone. Mya lowered her voice to a whisper.

"This is not the time, and before you do any more talking, you need to produce a DNA test. Just because you say you are . . ." Mya didn't even want to say it, just in case he could hear. "Get the test, then we'll talk. I need to talk to him first," Mya told Coach Riley.

"Believe me, I'm not trying to tell you how to handle this. I'm just asking you to not push me out. Have I not wasted enough time?" Mya watched as Judah got up and walked over to the caller ID.

"What does Coach want?" Judah asked.

"Baby, give me a second please," Mya said, putting her mouth back to the phone.

"What do you expect? You can't just drop something like this on anyone. I need proof first, and then I'll consider everything else," Mya said, choosing her words to Coach Riley carefully.

"What proof do you need to consider? He better not be coming at you incorrect," Judah blurted.

"That's what I'm saying. What do you need to consider? And who are you on the phone with?" Sway walked into the kitchen unexpectedly. Mya felt a meltdown coming on as she looked from Judah to Sway.

"Coach Riley," she answered Sway.

She then addressed Coach Riley. "I don't mean to sound unsympathetic, but I have to go. I apologize for not being able to assist you at the moment."

"Don't try to clean up y'all conversation now. Just a second ago you were whispering and being all secretive. Now you want to talk so I can hear you. You must think I'm lame." Sway's tone suggested he thought the conversation was less than civil.

"Mya, are you okay? Is that Jermal that I hear in the background? I hope this call isn't creating a problem," Coach Riley stated, apologetically.

"Calling me earlier asking me to go to lunch with you to meet him. That's probably why you got that dress on. Did you get an eyeful, Coach?" Sway yelled into the receiver.

"Coach is who had you so upset earlier?" Judah asked. "And now he's calling here?"

Mya couldn't say a word. She just wished somehow she could get away from the entire situation. She wished she had time to go pray, or know what to say. That God just magically calmed the storm that was surfacing.

"Mya, you've got one more time to act like you don't hear me. Why do you need him to give you more time?" Sway invaded her space. Mya felt as if she was at her breaking point.

"Sway, now is not the time. I'll discuss this with you later," Mya responded, matching his tone.

"No, we're going to talk about this now!" Sway grabbed Mya by her wrist as she attempted to walk away.

"You might want to let her go, homeboy." Judah didn't miss a beat.

"Judah, this don't have nothing to do with you, homeboy. Step aside," Sway replied.

Unfazed, Judah moved in closer. "I said let my auntie go."

"Y'all, please don't do this," Mya began pleading.

"Boy, you messin' around in grown folks business. If you want to act like a man, I'm gon' treat you like one," Sway threatened.

"All I know is you better let Aunt Mya go," Judah responded.

Sway used the hand he held Mya by, and pushed her as hard as he could. She lost her balance and fell. Judah wasted no time landing a clean uppercut to Sway's stomach, then he kneed him in the head. Sway got right back with him, but a knot formed in the center of his forehead. Judah's nose was bloodied from Sway's right hand jab. It didn't deter Judah from counterpunching each of Sway's forceful blows. Blood sprayed from Sway's mouth after Judah hit him with a quick mouth shot.

"Oh my God! Y'all *stop!*" Mya screamed. "God please!" She crawled the short distance to the phone that skidded away as she fell. She was trying to call the police when she realized Riley was still on the phone.

"Hello? Hello?" Mya panicked. She saw blood, and wasn't sure where it had come from.

"Mya, calm down. I'm almost there. I'm coming. Call the police." Coach tried to comfort her.

"Oh my God! He's bleeding!"

"Call the police, Mya!"

Mya didn't have time to call the police; she had to get this man off her baby. "Sway, *stop!*" Both men were locked up on the floor, wrestling more so than fighting. "Sway, if you love me, stop it!" Mya screamed at the top of her lungs. She ran over and started trying to pull Sway away from Judah.

"Mya, get off of me!" Sway demanded. Mya wouldn't let up. She was hitting him and yanking at the same time.

Coach Riley was at the front door, banging. Mya didn't want to leave them, but it was clear she needed some help. She ran and opened the door and took off back down the hall where they were still tussling on the floor. Coach Riley calmly walked up to Sway and put a pistol to his head.

"Get off my son!" Sway didn't move; Coach Riley put one in the chamber.

"Jermal, if you're as smart as you think you are, get off of my son!" The impact of what he said hit everyone. Mya froze. Judah looked to her as if he was asking what Coach Riley meant.

"Mya, this wasn't my fault," Sway said, as he stood to his feet.

"Get out of my house!" Mya demanded as she tended to her nephew, who was now on his feet. "Are you okay, baby?" she asked him. Judah looked at her lovingly, but she could see the pain in his eyes. Mya looked at Judah, then at Coach Riley who still pointed the pistol at Sway.

"So you just gon' put me out like this? Mya, if you love me, you wouldn't do me—"

"Sway," she interrupted him. "Get out! I won't say it again." Mya was pissed, disgusted even, and had no intentions of repeating herself.

Sway looked around at the mess they had made: a chair broken, a place in the wall caved in, blood on the floor, then at Coach Riley, suddenly looking like an older version of Judah.

"You heard the lady." Coach Riley pointed toward the door, then escorted Sway out.

"Mya, we can't end like this," was the last thing she heard Sway say.

She would cry, but not now. There was another issue at stake. She looked into Judah's eyes, who now looked so vulnerable.

"Baby, I'm sorry. I'm so sorry." Mya wrapped her arms around Judah, who rested his head on top of hers. "He just told me today. I wanted to make sure there was some truth to this before we even discussed it." Mya felt the need to explain herself. She could feel the weight of his heaviness as Coach Riley walked back into the kitchen.

"Yo, you a coward!" Judah said.

"Son, listen." Coach Riley took a step closer

"My name's Judah to you! You don't have the right to call me that."

"I know you're angry, but I need you to at least hear me out." Riley made another attempt.

"You don't know what I feel, so don't start acting like you do. If you

105

did, you would have been manned up. Dude, you been pretending like you give a—"

"Judah!" Mya interrupted him. "Baby, calm down." He wore that same look in his eyes, as he had just minutes ago, right before he swung on Sway.

"Auntie, this dude been gone my whole life, and now he want me to hear him out!"

"I know, baby . . . just . . ." Mya felt herself about to break down. "Just go upstairs and clean yourself up. Can you do that for me? Let me talk to Coach Riley alone." Mya watched as Judah disappeared upstairs. Her cell phone rang. She didn't have to check the number to know it was Sway.

But I say unto you, That ye resist not evil: but whosoever shall smite thee on thy right cheek, turn to him the other also

Matthew 5:39 (KJV)

CHAPTER 14

Mya's residence (6:18 p.m.)

"Well, looks like you ended up joining us for dinner anyways, huh?" Mya said to Coach Riley as she shifted her weight nervously from one foot to the other. The locksmith gathered up his tools and handed her the new house keys.

"Yeah, I wish it was under different circumstances, but I suppose things have a way of working themselves out." Riley guided Mya back inside, then closed the door behind them.

Things have a way of working themselves out. Hmm . . . God has a way of carrying out his will, Mya thought. She probably would never admit it, but she was grateful for Coach Riley being there. She wasn't sure just how things would have ended if he hadn't come, even more if he hadn't put his own life on the line. Sway was known on the street for being top dog. "Lord, I know it was you who sent this man for this appointed time. Thank you!"

"All right now, Mya. Now that you got your new keys, don't forget to change your alarm code," Coach Riley instructed."

Mya stood in the foyer of her house trying to decide what to do next. Judah descended the stairs. They locked eyes. Judah had sustained a few cuts to his cheek and his nose was a little red. *God, I just ask that you come to sit amongst us. I ask that your hand be upon us this night*, she prayed as she met Judah at the last stair where she wrapped her arm around him. They then headed for the living room.

"Thank you, Lord," Mya said. Immediately, God brought back to her remembrance how willing Judah was to her request to go shower and give her a few minutes to get things cleaned up and situated downstairs. God was showing her that he was in control.

"What was that?" Judah asked.

"Oh, you heard me?"

He nodded yeah.

"I just thanked the Lord."

"For what?" he asked, more out of curiosity than sarcastically.

"For being who He is, and having his hand upon us."

She set the table at 7:40 p.m., grateful for the temporary distraction. Judah normally sat at the head of the table, but tonight he settled for the seat next to Mya's. Coach Riley did not want to imply he was trying to run anything, so he sat across from them. Somehow, a single tear escaped Mya's eye. She thought about how hours ago, this same meal had brought so much joy.

Judah reached over and wiped her tear away. They bowed their heads as Mya prayed.

"So, Coach Riley, the mic is in your hand. Do you have something you would like to tell me?" There was definitely a bite to Judah's question. Mya wasn't surprised though. She remember how she had felt.

"Ju," he started.

"Judah to you. My friends call me Ju." Mya knew he wasn't going to make this easy for Coach Riley. She placed her hand on top of his to bring him some form of comfort. He looked as if he was trying to pierce a hole through Riley.

"Judah, your mother and I started dating back when I was in high school. I met her back at the theatre when New Jack City was popular. Starter jackets and herringbone chains were the thing to wear. Yeah, that was a long time ago. I can remember that night so clearly; she was with her girlfriends. She was tip-toeing out to go get some more nachos, and I practically ran into Honesty. I almost spilled cheese all over her cashmere sweater. It was some peach color. Anyway, I was so humiliated. There I was, standing in front of the most beautiful, chocolate girl I had ever laid eyes on. For a second, I couldn't even put my mack down. She was so cool about it. She was like 'That was so nice of you to go out and get these for me. Thank you.' Then she took my nachos and started to strut her stuff back to her seat. Boy, your mother was wearing them j—. . . And she had heart . . . Like you do. Not easily intimidated, of course, you know I was running to catch up with her. I missed most of the movie, trying to watch her from a distance. What I loved most about her was she was unpredictable. You never knew what Honesty would do next." Riley smiled at the memory. "She was something else; she had this way of setting the atmosphere."

"Okay, thank you for taking me down memory lane, but how does that clarify you being up in my house saying that I am your son?" Judah showed no emotion. Riley looked over at Mya, barely moving her head. She gestured for him to continue.

"Honesty and I ended up making things official. We had already been together a few months before she told me the truth about being two years younger than the age she claimed in the beginning. By then, my feelings for her were serious, and I was willing to wait until she was of age, but too many opportunities of being alone, too much time available to count, got me in a whole lot of trouble. Needless to say, I was her first, and based on how she put it, her only. She and I were pretty much a secret because of the age difference, well that was only until other dudes started to get at her. And I had to make my presence known, to put a few of them in their place. I mean, we both were young and wild. Not really thinking about the consequences of our actions. We were having fun. After I graduated, Honesty found out she was pregnant. To me, this was a perfect opportunity to man up and ask Ms. Pearl if she would give me permission to marry your mother. Even if she said I had to wait, at least she would have allowed me to be active in you all's lives. I was in love with her and proud to be a dad. But Honesty preferred that I remain a secret. She didn't even want to be seen in public together . . . not even around you, Mya. Truthfully, on the other hand, I was in love."

Something just doesn't sound right. Why would a young, beautiful girl not want everyone to see her handsome guy? Mya sat on the edge of her chair.

"I mean, let's be serious. You are a child molester," Judah bluntly stated.

"That's where you got it twisted. I was not and never will be a child molester. I thought she was seventeen. That's what she told me. There was no mistake about that. When I learned the truth it was too late. I was in love with your mother. I would do it again if I could. The only thing I would change is allowing Honesty to talk me into agreeing to go away to college with the intentions of getting established so one day I could provide for you two."

"So you're saying your decision to leave us was my mother's idea?"

"That's exactly what I'm saying. I had a scholarship to play football, and Honesty told me to take it. We agreed to spend time back home together, and I would send money as much as possible. We had a three to four-year plan mapped out, and then I would send for y'all."

"So when things changed and my mother came up missing, what did you do?" Coach Riley looked like he wasn't sure of an answer.

"What do you mean *what did I do*?"

"Did you try to contact my family? Did you think for a second, my son needs me? Did you think how I would feel growing up without my mother and father? Did you think about how I must have felt like I wasn't good enough to be loved? Or how I must've felt never being able to ask my father to teach me how to fight, or how to handle a crush? What to do when my heart is broken? Or how about how to sex my lady?" Judah stood to his feet. "Were you so wrapped up in your life that you couldn't think about me?" He punched himself in the chest, emphasizing his point.

"Actually, Judah, I did." Coach Riley's voice was calm and even-toned. I sent Ms. Pearl several money orders addressed to her with made-up names because I did think about your well-being. The only reason I didn't come back was because word on the streets had me believing that I was a suspect in Honesty's disappearance. I wasn't trying to go to jail, or get killed. As the years passed, the loss of her and what seemed to be you as well, was too much. I lost focus, started partying. Taking pro football as a joke, gambling, sleeping with different women, trying to fill a void that I discovered after many years that only you could fill. Finally, someone brought me before the Lord, and that's when I began to believe that somehow I would have my son again. Judah, I wouldn't ever marry another woman and have children because I felt like I didn't deserve another child, when I haven't seen about the one I already have."

"Coach Riley, I remember Big Momma getting those money orders in the mail. They always came when she needed them too. She would always say, 'God always supplies our every need. We just have to trust Him,'" Mya said, remembering how Big Momma would suddenly get money orders in the mail for three to five hundred dollars. "She thought they might have been coming from Honesty."

He looked a little relieved. "Judah, the only reason I didn't come back sooner was because I didn't feel like I was the kind of man you could look up to."

Judah pressed his lips together, not buying Riley's excuse. "Nah, you didn't come back because you're a coward. For almost two years you've been in my life acting like my mentor because you didn't have the heart to tell me: 'I am the sucka who ditched you, left you in pain, and acted like you didn't exist!'"

"Judah, I can't change my mistakes. I didn't think about the overall effect. But I'm here now, I want to be a part of your life."

"Do I look like I care?" Judah was yelling at this point. "Do I look like I care about what you want? Am I supposed to take your word and trust you?"

"Judah, I love you. I love you with everything that I am."

Bam!

Judah swung and punched Coach Riley in the mouth, knocking him out of his chair and onto the floor. "Coward! You don't know what love is!" he yelled from across the table. Coach Riley quickly gathered himself and stood. He knew he deserved every blow.

Mya jumped up. "Ju, baby. Calm down! You're better than this! Calm down!" She stood in front of Judah, trying to keep him from going around the table to get to Coach Riley.

"Aunt Mya, get out of my way! Everybody's running around talking about they love me and they love you, but look how they treat us. This love!" He pointed at Mya, directing his remark toward Coach Riley. "This is love! She been down with me from day one. Sacrificed her own life for mine. She was there when I couldn't sleep from the heartache you left me with. You sitting up in here claiming you love me."

"Judah, calm down, baby. Please!" Mya wrapped herself around him, but it was no use; he broke away and managed to get closer to Riley.

Bam!

He made body contact again. Mya ducked to avoid getting hit.

"It's cool, Mya. Let him get it out."

Bam!

He punched him again. Then Coach Riley locked up with him, controlling Judah's ability to hit him hard.

"It's okay, Judah. Get it out. Get it out, son. I'm not leaving this time. I promise you I'm not leaving."

The sight of it was all too much. Judah just kept punching until he was out of breath. Through sweat and tears, he kept repeating, "You should've been there!" Coach Riley wrapped his arms around Judah as tight as he could. Judah's body shook from the impact of his sobbing. Finally, he hugged Coach Riley. Mya stood only inches away from the two, trying to keep her composure. The sight of her nephew in such a state made her feel helpless, but the possibility that Judah was going through this and the possibility of Coach Riley not being his father, infuriated her. Now as she stood there observing them, she was willing to admit that there was some resemblance, but she needed proof. Judah needed proof.

"Judah, come here. Baby, come here." Mya set her attention back on Judah and extended her arms to embrace him. It took a few seconds for him to compose himself, but slowly he pulled away from Coach Riley and stepped into her embrace. She prayed silently, caressing his back until his weeping ceased.

When they finally made eye contact, she intertwined her arm with his and led him upstairs to his room, leaving Coach Riley alone.

"Do you want to talk?" Mya asked, sitting on the edge of the bed. Judah stretched out on his back, grabbing his iPod.

"Not really," he replied, still sounding full of emotion.

"All right, I'll be back to check on you, okay?" Mya replied.

He nodded yes. She leaned over and kissed his forehead. "Baby, I want you to keep in mind that we still have to get a DNA test done to confirm his allegations."

Judah opened his mouth to speak but nothing came out. Mya reasoned if she should let his response go, or try to pull it out of him. Judah's brows narrowed, and his lips began to quiver. Without his consent, she crawled in bed next to him and put an arm around him. They lay there in silence for a few minutes.

"So . . . you . . . you don't think he's my dad?" Judah finally broke the silence.

"Honestly, I don't know what I think right now, but we must be one hundred percent sure before we completely open the door for that possibility. You just never know about people these days." She raised up to rest her weight on her elbow. "What I do know is, I'm going to be his worst nightmare if he's on some BS and isn't your father!"

"I know what you mean," Judah stated, and then drifted off into his own head space.

"If you're up for it, we can set up an appointment to get this test done, or possibly find a place that will permit y'all to just walk in."

"Yeah, I want to get that ASAP."

Thirty minutes later, Mya walked back down the stairs and found Coach Riley in her kitchen finishing up the dishes they had just used.

"So . . . is Judah all right?" Coach Riley asked with his back to Mya, catching her by surprise.

"He's listening to his music." Mya sucked her teeth. She knew she should have been more mature about the situation, but she just couldn't accept that Coach Riley was really that concerned about her nephew. "What do you want to do, Riley?" she blurted out before she knew it.

"What do you mean?" he asked, setting the last plate in the dish rack. He grabbed the dry cloth to dry his hands and turned to face her. Just looking at his pitiful sad eyes, and droopy bottom lip, cut her tolerance short. She was not in the mood.

"What the heck you looking down and out about? *You're* the one who caused all these things!" She got up in his face. "I could slap the breath out of you right now." Her mind raced with how fast things had just spiraled out of control. Her cell phone rang again from inside of her purse. She had placed it on the countertop next to the microwave, when she came in with the groceries.

"Not now, Sway!" she shouted, knowing it was him. Mya set her annoyance back on Coach Riley, who just stood there looking pathetic. "Let me tell you how this is going down. First thing in the morning, you are going to call and set up an appointment for a DNA test."

"Mya, I would love to, that's the least I can do. Is there anything else you recommend I do?"

Ring, ring, ring.

Before Maya could answer, the house phone began to ring. Mya looked at Coach Riley and thought about Judah answering it. She ran over to the same phone that broke out the war in this same room just hours ago.

"Hello!" she yelled.

"Baby, I need to talk to you," Sway said on the opposite end.

"Sway, I don't have time for this right now." She hung up.

116

"Now, back to what I was saying." She directed her attention back to Coach Riley. "If this test comes back that you are not his—"

The phone rang again. He was really beginning to piss her off.

"What!" she snapped into the phone.

"I need to talk to you, Mya. We're supposed to be family."

"Jermal, you put your hands on a minor . . . You disrespected my home! If you love me like you say you do, respect my request and give me some space."

"Baby, I need you . . . I want to come home."

"Bye, Jermal!"

"Okay, okay. Just tell me you love me. I just need to hear it."

"If that was your concern, you would not have done what you did." With that, she hung up and dropped her head. Her heart ached! He sounded so pitiful and lonely. She hated it had to be this way, but her nephew came first in her life. Right before she walked away, she lifted the phone from the receiver and left it off the hook. Knowing Sway, he would call all night.

"Mya, I think you have had enough for one night. We can finish this discussion tomorrow," Coach Riley suggested. Although didn't want to admit it, he was right. She was spent. "I'm going to make sure all your windows are locked and secure your back door. You can wait for me right here." Coach Riley made his way around her first level, as if he was familiar with the space. Under normal circumstances she would have declined, but nothing about today was normal. She grabbed her phone and checked her messages and texts, hoping to have one from King. She needed a calm after the storm.

Sway left over twenty texts, and she deleted them all without reading them.

"You are squared away," Coach Riley announced as he walked back into the kitchen.

"I'm going to walk you to your car," Mya offered, easing off the barstool that was stationed at the island.

"You don't have to do that," he replied sincerely.

117

"I want to . . . catch some fresh air real quick."

The two made it out the front door and were descending her front porch. A black Acura Legend suddenly took off, speeding down the residential street, tires burning rubber. Coach Riley stepped in front of Maya, causing her to lose her balance. Once the car was out of sight, he turned to help her up. "I'm so sorry. I didn't mean to knock you down."

"It's okay." Her nerves were shot, and her hands shook as he reached out for her. The realization that her house was being watched made her uneasy.

"I tell you what. If it's okay with you, I think I'll just stay tonight." Mya looked up the street in both directions. Whether it was Sway watching, or someone he sent, she was afraid of what might happen if Coach Riley left.

"You can sleep in my guest room."

I knew it! I knew that man would be still hanging around here or having one of his do-boys watching the house. She shivered, and couldn't shake the uncomfortable feeling that this would be her reality for as long as Sway was gone from her home. Mya would probably be watched by someone every second, minute, and hour of every day. The thought of Sway ducked off outside peeping through the windows sent cold chills down her back. She was too unsettled to even walk over and make sure he wasn't.

And it shall come to pass, that before they call, I will answer; and while they are yet speaking, I will hear.

Isaiah 65:24 (KJV)

CHAPTER 15

Mya felt as if she had been running all night. Her left side was sore, her eyes a little swollen, and her dress felt as if it was clinging to her. She hoped never to be in the middle of two men tussling ever again. She desperately needed a shower and forced herself to sit up.

To her surprise, Judah was stretched out at the place where her feet had been. Mya was amazed that she hadn't realized he was there. But how could she? She didn't even remember coming upstairs, nor getting in bed. *Lord, this child is something special,* Mya thought about all that Judah had to be going through, but here he was still trying to protect her, to comfort her. For a split second, she saw her four-year-old hero again, who, after hearing ominous thunder and lightning outside Big Momma's house, snuggled up next to her as close as possible and said, "I got you, Tuntie. I got you." She knew from that day forward that Judah was God-sent.

Lord, I wish I could take Judah's pain away, Mya prayed as she positioned herself prostrate on the carpet. She wasn't sure what the day would bring, but she needed the Lord to keep Judah in a deep sleep, just as He had done when she prayed for Sway to remain in a deep sleep a few times. "Oh Lord God, who has always comforted me; Judah and I need you to strengthen us both for what lies ahead on this day." Mya found the courage to pray, knowing her God was greater than the concerns of her life.

After she showered, she dressed in a black skirt and black sheer blouse with an electric blue tank beneath. She pulled her hair back into a bun and went downstairs to prepare breakfast. Mya sat at the table drinking a cup of tea while conversing with Coach Riley. He wolfed down several pancakes, eggs, and turkey sausage.

"Mya, I want to thank you for making me feel so welcomed and for cooking that delicious breakfast!" He rubbed his stomach as he smiled from ear to ear.

"No, I'm the one who needs to express gratitude. Thank you for staying over to keep an eye on us. I bet you think our lives are full of drama." Mya felt a little ashamed just thinking about the previous day's mishap.

"By no means do I think such a thing. You are a beautiful young woman, and some men are not confident enough within themselves to handle and keep a woman with your type of values and upbringing."

Mya really wasn't sure how someone like Sway, who lived a life of luxury and was good-looking, would struggle with insecurity, but she did her best to receive Coach Riley's remark as a compliment.

"If you need me for anything, just call. You won't be a burden, I promise." Riley stood to his feet. "Thank you again for breakfast. I'm ready to start the day now."

Looking at his empty plate, Mya smiled. "You are most definitely welcome."

"You wouldn't believe the last time I had a home cooked breakfast." Mya could tell he was genuinely grateful.

"Judah." Coach Riley acknowledged Judah coming into the kitchen dressed in red and black checkered pajamas. "Good morning."

"Good morning," he responded plainly as he kissed Mya on the cheek.

Mya hurried over to the stove, fixed his plate, and poured him a glass of orange juice and set it before him.

"Baby, why aren't you ready for school?"

"I'm not going today," Judah responded nonchalantly, then bowed his head and silently prayed over his food. Mya stopped in her tracks, amazed by the sight. Judah had never blessed his food on his own accord. *Maybe he is beginning to believe that God cares for him,* she thought.

"Ju, now you know how I feel about school. You have never missed a day. Nothing changes today." Her voice was loving, but stern.

"Aunt Mya, someone needs to be here just in case Sway tries to come back." He looked into her eyes.

Her heart ached. *Why did I have to put my nephew in this situation?* "Ju, I will be fine. I promise. Besides, I'm going to get my hair done today, and I have to meet with a client. Then after practice, we can go by the sports store." She glanced at Coach Riley, her eyes pleading for his help.

"Judah, you know Mya is a smart woman. She'll be fine," Coach Riley stated.

"That may be the case, but I'm going to make sure. I'm not going." Mya sat next to him, silently asking the Lord to help her. After a few seconds she spoke.

"Judah, look at me. If I didn't care about your future, I would let you do whatever you wanted, but baby, you have had to endure some very powerful things in your short life. God has us in the palm of His hands. You don't have to live each day worrying about me."

"But you are all that I got!" Judah yelled unexpectedly, slamming his fist on the table. Mya knew his aggression was deeper than yesterday's incident. Her nephew was in torment. Tragedy was a little too familiar for him, and no matter how hard he tried, she couldn't tell him how to cope with what he felt. She could only direct him to the one who healed her heart.

"I tell you what. Finish eating, then get dressed, and we'll leave together. I'll follow you to school, then go get my hair done. We'll meet up after your football practice. We can hit the store, get something to eat, and come home together. I'll keep my phone near, so you can text me anytime you feel the need, and I'll get right back! How does that sound?" It was obvious he wanted to protest. "Good. That's the plan." Mya didn't give him time to respond. "Finish eating, I'm going to go straighten up my room and grab my handbag."

Mya stood to her feet, kissed Judah on the forehead and was headed down the hall toward the stairwell when Judah called after her.

"Auntie, you got a deal, only under one condition." His tone touched her heart. It's like the young man she'd just faced, was suddenly a boy.

"What is it, baby?"

"I'll only agree if my dad agrees to spend another night." Judah looked over at Coach Riley, who swallowed to keep from getting emotional. Mya felt herself wanting to cry, just seeing the hand of God bond their relationship. "Well, my possible dad . . ."

"Mya, if you're okay with it, I would be more than honored to sleep in that cozy king-size bed again," Riley replied, looking just as hopeful as Judah.

"Baby, if that's what you want, then you got it." Mya turned on her heels and put on her leather moto jacket, and a pair of electric blue suede boots.

Twenty minutes later, they all were standing in the foyer. As they waited to exit the house, Mya's heart began to pound. She thought about someone sitting outside her home like Sway had done last night.

"Judah, baby, can you do me a favor?" she asked as she unlocked the front door and turned the knob.

"Yes, Auntie."

"Can you run into the kitchen and grab me a cranberry juice? I forgot to get one, and I don't want to stop on the way." She needed an excuse to make sure the street was clear before he stepped outside. She wasn't up for any surprises or altercations this morning.

"Coach Riley, make sure he locks up the house and sets the alarm," Mya instructed as she slipped out and closed the door behind her.

She held her breath as she descended the steps and looked up and down the street. Everything looked normal. The trees were green with leaves and still; the streets were empty, except for a neighbor's cute little Pomeranian roaming into another neighbor's yard. She was just glad their pit bull wasn't able to sneak out of the gate as easily. It was strange that a pit bull and Pomeranian were able to live peaceably within the same household. The garbage truck rode by slowly, as workers picked up the trash bins to dump them as usual. She exhaled.

"Thank you God!" She praised aloud. The cool morning air almost made her want to grab a heavier coat, but she decided against it, knowing it would warm up. Instead, she rushed to the car and stood there mystified. Her doors were already unlocked. *I never leave these doors unlocked,* she thought. Mya peeked in the back passenger window to make sure no one was lying on the floor or hiding in the back, but the tint made it hard to see. She turned to look behind her. Judah was coming out of the house. Against her better judgment, she hurried inside the car, and then looked in the backseat. A single rose lay on the seat. The three quick knocks on her window frightened her, especially once her door opened. She gasped and turned toward the driver's window.

"Auntie, here you go." Judah handed her two bottles of cranberry juice.

"Oh thank you!" She leaned forward slightly, not wanting Judah to look past her and see the rose. Panic had set in, but she wouldn't let it become apparent to Judah.

"Come on, Ju! Let's get out of here. I'm waiting on you! You got me blocked in." She tapped the steering wheel lightly.

Judah didn't respond right away. His brows wrinkled, as if he could detect something was up. He just stood there looking at her strangely.

"Judah, can we go?" she asked in an irritating manner.

"Yeah." He finally spoke and strutted to his vehicle and got in. Once he started his engine, she reached back and grabbed the rose. There was a note attached: **I WON'T LIVE WITHOUT YOU!**

Thou shalt not go up and down as a talebearer among thy people . . .

Leviticus 19:16 (KJV)

CHAPTER 16

Hair Couture (8:45 a.m.)

"Yes, girl! I love a woman who knows how to operate on schedule. It's still early, so I can get started with you at exactly 9:00 a.m. on the dot, *after* we spill a bit of tea. Girl, look at you walking up in here glowing! Sway must be handling his business!" LaTanya sang. She rushed to the front of the salon as Mya signed in. The mention of Sway made Mya's heart ache.

"LaTanya, I'm going to need you to do better." Glowing was the last thing Mya felt like she was doing.

"Me . . . do better? No, hon'. You know I tell it like it is. I mean, look at you, you're killing that skirt. You have a certain glow. You got that got-a-good-papered-up man glow written all over you!"

"The only man that's been on me, or in me is God." Mya let her remark linger in the air for a minute. She wasn't surprised to see her beautician's excited expression change into a saddened one.

"Girl! We most definitely got a lot of catching up to do." She gently led Mya by the hand to her station. "Honey, I'm so glad you took those braids out. It's been too long since I've seen you."

"LaTanya, stop acting. It's only been a month."

"That's still too long." She wrapped a smock around Mya. "Now what's all of this God business you're talking about? Did somebody die?"

"What? Why would you think somebody died?"

"I'm just saying, you're talking about God touched you. I figured something must've happened." She began applying the cold, creamy substance to Mya's head.

"People can give their lives to the Lord without some type of misfortune happening."

"Really? I don't know none."

"Well, you just met one." Mya's cell phone began ringing. She looked at it. *Sway.* She sent him to voicemail, and then put it on vibrate. She wasn't ready to face him. He had left four messages already. She knew better than to listen to the messages because she just might have fallen for them.

"Since when you stop answering your phone?"

"Since I didn't feel like being bothered." *Whoo, this girl is so nosy!*

"Mya, you trippin'! A man that fine can stay on my—" LaTanya stopped mid-sentence. "Mya . . . what in the heck happened to your hair, girl?" she asked, sounding distraught at the sight of a few bald patches throughout Mya's scalp. She turned Mya around to face her.

"You have no idea what a man that *fine and papered-up* has been taking me through."

"He did this? Looks like alopecia areata to me. Is this stress related?"

"Girl." Mya looked up into LaTanya's watery eyes. "I didn't come here to talk about Sway."

LaTanya bent her knees slightly and hugged Mya tight for several seconds. She wiped away the tears that had fallen from her eyes. "I'm so sorry to hear that, Mya. Y'all are one of my favorite couples. But you and Sway seemed so happy. He's always so sweet, always taking you somewhere and buying you stuff. I wondered what happened."

Me too, Mya thought, remembering how happy she used to be, how she and Sway and Judah would watch movies together or just hang out having a good time. Or those long late night talks she'd and Sway would have every now and again about their future. A wedding, children eventually, Sway finally going legitimate and opening a couple of businesses. Going to church and serving God and raising a God-fearing family who loved God before everything else.

LaTanya gently patted her shoulders. "Is it burning or anything?"

"No," Mya said and nodded.

"This just makes me so sad that you're this stressed out. Let's get this out of your hair right away." She kept her voice lowered. "I wasn't gon' say nothin', but he called here early this morning asking if I needed something. And if you were coming today."

Mya felt the elephant in the room and her body stiffened. LaTanya urged her out of her seat and directly over to the sink. Mya sat in the shampoo chair in front of the sink and leaned her head back. LaTanya turned on the hot water and adjusted the temperature.

"Oh my God! I thought he was just trying to surprise you with something because you know how he's always looking for an opportunity to show off." She rinsed the chemicals from her hair in no time. And rinsed it twice more before gently applying conditioner.

"Did you tell him what time my appointment was?"

"Of course I did. I know how much you love those surprises too. But I didn't know about . . ."

"I wish you would've told me this before you started putting in my relaxer."

"I'm so sorry, sweetie. I'll rinse this out right away." LaTanya kept a gentle hand on Mya's scalp. "You need to see a doctor right away, hon'. I'm low-key worried."

They returned to her station. LaTanya used the cool setting on the blow dryer to dry Mya's hair. Rather than close her eyes like usual, Mya kept her eyes trained on the front door. "I'ma need you to speed it up with the flat ironing, okay?"

"I gotchu. Girl, I know how much Sway loves you though." She dragged the flat iron across a small section of Mya's long, dark strands.

"Whatever y'all going through, y'all will get through it. He probably didn't mean it anyways."

How do you know what he meant? Mya thought, offended by LaTanya's comments.

"It just doesn't seem like the Sway I usually see. And it's never happened before, right?" She leaned over to get a good look at Mya.

Mya didn't want to answer, but she knew her beautician well enough to know she wouldn't stop questioning her until she responded. "Right," Mya barely uttered.

"Plus, the way he spoils you, if it were me, I would overlook a temper tantrum. As long as he got some counseling though."

I need to find another beautician, Mya decided right then.

LaTanya had been dressing her hair for the last four years, and apparently, they had gotten a little too close. Mya could only imagine what Sway was cooking up. She sat there praying, on the verge of tears, as LaTanya went from subject to subject. She felt a little relieved that there had been no sign of Sway.

"Girl, I hear your nephew is about to go pro!"

"He has to go to college first."

"Chile, you and I both know they gon' try to draft him ASAP. He made the paper."

Mya smiled.

"So, what are you gonna do with him gone off to college?"

"I don't know. I might go with him." Mya was surprised to hear herself say that. She hadn't even thought about that as an option.

"Mya, I ain't feeling that. What about me? You're supposed to be my girl."

"I'm sure you'll manage without me." Mya cut her eyes. "You have more than enough clientele to get by." LaTanya poked out her lips.

"So, listen, I have a DVD about how to grow your hair back. I want you to watch it. Another client of mine got her weave pulled out, out there fighting over some man. It's been three months, and her hair is coming back in thick and shiny like the rest of her hair."

"Girl, I believe you, but I don't have time today. I have to meet a client about the number of artists and the available space for my next art gallery event. We're also incorporating body art and interpretive dance."

"Oh wow! Sounds fun. Where are you having it?" she asked. Mya almost told her, but it was as if the Holy Spirit was reminding her that Sway had LaTanya in his favor. If LaTanya showed up, so would Sway.

"Someplace where I can get something decent to eat," Mya responded cryptically. LaTanya didn't ask any more questions, so apparently, that was good enough. Mya was kind of tripping about how God had intervened. LaTanya spent the rest of their time working her magic. She definitely had a gift for styling hair.

"Okay, girl. I'm all done," she finally said.

As soon as Mya gathered her purse and stood, she could see Sway confidently sitting in the plush leather salon style chair. An uncertain smile graced his lips. He spotted her before she had a chance to turn back. Her heart raced. His smile seemed weak, but she was the only one to notice because she knew him. As she sat back down in the chair next to LaTanya's station. Sway stood to his feet. The brother looked like he stepped right off an Armani advertisement. An expensive-looking black leather coat was draped across the chair he was just sitting in and the black shirt highlighted his bulging arms and chest. His snakeskin loafers matched the cover of his cell phone, and that cologne . . . *Lord!* The brother smelled good. Mya wasn't crazy; he knew she loved when he wore all black. *Do not fall for it.* She tried to avoid contact with him, but he was swift on his feet.

He stood in front of the chair holding a single purple rose, her favorite color. "Good morning, baby." A few women who were now present began cooing.

"Thank you. Good morning, and excuse me." Mya was very short. He didn't move. "Jermal, this is not the place." She knew that he would have to take her seriously, after hearing her call him by his government name.

"Well, being that you didn't call me back nor answer the phone, I had to see you."

"Come with me," Mya instructed him, directing him to the restroom. Although she didn't feel all that comfortable being alone with him, she knew he wouldn't leave the shop without talking to her. He followed. She decided that if he even looked like he was going to put a hand on her, she would scream bloody murder. At least one of the six women in the salon would call the police.

"Jermal, this is not the time or place for our issues to be put on display." Mya leaned closer, so only he could hear her, even though they appeared to be alone. Sway wrapped his arms around her, pulling her into him.

"Girl, you just don't understand just how bad I needed to touch you." Mya refused to allow her body to relax; she started to push away. "Mya, please don't do me like this."

Just as LaTanya knocked on the door, Mya managed to get out of his grip. "You two lovebirds all right in there?" she asked. Mya opened the door. God had intervened.

"We're all right." Sway acknowledged her. "I just need a minute."

"Now, unless you are about to get a haircut, I advise you to vacate this room, so I can finish making this money, Sway. My client needs to use it, and she has to hurry so I can finish styling her," LaTanya lied.

Sway looked at Mya from head to toe. Mya tried not to make eye contact, but he wouldn't stop staring.

"My girl does look good though, doesn't she?" LaTanya said.

"Good enough," Sway replied.

"Save it," Mya cut him off.

"Can you step outside with me for a moment?" Sway asked, looking from Mya to LaTanya.

"No, I cannot. I'm not up for conversation."

"Mya, I just need a second."

"Please, not here. Not now, Sway." She was getting frustrated.

"Child, y'all holding up my bathroom," LaTanya began to rant. "I

132

don't understand why you just won't go talk to the man real quick. So I can do this last little section." LaTanya winked.

"Mya, don't do me like this." Sway pulled her back into his arms. "Baby, I am sorry. I know I made a mistake." He was whispering in her ear and caressing her back. "Baby, I should have never allowed things to go down the way they did. I mean, you're family. Baby, I miss you. Can you understand that?"

LaTanya started to say something about her time being wasted, when Sway reached into his pocket, pulled out a roll of money, and peeled off two crisp hundred dollar bills and handed it to her. "Look, Sway—"

"This is for her, keep the change." LaTanya shut up real quick.

"Amen, take all the time you need. I'll just wait out here with my other client." Mya shook her head as Sway closed the door. LaTanya had always been a character. He turned his focus back to Mya. "I know I messed up. I know I did. But I know you can find the strength to forgive me."

Although she tried to resist, Mya felt herself melting in his arms. Becoming vulnerable to his touch. Obviously, he felt it too. He lifted her chin with his fingers so she would look into his eyes. "Baby, I really do need you. I am sorry." He leaned down to kiss her. She caught herself kissing him back, and then turned her head away. "Mya, I want you." His erection pressed up against her body. "Baby, I have to come home. I can't live without you. She thought about the rose in the car. His written words sounded more like a threat, but his gentle expression didn't look like one, nor did it feel as such. *Mya, keep it together, you better not give in,* she told herself. *I need to get away from this man.*

"Sway, I need time to think. If you mean what you say, then give me some space. Okay?"

"Okay. Okay, baby." He leaned forward and kissed her on the cheek, and then headed for the door. Mya didn't move. He stopped and turned around. "Mya," he called to get her attention. She looked up. "I love you." He didn't give her time to respond, but just strutted out the door like he dominated the turf he walked on.

Mya finally walked back into the salon and picked up her things, feeling like she had betrayed Judah. Herself. Why did she still want this man who had purposefully provoked her nephew? The only family she had left. She wished that she hated Sway, but hate didn't even fall into the category of what she felt for him. She knew better than to express to LaTanya how she felt. Instead she did what had become routine for her. *Lord, I don't know what to do. Should I forgive Sway and let him back in?*

For the flesh lusts against the Spirit, and the Spirit against the flesh: and these are contrary to one another, so that you do not do the things that ye wish.

Galatians 5:17 (NKJV)

CHAPTER 17

Wednesday (12:07 a.m.)

For the past hour, she had been lying in bed alone, praying just to fall asleep. Mya buried her face in her pillow to muffle the sobs. She missed the warmth of Sway. But tonight, the heaviness of her heart wouldn't allow her to do anything but cry.

It amazed her how God had given her exactly what she needed all day and not just her, but everyone she came into contact with. But somehow, now that she was alone, her heartache overwhelmed her. Deep, painful sobs found their way out. She could still see Judah as he sat next to her and across from Coach Riley, drilling him with question after question. He had never seemed more serious, but she knew him well enough to know he was processing his feelings.

It didn't help the situation that she kept playing over in her head why she needed to let Sway go on his way, but none of that made a difference to her heart. Plus, she felt slightly guilty about not going to Bible study, convincing herself that she just didn't have the strength to look anyone in the face. As she inhaled deeply, she closed her eyes. Her pillow smelled like Sway, and so did her sheets and comforter. *Maybe I should call and see how he's doing.* She looked over to her phone on her nightstand.

Mya, don't be stupid. She buried her face into the pillow and flashed back to her salon visit where he had been standing over her, smelling so doggone good, and rocking a fresh cut. How comforting his muscles felt as he pulled her into his embrace. It was almost a shame for a man to be that fine. "I can't win this battle like this," she spoke aloud.

Wasting no time, she got up to change her bed linen, but once she finished, her longing for him grew even worse. As if something stronger than herself possessed her limbs, she picked up her phone.

The second she heard him answer, tears fell from her eyes. She knew she had made a mistake, but she missed him.

"I was hoping you called," Sway said, sounding so sexy to her.

"I shouldn't have." She wanted to hang up, but didn't have the willpower to do so.

"I need to see you."

"I just called to make sure you were all right and to say good night," Mya lied.

"No you didn't. Meet me somewhere."

"Sway, I really just wanted to say good night."

"That's fine. I'll be in front of your house in ten minutes. Come sit in the car with me then."

"Jermal, please don't. It's not a good idea," Maya pleaded.

"I need to smell you, touch you . . . taste you. I miss you. I'll call you when I'm turning on your street." He hung up.

The way her stomach turned had confirmed that this was truly a bad idea, but the longing in her body spoke louder than her logic. She wanted to be with him. She rushed to her dresser and moisturized her skin and sprayed on perfume by Calvin Klein. Then she combed down her wrap so her hair hung inches past her shoulders. Her cell phone rang after a few minutes had passed.

"I'm in front of the house," Sway announced as soon as she picked up the phone.

"Okay. Pull into the driveway. I'll be out in a second." Mya set her phone down on the charger, and then thought a second. *Someone might call, or I may need to call someone!* She picked it back up. Dressed in an ivory silk night gown, she rushed down the stairs, ignoring her conscious that screamed, "Stop right in your tracks and go back upstairs!" Mya opened the closet in the foyer and pulled out her chestnut-colored trench coat.

"God, please forgive me." She unlocked the door and stepped out into the cool night air. Her heart raced as she skipped down each step. Sway already had the passenger door open. Mya slipped into the plush leather seat and closed the door.

"Is it warm enough for you, baby?" he asked. She nodded yes. Sway leaned over and gently grabbed her by her neck and pulled her closer. Breathless, she stared into his eyes as their lips locked.

"You smell so good," Sway said after their kiss was broken.

"Thank you. I was thinking the same about you."

"You miss me?" He let her seat back.

"What do you think?" Mya teased, feeling like a high school girl sitting beneath the adoring eyes of her first love.

"What's this that you got on?" he asked.

"Just my gown."

"Take it off."

"Sway. I am not taking my gown off." She punched his arm tenderly.

"Well, I want to see what's underneath." He removed his coat, gazing at Mya with overwhelming desire.

"What are you up to, Sway?" Mya played dumb, ignoring her own arousal.

"I told you I need to touch you." He rubbed her left leg and slid her gown up to her thighs. "That I need to smell you." Sway leaned over and kissed her neck, inhaling her aroma. "That I need to taste you." He looked at her, allowing his words to register.

"Sway, are you saying . . ." She wouldn't vocalize it. "Jermal, I miss you and all, but I don't think we should rush things." Silence answered for him as he let his seat back. "Maybe I should just go." Mya closed her coat and placed her hand on the unlock button, trying to fight off the temptation.

"Mya." He reached for her hand. She refused to look at him. Her body had already betrayed her. She wanted his touch. Wanted it bad.

"Jermal, I love you, but I have to go. Your actions caused a reaction and that's a situation you have forced me to live with. I really do need time."

"Baby, look at me." She refused. He leaned over and turned her head toward him. Mya closed her eyes. "I know I messed up, and I respect what you are trying to uphold. That's why we're out here and not in our bed. But I need you to understand that I need you too." Mya swallowed the lump in her throat and fought off the tears welling in her eyes. "Baby, just look at me. Please!" he begged. "Look at me."

Slowly, Mya opened her eyes and glimpsed a teary-eyed young man who was filled with hurt and pain.

"I need you too, and I need you right now." He reached for her hand and she yielded. "You gonna give me what I need? I need to be close to you." His eyes penetrated hers.

"Yes," she whispered with a nod.

"Take that coat off." Slowly and hesitantly, she removed the trench coat.

"Come here." He leaned back as far as the seat would allow. A part of Mya screamed no, but a resounding YES! YES! YES! overruled her reasoning. She pulled her gown up to her waist and crawled over to his seat and straddled Sway. His manhood expressed his approval.

"Come here," he said. Immediately she recognized the tone. Sway was intoxicated with lust. "Come sit on my face," he said.

"Sway, are you serious?" Before she could protest further, he used his strength to ease her into a new position—just where he wanted her to be, where he needed her to be, where he could taste her.

Mya couldn't deny the smile that was glued across her face as she snuck back into the house. Sway had a way of making her feel as if she would lose her mind. But no sooner than she shut the door and locked it, the reality of her double mindedness mounted her shoulders. Guilt became the most dominant emotion.

"God, why does the wrong thing feel so good?" she asked aloud. Mya slipped her coat off and hung it back in the closet. She tiptoed upstairs, hoping no one caught her in the hallway. The last thing she wanted was to answer for her whereabouts at this hour. Especially wearing a nightgown.

She tiptoed to her guestroom and put her ear to the cracked door, listening for any sound. There wasn't any, other than Coach Riley's deep snores. She pulled the door shut and sprinted the short distance to her room. She closed her door hoping to find refuge, but the moment she sat on her bed, bad thoughts of the pleasure she just received flooded her mind. Guilt rained down fiercely on her conscience. For enjoying herself . . . for obtaining such pleasure.

"I can't do this all night." She grabbed her silk housecoat from off the bathroom door, unsure of where she was headed. For a moment she paced through the house until she found herself standing at the door to Judah's room. Slowly, she turned the knob to let herself in. To her surprise, he lay stretched out the exact same way that Coach Riley was. Amazing, how much alike they are. She grinned slightly.

The light from the hall enabled her to see the pictures of Big Momma and her father. They looked so happy together. She wished her mother and father were still alive. Mya looked over at Judah, who had a trail of dried tears on his face. Her eyes misted over. He must've cried himself to sleep. She noticed a little bulge beneath his covers and forgot to breathe as she considered what was just inches away. *Where this boy get a gun from?* Mya thought. *And why would he need one?*

At first she considered that he may have felt the need to protect his family, but then as she analyzed the trail of dried tears, she wondered if he had contemplated suicide. The suicide rates had recently doubled for African Americans. *Oh God! No!* Mya screamed in her heart as she tiptoed over to his bed. *I've got to get this away from him.* Carefully, she peeled the covers back and finally released her breath as she discovered

141

Big Momma's Bible beneath his hand. Her heart was filled with gratitude, yet she couldn't believe it. She stood there blown away by the God she served, wondering how long he had been reading. This touched her soul and even increased her faith. God had been listening to her heart cry. The Lord was obviously dealing with Judah's heart.

Suddenly, she felt the urge to pray. But the thought of her behavior just minutes ago made her think twice. *How can I ask God for anything when I just . . .* She bowed her head in shame. *God, I'm sorry. I am so sorry.* Her knees hit the floor, and tears streamed from her eyes. "Please, forgive me," she pleaded as chills washed over her. Without any conscious effort of her own, words began to spill from her lips. "Oh Lord God, who never fails. You promised me in your word that you would pour out your spirit on all flesh," she whispered. "Our sons and daughters shall prophesy and our young men shall see visions. Lord, I know it's in your will for Judah to be established and grounded in your will for the edifying of your kingdom. Lord, I know you have a plan for His life. You promised in Jeremiah that you know the plans you have for him. Thoughts of peace, not evil, to give him a future and hope.

"My nephew has had a bitter pill to swallow, but by your grace, he still stands. I don't know what awaits him, but I'm just asking that you protect him—please watch over him." Mya wept quietly, but she didn't want to disturb Judah's sleep.

Finally, after getting off the floor, she was humbled that God, our creator, would take the time to speak to her heart, concerning the one who was her heart. She wasn't sure just how long she had been on the floor, nor did she even care, but she got up knowing deep down in her heart that she was loved and revived. Determined to be done with Sway, she knew she could no longer straddle the fence. Judah hadn't moved an inch. Pushing the door closed, she walked around and curled up next to him on top of his comforter. She wasn't concerned with what the sunrise would bring; God was watching over them. But what she didn't know was God wasn't the only one watching them. Sway's vehicle had never left her driveway.

For we are saved by hope: but hope that is seen is not hope: for what a man seeth, why doth he yet hope for? But if we hope for that we see not, then do we with patience wait for it.

Romans 8:24-25 (KJV)

CHAPTER 18

Judah's room (6:00 a.m.)

Judah slowly rolled over, just in time to see her head sliding down from the mount of his pillow. The sight was funny to him. With no effort, he repositioned her and covered her up. For a few minutes, he kept staring at the woman who loved him unconditionally. He knew Big Momma loved him and would stop the world for him . . . But Mya . . . there were no restraints, no boundaries, and no excuses when it came to her loyalty to him. Even as she slept, he felt her love clothe him like a cape. She always knew how to be there when he needed someone the most. Last night had been one of the hardest nights for him. He respected Coach Riley for the man he is: one who is understanding, down to earth, and well-respected in the community. For being his role model for the last two years. He was trying to love him as his father, but alongside that was an inkling that Coach Riley was making excuses about his absence from his life in the past. A feeling that made him question why the coach suddenly wanted to be in his life. A feeling that cast blame on Coach Riley for Judah's secret insecurities.

He really didn't know why, but he found himself kneeling and praying to the God he once loved as a small child.

"Father, whatever heartache Mya is carrying, please take away her pain. I also need you to help me with getting rid of this raging anger I have deep inside of me." He sighed deeply. "Lord, I feel a little stupid praying to you after believing I truly hated you for all the bad things in my life. And I'm very sorry. But just thinking about how you have blessed me with Aunt Mya, and how much she loves me lets me know just how much you have to care for me. I am grateful to you for putting her in my life and making it as full as it is—even though it is far from perfect. In Jesus name. Amen." He was about to get up when he spotted Big Momma's Bible. He had pulled it out days ago. Judah closed his eyes and randomly opened it. He figured wherever he opened the Bible is where God wanted him to read. Judah had seen Big Momma do the same on several occasions.

When he opened his eyes, he was staring at the face of a woman that looked exactly like the woman he loved. He had never seen this picture before. His eyes darted from the picture, and then to his aunt Mya. He was amazed at how identical his mom and aunt looked. It made him want to cry. Down beneath the picture was Big Momma's penmanship. Acts 16:31 was scribbled on it:

And they said, Believe in the Lord Jesus Christ,
and you will be saved; you and your household.

Judah dropped his head in disbelief. He couldn't believe that Big Momma had gone to her grave still trusting God to save them. His mother included. *Does that mean that Big Momma still believed that my mother and father were still alive?* he thought. *Only God knows.* He put the picture back in the Bible and placed it into his nightstand, then headed to the shower to get ready for school. All the while, thinking about everything.

If you care about me, Father, I need you to direct my steps. In Jesus' name. If Riley's heart isn't in the right place, and he's only stepping up as my dad because of the possibility of me playing pro football after college, then please reveal his intentions to me directly.

Amen.

. . . but he told me, My grace is enough for you, for my power is brought to perfection in weakness.

2 Corinthians 12:9 (CJB)

CHAPTER 19

The following day . . .

"Yes," Mya answered the caller dryly.

"Well . . . hello stranger," a familiar female voice sang.

"Hello," Mya answered, trying to perk up.

"I'm starting to think you either don't want to be bothered, or you don't know who this is."

"Janelle? . . . Girl! I know who this is! How could I not! You just caught me right after I sat down. I've been cleaning like crazy. The stuff that's usually reserved for spring cleaning."

"Oh, tell me something because you already been acting funny . . . like you can't call nobody," Janell snapped.

Mya wasn't surprised at Janell's words. Although Janelle was beautiful and intelligent, at times she had the tendency to get ratchet would pop off if the conditions were right. "You would think your little short butt would be the one to keep the peace, but you flip into beast mode in a heartbeat. Always wanna throw the first punch. I am truly sorry, Janelle. I just got a lot of things cooking right now. Too many, in fact."

"That's all well and good, but it only takes three minutes to dial a number and say what's up. So why haven't I heard from you? It's been an entire year since we've hung out. That's making me feel some kind of way. I believe in giving people space, but this is cray. Twelve months is too long. I know we're both busy, but not that doggone busy."

"Girl, it has not been a year."

"Mya . . . Oh, yes it has! That's why you think you can't talk to me about everything anymore?"

Has it been a year? It couldn't be. When was the last time we talked? "It's not like that at all. And why would you say that?"

"Because I ran into LaTanya at the beauty supply and she told me that you and Sway are having problems."

"What? I can't believe her. But it's not even like that." Mya had a mind to go slap the crap out of LaTanya.

"Well, if it's not, let's meet up."

Three hours later, Mya was pulling up in the parking lot of Jacksonville's River Walk. The lot was built on top of the river. Wherever you stood, the river was visible from beneath or beside the historic site. During the weekdays, a small museum on the landmark would be open for tourists. Once the sun set, the placed served as an intimate setting. Today it would serve as the backdrop for a private conversation. Mya would pour her heart out to Janelle, the only person she trusted outside of her family. Janelle knew everything there was to know about Mya, except the latest with Sway and King. She texted Janelle to let her know she had arrived. A text message was waiting her response. *I didn't hear the phone vibrate or make any noise,* she thought.

KING: *Hello beautiful. This is King. I haven't heard from you, but I trust in God and know that all is well with you. I've barely slept since I last held you. Your well-being is more necessary than sleep. I'll spend the rest of my life interceding for you, by God's grace. I'll be at work by the time you get this. I just hope today you discover that your existence makes the darkest night seem as if the moon shines like the sun. I miss you and know that God is able to be whatever you need him to be.*

Mya read the text message over and over again until she heard a knock at the window. It played in her mind as she showered and then dressed.

"Girl, you going to spend the day in there, or you going to get out and hang with me?" Janelle stood with her hands on her hips. She'd put on a few pounds, but looked very casual in jeans, a cashmere sweater and suede booties.

"Hey, girl," Mya said with a smile as she opened the door to exit. She hugged Janelle tight the moment her feet hit the pavement and she closed the door. "You look great, Janelle. You wearin' those jeans, girl. They ain't wearin' you. Cute sweater too." Mya open the back door on the driver's side and grabbed the picnic basket.

"Girl, I'm trying to catch up with you." Janelle eyed Mya's designer sweater dress and thigh-high boots.

"Please, with all the stress I've been under. I have lost a little weight."

"It obviously didn't fall off from your butt because that thang still sitting nice," Janelle teased as she reached for the basket.

"Shut up, chile!" Mya beamed, secretly appreciating the compliment. They had only been in each other's presence for less than five minutes, and she was already feeling like this is exactly what she needed. "I miss you so much, Janelle!" Mya admitted.

"Mmm hmm, who wouldn't?" Janelle replied.

"So, what's been going on with you?" Mya asked before they got into the mess that was her life.

"Business is great! I made partner!" Janelle beamed with pride.

Mya gasped. "Oh my God! Janelle! Congratulations, girl!" Mya hugged her tight and grinned just as wide. "That is awesome. I am so proud of you." They spread their blanket across the table and set the picnic basket on top of it.

"Now how many Black Americans can say they've accomplished that at your age? God is good."

"Yeah, I know. Not bad for thirty-one, huh?" Janelle looked away.

"What's that look you just did? What's up? What aren't you saying?"

Janelle told her the partnership came with a relocation to Atlanta, but her boyfriend Simon wasn't onboard with the move. Although Mya rarely drank, she poured wine for them both. The wine made it easier for Janelle to share her dilemma. After pouring her heart out about her relationship, Janelle waited for Mya to respond.

"So, you're saying . . . not only is he married with a kid. He also isn't an American citizen?"

"Correct. Simon AKA *See-mon* is from Ethiopia. And he lied about attending Morehouse College when we first started dating."

"Girl, stop playing!" Mya couldn't believe it. "So, how does your coworker know?"

"She just so happens to date the guy who co-owns the club with Simon. Since we traveled to ATL for work, she took me out to that evening to see the sights. Wouldn't you know we ended up at Simon's club! I'm sitting there wondering, *What the heck is he doing here?*"

"Wow! That is so crazy!"

"He also proposed, had his family come down here under the pretense of announcing our engagement. His family did come here, but he whisked them away to a restaurant that I had no idea about. I mean, he just up and left me without a word." Mya shook her head. "I called his cell and was like, See-mon, where you at?'" They burst out laughing.

Janelle ended the tragedy by telling Mya how she tracked him by using GPS and went into the restaurant to confront him, but she found him seated comfortably with his wife and daughter. She eventually left him and hadn't looked back since.

"How can you be so certain that you're done with him?" Mya asked, more for herself than for Janelle's full explanation.

"He lied to me. It's simple. He was deceitful when he didn't have to be. We could've been friends perhaps. But not now."

"Do you miss him?"

"Of course, but I'm not about to settle and be some weak dummy walking around accepting anything in the name of love. Heck no! There are plenty of fish in the sea. And it's cool that he didn't recognize my worth, because someone else will. All I've gotta do is chill out and be patient."

Mya grabbed her glass and guzzled. She wanted to disappear just like her drink. *Man! I must be one of the weakest women on earth!* She poured another glass of wine as they began making their plates.

"When did you start drinking?" Janelle asked, looking intrigued.

"Since we sat down," Mya confessed.

"So what you got going on?" Janelle moved the bottle to her side of the table. She tilted her head slightly. "You feel like you can't talk to me anymore?"

"Oh Janelle! Girl, where do you want me to start? With the day I decided that what my man wanted was more important than what God wanted? Or the day I allowed my boyfriend to demoralize me? Or the fact that my nephew's life may change forever?"

Thou shalt not be afraid for the terror by night; nor for the arrow that flieth by day;

Psalm 91:9 (KJV)

CHAPTER 20

"For real? That's how you do me?" Judah addressed Mya as he opened the door before she had the opportunity to unlock it. "Yo, it's after six. The sun will be setting in a minute." He followed her as she stepped into the foyer and hung up her coat in the closet. "I been worried sick, calling you all day, only to come home to an empty house. No note and an answering machine full of my messages."

"Ju, I'm fine! I've been with Janelle. I didn't realize so much time had passed." She made her way into the den, sat on her contemporary designer sofa and removed her boots. Her head spun a little, tipsy from the wine she drank, but she wouldn't ever admit it.

"Janelle? I haven't heard you say her name in a while." Judah picked up her boots and placed them in the closet. He retrieved her slippers and set them at her feet.

"You didn't have to do that." She beamed with admiration. "Thank you." She stroked his cheek. He playfully stepped out of her reach.

"You ain't getting off that easy. So . . . you didn't think to text me, leave me a message, or even call?" Judah sat back and put his feet up on the ottoman. "I've never gone an entire day without hearing from you."

155

"It really wasn't my intention to make today any different. I do, however, sincerely apologize. I'll make it up to you." She tried to stifle her laugh.

"I'm glad you think I'm funny." He picked up his laptop from the cocktail table.

"I don't!" She held up both hands to surrender. I see you found something to eat." She glanced at the empty plate of what had been lasagna.

"Yeah . . . come here. Let me show you something. Check this out, Aunt Mya."

"Did you save me any?" she asked, testing him.

"Nope. I was stressed out. Emotional eating." He burst out laughing.

"Whatever, Judah!" She stood behind his chair and watched him pull up a newspaper article. Mya leaned in closer. "Is that . . ." She couldn't believe her eyes. "Is that Big Momma's house?"

"I guess," Judah politely replied.

Mya grabbed the other chair and placed it next to Judah. "I've been trying to find out what happened to my mother." Mya stole glances at Judah, to see if he was getting emotional.

"What disappoints me is that when I type in her name, my name and her name comes up, and it only shows me as a relative."

"That's it?"

"Yeah. Can you think of anywhere else I can look?" he asked, trying not to get discouraged already.

"Let me ask you something. Do you really believe she is still alive?"

"I do . . . and Big Momma died believing the same thing."

Mya was silent for a minute. "Well, I'll tell you what. We could go file another missing person's report. Maybe they'll put somebody new on the case. Maybe a newly hired detective who's hungry enough to solve a cold case."

"Okay. That sounds good. I didn't think about that. Thanks."

"You're welcome."

"If you don't mind me asking, have you ever tried to find my mother? Or did you just assume that she didn't want to be found, or that she was dead?" Judah closed his laptop.

"Aside from reporting her disappearance and talking with Detective Fritz for a few months, there wasn't much else I could do. I did check the missing persons' website and call the detective over several years, but he was never able to find any solid leads."

"I read that sometimes they don't want to be found and take on a new identity. It just makes me even more curious why she stayed away, or who took her."

"When the neighborhood started getting really bad, Big Momma sold the house and told the new owners to give our new number and address to anyone who might come by looking for us." Mya stared ahead, remembering how weird she felt during the move, as if they were giving up on Honesty. "A part of me still believes she's alive, but another part just feels like something happened. I can't ever see her just leaving you like that. Shoot, she took me with her everywhere and wouldn't let me out of her sight. Until she started dating . . . that's when she became secretive." They both let silence occupy the room. "So, what you want me to fix you for dinner?" he said, lightening the mood.

"Dinner? Boy, I've got two more days until your birthday. I'm trying to live to see it." Mya grabbed a toss pillow and hit him with it.

"Whatever! I throws down in the kitchen." He began tickling her. Mya almost fell over the table trying to get away. They were like two kids running around the house, wrestling.

"Aunt Mya, I'm hungry."

"Are you serious, Judah?"

"Yeah, you worked off all my food."

"That's a shame. You didn't save me any food, now you want something else."

"I'll rub your feet," he said, smiling, knowing she was going to make him a meal.

"Good, because I was on them a long time cooking that lasagna. Decide what you want to eat. I'll go change." Her head was still spinning and she kind of liked it. Things that had once been her concern didn't seem so worrisome now.

Mya walked into her room and slid out of her slippers. She loved the way the thick carpet felt against her feet. She undressed and took a quick shower. She didn't intend on cooking a huge feast, nor did she plan on being up all night. Tonight Judah was getting a twenty minute meal. After wrapping herself in a towel, including one around her hair, she headed into her bedroom and stopped in her tracks. A single purple rose lay on her bed in between two pillows. Her brows lowered.

"Why didn't I notice that this was here when I walked in the room?" she asked aloud. Chills raced up her back. She turned right and left to inspect her room; her space had been invaded. However, nothing seemed out of place. Her eyes darted toward the windows, but instead she rushed into the closet and grabbed her housecoat and put it on. She wasn't that much under the influence.

"I know Sway wouldn't be in here hiding, would he?" *Probably.* The answer came swiftly. She canceled her window theory; her room was on the second story. Getting down on her knees, she checked beneath the bed. Nothing. Considering the huge blow up between Sway and Judah, Sway had no right coming up in the house. He represented a threat toward Judah, and he also disrespected her wishes when she asked him for more time. She tiptoed to the nightstand and grabbed her phone, prepared to call 911, just in case Sway wasn't the person responsible for the rose. But who else would be creeping around in her house while she was unaware? Mya cracked her room door, strictly for the purpose of getting the heck out of there swiftly if the intruder suddenly appeared. She felt as if she were in a thriller and slowly made her way to the closet. Her heart beat tripled. *Calm down before you beat yourself right out of my chest,* she thought, touching her heart. She placed her hand on the closet door and turned the doorknob. Nothing. Relieved, she closed her eyes and took a deep breath, squatting at the entrance of the closet. Yes, she was looking for a pair of feet. "That rose didn't get here by itself," she spoke aloud, giving the closet a thorough search. Growing agitated rather than fearful, she headed toward the windows and was somewhat surprised to find that it was unlocked and opened easily. "Now, I know this dude ain't gone through the trouble of getting a ladder just to climb through my window!" She looked down toward the ground, only to see grass. "He must think that this sick game is actually cute to me. My patience is running thin," Mya snapped as she locked the window and closed the curtains. She rolled her eyes. "If he thinks this is going to win me back, then he got something else coming." She dialed his number.

"Aunt Mya, some dude named King is on your cell phone." Her heart jumped as she heard Judah yell from downstairs. She hung up the house phone. Sway's cell had only rang once.

"Do you want me to tell him you'll call him back?"

"No. Do you mind bringing it to me?" Mya stuck her head out of the door.

"Who is King?" Judah asked as he mounted the stairs.

"Not now, Judah," she replied.

"What do you mean? You've never mentioned anybody named King to me. Is this a business call or personal?"

"Judah, I said not right now. I'm grown. Quit questioning me. Dang! Just hand me the phone," she said.

Once he managed to reach her room and pass her, her cell phone, she whispered, "Close the door for me on your way out. Thanks." He scrunched his face up, but did as she had asked.

"Hello!" she said as if King had been the one to irritate her.

"Hi uhhh, Mya. I must have caught you at a bad time," King replied.

"Kind of, but what's up?" Mya walked over to her dresser and put on her underwear, a pair of jogging pants, and a T-shirt.

"I really just wanted to hear your voice," he said plainly.

"I'm sorry, King. I'm pretty annoyed right now. Do you mind if I call you back?"

"It's all good. I'm cool with that," he responded.

"Thanks. Good night."

"Have a better evening, Mya. Good night."

She heard the front door slam and raced down the stairs and out the front door to catch up with Judah to apologize for her rude behavior. His truck was still parked in the driveway. She glanced from left to right, giving her block a half panoramic view. Sighing deeply, she went back inside and ran toward Judah's room and opened the door. He lay in bed with his Beats by Dre headphones on blast.

"Judah!" she yelled. His eyes were closed. "Judah!" She finally shook his arm. He removed his headphones, looking at her curiously.

"Did you have company?"

"No."

"You sure?"

"Yeah, I'm sure. Why?"

"'Cause I heard the front door slam."

"We're the only two people in here, Aunt Mya. Let's go check the house," he said seriously. He grabbed a flashlight. Together they checked each room and the basement and found absolutely nothing. As they made their rounds, Mya apologized to Judah and he accepted. They made sure their house was secure.

"I'll go start your dinner. I know I heard a door close, Judah. I'm sure of it," she said. Either Judah had just snuck some girl out of the house, or Sway had just made his exit.

Confess your faults one to another, and pray for one another, that ye may be healed. The effectual fervent prayer of a righteous man availeth much.

James 5:16 (KJV)

CHAPTER 21

Friday (6:50 p.m.)

"Coach Riley, you got everything in place?" Mya asked.

"Yes. Mya, everything is set," he replied.

"Good, because I'm almost there. How's my baby?"

"He's fine. A little nervous, but the boys are keeping him distracted. Do you know practically the entire school has been showing this boy love all day? You should see the gifts he received."

"Yes, he texted me during lunch. I'll see you shortly."

"Okay. See you in a minute."

Mya rested her phone in her lap and concentrated on the road. She didn't want to jeopardize tonight. Her cell rang. She started not to answer, but it might be Judah. Without taking her eyes off the road, she answered.

"Hello?"

"Hi, sunshine." It was Sway; she knew without question.

"Good evening." She kept her tone flat, avoiding mixed signals.

"Are you busy?"

"Actually, I am. I don't mean to seem rude, but can you make this quick?"

"I miss you, Mya. I want to be with my family."

"Sway, I can't do this right now."

"I know. I was hoping you and Judah would allow me to be a part of his birthday celebration."

Is he serious? Mya thought. "I don't think Judah would like to focus on you tonight. Look, if you think there is any chance of redemption, just give it time."

"Mya, everybody makes mistakes!" he yelled into the phone, trailing a line of curse words.

"Sway, I'm not doing this. I'm not going to fight with you. That's what got you in this position in the first place. Good night." Mya dropped the phone in her lap as she stopped at the red light. She placed her head on the steering wheel and began to pray.

The driver of the car behind her blew the horn. Out of instinct, she placed her foot on the gas and accelerated forward. The car in the opposite lane cut her off. Mya slammed on the brakes. Tires screeched. She ducked her head in her arms and squeezed her eyes shut as she screamed, "Jesus!" Her car spun out of control and Mya prepared herself for impact. A few seconds passed, and finally the car stopped moving. She opened her eyes and looked around. The vehicle she expected to hit her had stopped inches from the passenger side. A man was getting out of the vehicle.

"Ma'am, are you all right?" he asked, approaching the passenger window. Mya snapped out of her shock and jumped out of the car, amazed that she wasn't hit. She ran around to look at her car.

"Oh my God!" was all she was able to fathom. She knew this could've ended differently.

"Ma'am, are you okay?" the other driver asked again.

"Yes! Yes, I'm fine!" Mya rushed over to him. "I'm so sorry . . . I am so sorry. I almost caused you to wreck." Mya was very apologetic.

"It's okay. I'm relieved no one got hurt."

She could hear her phone ringing in the distance. Angry drivers glared and honked as they drove around the awkwardly positioned cars that had slowed down traffic. Suddenly, the unwanted attention made her uncomfortable. She apologized again and rushed back to her car. Her phone lay on the ground. "It must have fallen out of my lap and out of the car once I opened the door. Geesh!" Mya picked up her cell phone, hopped in her ride, and maneuvered back into the flow of traffic. At the stoplight, she glanced at her phone. Two missed calls from Judah. She considered calling him back, but reasoned she would see him momentarily. Her phone rang inside the cup holder where she'd just set it. It was Sway. Glancing up, she saw the car in front of her moving and proceeded forward as well. She had turned out into traffic without signaling, and noticed too little too late that the traffic light wasn't in her favor. Again, she slammed on brakes to avoid another collision. The phone kept ringing and ringing. Sway wouldn't let up. It seemed like a revelation from God. *Anything dealing with that man throws everything off balance. Not good,* she immediately thought as she drove slowly and cautiously toward her destination.

Minutes later, she pulled into the high school arena where hundreds had already gathered. She jumped out of the car with a smile stretched across her face without effort. Sway wouldn't ruin this night. If Judah could press beyond the mishaps in his own life and still give his all every single day; then she could set aside her personal drama and make this night a celebration to remember! As Mya caught a reflection of herself in the window, she couldn't help but see that she'd put on a couple pounds since Sway had left, and her backside was protruding a little more. Between eating with Riley, Judah, and King, she'd have to start working out. She secured the car and was crossing the street when she noticed King.

"Heyyyyy! I didn't know you were coming to the game."

"Well, I didn't want to miss seeing Judah in action, and of course, the biggest high school rivalry of the year."

Mr. Springer, Andrew Jackson High School Assistant Coach spotted Mya and got her attention, motioning her and King to come ahead of the line. They declined the offer, but thanked Coach Springer, knowing they did the right thing because angry glances from anxious football fans would have been all over them. Once they entered, they stopped by the concession stand, not wanting to get up during the game. King was such a gentleman. He didn't want her to carry anything. Nothing like Sway. She would have had to carry her food and his food.

She got her same spot, the seat in the bleacher next to the band. They were just marching in. About three minutes later, the band eventually got settled; the game would start in a few minutes.

"Mya! Mya!" Coach Riley waved, motioning her to come here.

"I'll be back in a moment," she told King.

"Mya, you've got to come to the dressing room. He won't come out until he sees you."

"I'll be back," she told King and followed Coach Riley to the entrance of the dressing room. And once the team saw that she was outside, they started shouting and clapping.

"Guys! Guys. There is no need for the uproar. Y'all are the stars tonight. Y'all are going to send Wilson back across town, wishing they had not stepped foot on your field. Plus, those recruiters will be trying to get all of you into their colleges." They began to cheer again. Coach Riley told them all to line up in the hall and led Mya into his office. Judah was sitting there, dressed from the waist down, right leg shaking and looking worried.

"Hey, love of my life."

"Auntie! Aw man! Man I was so scared. I was so scared!" He sat her down. "I was sitting here getting dressed when this feeling came over me. Then I had a vision of you spinning in the middle of the street in your car, screaming." He looked intently into her eyes. "I don't know what I'd do without you. I didn't know if I was having an anxiety attack or was just trippin' in my head. Something just didn't feel right. So I just started praying." Mya hugged him. The scene at the red light flashed in her mind. It gave her chills.

"Judah, I texted you when I arrived."

"I made a bet with the guys and lost, so I have to get a new phone."

166

"Who makes those types of bets?" She shook her head. "I'll tell you what. Finish getting dressed, and then I'll tell you what happened later."

"Give me the thirty second version, Aunt Mya. Go." He jumped to his feet. Mya elaborated about the phone call and the incident at the light. Judah bunched up his face like he had a sour taste in his mouth.

"Dude almost cost you your life."

"But guess what? Your prayers saved me."

Her words had to be as heavy as the profoundness of the situation. For a series of seconds he didn't say anything. "So what you're saying is God hears my prayers?" Judah said.

"That's exactly what I'm saying. Baby, it's all good! Now go on and show these rich boys how this praying man runs the ball."

"Auntie, you a trip!"

"I get it from you." Mya hugged him.

"Aunt Mya, would you pray for us?"

"Okay, let's do this." Without any more delay, she consulted with God. She finished her prayer and felt a sense of peace.

"All right then, I'll see you in a minute." She left while he headed toward the locker room to finish getting dressed.

"Aunt Mya!" Judah called after her. "I love you."

"I love you too!" She could hear them hyping themselves up as she practically ran back to her seat. She had a feeling tonight was going to be like no other night.

"Everything all right?" King asked, standing up and taking Mya by the hand and leading her back to her seat.

"Yeah. Judah asked me to pray with the team. Can you believe it?" Mya looked at King, expecting him to say he couldn't.

"Yes, I can believe it. You're a woman of strong faith," King said.

Why does this man have so much faith in me? She set her attention on the field, trying to deny the rising feeling that she had to tell him why Judah was initially upset. Looking over at him, her eyes met his, and his fixed gaze made her feel as if he were looking through her. His stare compelled her to just spit it out.

"Sway called me on the way here. The call was upsetting me so much that I almost wrecked." She wasn't sure what his response would be, so she braced herself for whatever accusation he might make. He made none.

Instead he said, "Thank God! For his faithfulness! I'm so glad that you're here with me now. And you're well and sitting right next to me. I enjoy having your company in my life!" Mya felt herself wanting to cry. Was it because God had spared her life? Or was it because King was so understanding. It probably was a combination of things. She almost felt she didn't deserve it.

"Oh yeah, while you were gone, Shon, Judah's friend's mother sent someone to get the shirts. I asked them to leave you one." *This man is so thoughtful,* she thought.

"You know what?" he asked.

"What?" she responded, staring into his eyes.

"You're the sexiest, godly woman I have ever laid eyes on. I know sexiest doesn't fit with godly, but I am very much attracted to you. But there's just this . . . *energy* surrounding you that tells me that you truly love God."

"King, get out of here. Why would you put God and sexy in the same sentence?" Mya asked with her head cocked to right.

"What? It's a compliment. Shoot, I don't know." He laughed. "You've got some women wishing they could be like you. Mya, you are one bad woman!" He couldn't restrain his laughter. "I'm serious!"

They shared a laugh. "Look at that." He referred to her smile. "I could spend my life staring at that."

"King, you never cease to amaze me." She kissed her fingers, and then placed them on his lips.

"And now, ladies and gentlemen, give it up for the undefeated Andrew Jackson Tigers!" the announcer said.

Everyone was screaming. Maya and several parents of Judah's teammates stood in the bleachers with T-shirts of Judah's face that said "Happy Birthday" on it. Right after they announced Judah as the team captain, his schoolmates and the parent began singing Happy Birthday. By the time they finished, Judah was on his knees praying. He rose to his feet with one finger pointing toward heaven, acknowledging God. He had never done this.

Mya's eyes began to mist. She mouthed the words, "You're the best," like she did at every game.

Coach Riley called their play and they lined up. Mya didn't even know why she even sat down. Every time she did, she was back up. By the end of the first quarter, they were winning with a 14-point lead. Judah told her at halftime that they weren't ending the game until they had a 21-point lead. And by the end of the game, he made good on his word.

As a few spectators began leaving, Judah motioned Mya over to him. He picked her up and spun her around. He put her down just in time to avoid the cooler of ice water being dumped on him.

"Oooh! Y'all going to pay for that!" Judah threatened the team as he jumped up and down, trying to shake off the chill from the ice.

"Boo, you showed out, didn't you?" Mya said as she handed him the towel the water boy had just handed her.

"Thank you!" He rested his wet and sweaty arm over her shoulder.

"I've been watching you. Who is that little dude you been hugged up with? Is that King?"

"Judah, we are not talking about this now, and you didn't see me hugged up."

"You're kidding me. You've been grinning since I saw you." She burst out laughing.

"Oh, you think it's funny?" Judah stopped in his tracks.

"The only thing funny about the entire situation is that lil bitty dude got your head spinning."

"You're pushing it." Mya felt herself blushing. She was relieved when Coach Riley approached with two scouters.

"That was an outstanding performance, young man. You make football worth watching. You're full of surprises." The man extended his hand to Judah. "My name is Chase Wilmot, University of Alabama."

"And I'm Andre Foster, Georgia State." He then proceeded to shake Judah's hand.

"Mya Jenkins." Judah directed their attention to his aunt.

"Your son is truly talented," Mr. Foster addressed Mya, extending his hand to her.

"Oh no—" Mya attempted to correct him.

"If I did my research correctly," Mr. Wilmot interrupted her. "Your aunt is listed as your guardian." He addressed Judah.

"Yeah . . ." Judah answered shyly.

"So . . . would this be her?" Mr. Wilmot further inquired.

"It is indeed." He perked up a little.

"It's a pleasure to meet you. I hope someday we'll have the chance to discuss what it's like to raise such a humble young man." Mr. Wilmot seemed proud of himself for taking time to familiarize himself with Judah's situation.

"If it's God's will, we will," Mya responded, smiling proudly.

"Young man, you grew up under some very unique circumstances, and the fact that you are doing so well, despite the odds is admirable," Mr. Wilmot sincerely admonished.

"Yeah, he is an amazing young man. Always has been, and he's been raised by some incredible women," Coach Riley chimed in.

The smile Judah donned disappeared. Mya could feel his muscles flexing in his arm, and she didn't have to look at him to know his temper was pulsing. It was apparent that Riley's speech upset Judah. Gracefully, she undid her arm and began stroking his back. She didn't want Judah to lose his temper in front of these scouts.

"Indeed. I have been blessed. Mya is my aunt, but her and my late grandmother were wonderful mother figures to me." Judah addressed the scouts but stared directly at Riley. "But I have no idea what it's like to have a father." He ended his statement coldly. Coach Riley blinked and looked away for a second.

"Well, gentleman . . ." Mya took over. "I'm sure we will both be seeing the two of you again."

"Of course, of course." Mr. Chase finally spoke. "Absolutely . . . I understand it's your birthday and tonight is a big night for you. So I won't hold you any longer." Mr. Wilmot gave Judah a jacket and a hat similar to the one he wore.

"Thank you, sir," Judah said.

"No. Thank you." They all shook hands again and Coach Riley excused himself. Judah watched as he escorted the two scouters off the field.

"Auntie, did you hear this dude? Acting like he has known me since I was a child. Like he personally knew my Big Momma. If it wasn't for them scouts, I would have laid him out! I'm starting to feel like I don't want him around until the test results come in the mail."

Favour is deceitful, and beauty is vain: but a woman that feareth the Lord, she shall be praised.

Proverbs 31:30 (KJV)

CHAPTER 22

Stadium (9:36 p.m.)

"This boy knows he takes a long time." A single glance at her watch showed it was nearing the time where they'd eventually end up at their destination much later than expected if Judah didn't get a move on.

"I doubt that you have to do much of anything besides wake up," King stated, stealing her attention.

"King, you are so sweet. You always know what to say."

"I just speak the truth."

"Do you really think that's all I have to do?" Mya said.

He took his time answering. "Do you listen when I'm talking to you? Your outer beauty is natural. Nothing you have to enhance with makeup. But your inner beauty is . . . breath-taking. Just by the way you care for Judah shows me how giving, kind, and loyal your heart is. It's all anyone wants when in search of the perfect mate. So yes, I'll admit it, I am enamored by your beauty. Girl, you are as fine as wine! But I can see way beyond that. I can feel what's inside your heart, your mind . . . I can sense your undying love for God. And it's, it's . . . it's so soul-stirring."

Mya felt as if she was about to break out in a sweat. She wanted to

173

rest her head on his shoulder, but she spotted Judah approaching and didn't want King to have to endure his height jokes.

"Good evening, Mr. King," Judah said.

"Please, call me King." King told him as he shook his hand. "Young man, you have a gift."

"Appreciate that," Judah responded politely, but he had a pressing concern on his mind. "So what's your intentions for my aunt?" Judah towered over King, his chest high and his hands in his pockets. Staring at King like his life depended on his answer.

Mya thought she would faint. She almost couldn't believe Judah, but after the drama with Sway, she should have known.

"I respect you for that, being that Mya is your leading lady. My intentions are to sacrifice my life so that she may have life. She's everything I've always dreamed of." King never broke eye contact with Judah.

Mya felt mixed emotions. He had to be the most considerate man on earth. She only heard of his type in fairy tales, which made her question if she could take him at his word. Judah, on the other hand, didn't seemed moved.

"I understand," King said after moments of silence. He and Judah gave each other dap.

"So where we going?" Judah asked Mya.

"You just follow me. That's all you need to know." She glanced at King, who was comfortable with Judah's dominance. Unlike Sway.

"Now I know why you wanted me to follow you. Give me the keys!" Judah exclaimed.

"Give you the keys to what?" Mya asked, confused. At that moment, she noticed the candy apple red Escalade. *This has Sway written all over it,* Mya thought.

"Happy Birthday, lil buddy," Sway said, stepping out of hiding and leaning against the SUV. Judah's facial expression changed.

"What's the matter? You don't like my present? This straight off the lot," Sway said, eyes filled with disappointment.

"Nah. No thank you. Dude, what're you doing around these parts? You *know* you're not invited."

Sway stood up. "Judah. Man, I didn't come to start no trouble. I'm just trying to celebrate with my family." He smiled, extending his hand for a peace offering.

"Family!" Judah yelled. "You forgot about family the day you put your hands on my aunt."

Sway approached Judah. Mya jumped in between them.

"Not tonight, Sway. I'm asking you to get in your truck and leave." Mya was surprised at how calm her voice was. Sway didn't say a word, instead he pulled Mya in and tried to kiss her. She slapped him.

Before Judah could respond, King did. "Brother, I think it's time you leave."

"Who is this dude?" Sway asked no one in particular.

Mya closed in the space between her and King. "That's all right. We will leave. If he wants to stay, he can." She cuffed her hand in King's and attempted to pull him away. He didn't budge. Judah stood beside him, mean-mugging Sway.

"Please, Father. Please let there be peace tonight for Judah's birthday celebration," she muttered.

Sway's eyes dashed from King to Mya. "You with him? This your dude?" The sound of his incredulity made her flinch. King stood his ground.

"Baby, y'all go ahead," King instructed her, never taking his eyes off Sway.

"Baby! Did you just call my woman baby?" Sway barked.

"Man, I believe in handling things in decency, but it turns my stomach when a man puts his hands on a woman. I'm gonna ask you one more time to get in your truck and leave." King stood inches from Sway, fists balled up. He had no doubt he could take Sway.

Suddenly, Coach Riley joined King and Judah. Then a few security officers stepped on the scene.

"Y'all ain't even worth my time. I'll catch you later. I will most definitely catch you later," Sway spat, glaring at Mya and King and Judah. Then he jumped in his truck and left.

"I think it was a good idea parking your car at my house. Sway will probably think we're inside," Mya told King as they pulled out of the driveway of her residence.

Holding her breath, Mya closed her eyes and anticipated the moment when their lips met.

Beep, beep!

The abrupt sound of Judah's horn suddenly brought her back to earth. The two of them looked back and started smiling. Judah had his all black F150 right up on her bumper. "He's one anxious young man, huh?" King asked as he finally pulled off.

"Promise to keep your eyes on the road?" When she didn't get a response, she repeated herself.

"I promise," King answered with laughter. "You know I will."

Mya climbed in the back to change her outfit, hoping Sway wouldn't do any more of his pop-up visits tonight.

A man hath joy by the answer of his mouth: and a word spoken in due season, how good is it!

Proverbs 15:23 (KJV)

CHAPTER 23

Beach House (11:00 p.m.)

The beach house Mya rented for Judah's eighteenth birthday was in full swing. Guests were in all white attire, and they were able to swim in the indoor pool if they chose. She was amazed at how well this house full of teenagers were conducting themselves.

She looked around the room and noticed Judah stealing glances at one young lady. The cute girl acknowledged his stare, but didn't step to him. *That's right, baby girl,* she thought.

It soothed her to see her chaperones, who were some of the teammates' parents and King, spread throughout the house keeping a watchful eye. Coach Riley challenged the teens on the pool table. While another parent busied herself with food and drinks, making sure the kitchen island stayed packed with snacks and finger food. King seemed to fit in playing cards, talking smack with his teammate against Shon and Alfred.

Everything was perfect. She couldn't have asked for a better turnout. Everyone looked content, except her. She couldn't deny the subtle longing for Sway, hoping that he was okay. Mya walked around for five more minutes, making sure that everything was going as planned. Yet

179

the urge to be alone overwhelmed her. She remembered the bottle of wine in her trunk that was left over from her picnic with Janelle.

She grabbed her car keys, a glass and her cell phone and snuck out the door. The second she stepped out, she knew it was a wonderful idea. The sound of waves crashing in the distance. The cool night breeze. It was beautiful. She walked the short distance to where she was parked. As she opened the trunk, her mouth watered at the sight of the wine bottle. Mya popped the cork and filled her glass. She leaned against the car, its trunk still open and tossed her head back, finishing the sweet tasting elixir in one semi-long gulp. *I just wanna be free from worry. At least for a few hours,* Mya thought with closed eyes.

"Mya, I really need to talk to you," Sway whispered. Mya opened her eyes to find Sway standing in front of her. She blinked, thinking she was trippin'. Again, she opened her eyes, and the wine glass slipped from her grasp and shattered.

"Sway, what're you doing here?"

"Mya, I'm not trying to cause any trouble!" Sway looked so pathetic, hands at his side and head held down. She glanced back at the house to see if anyone was peeking out of the door or a window.

She was undecided, but the thought of ruining the night was not up for discussion. "You've got three minutes."

"Do you mind sitting in my car?"

"Sway, I don't have time for this." Mya shifted her weight to her left foot.

"You said I only got three minutes, and I see you watching the house. If you get in my car, I might have your undivided attention for all three minutes." Again she peered around the trunk and back at the house. She closed her trunk and followed Sway to his vehicle, parked four cars down. They got inside and she kept the house in view and refused to close the passenger door. The thought of him being parked out here so close spooked her. She never heard him drive up. One glass of wine wasn't enough to make her miss someone parking so close. *How long had he been parked out here?*

"Do you love him?" he asked.

She turned to look at him. His eyes were red. Those crazy eyes appeared again, dancing around in his sockets. Sway couldn't focus on one thing. He glanced all around, paranoid. *His hair is too long. He hasn't had a haircut in a while,* she thought. *What is going on?* Mya looked away, refusing to acknowledge the decline in his appearance. Sway kept sniffing the air.

"You smell that?" he asked, rubbing his nose.

"Smell what?" she asked, sniffing just as he had done. All she took in was a breath of fresh air. *He's high!*

"Do you still love me?" He leaned in quickly and kissed her lips, startling her at first. His warm lips pressed against her wine infused lips and she kissed him back. His cell phone began ringing, breaking up the moment. It was as if someone had turned the light on.

"I've gotta go. Without delay, she pulled away, leaving her keys in his seat. She didn't quite run, but lightly jogged back toward the house. Her cell phone rang again.

"Yes, love?" Mya answered.

"Where are you? I haven't seen you in a minute," King said on the other end. It was 11:30 p.m.

"Well, I wondered if you'd notice." She had to think fast. Her hands were shaking. She seemed to only relax once she noticed Sway cutting on his lights and pulling off.

"I got a little jealous, seeing you giving the kids all your attention, so I stepped out. I'll tell you what, if you can manage to get away for about two minutes . . . I could use an 'I'm-just-fine embrace' right now."

Mya went to retrieve the wine bottle and towel and realized she didn't have her keys. *Dang! I must have left them with Sway.* She headed to the beachfront, anxious to get off the phone.

"Oh yeah! If you want, you can have all my attention for the rest of your life," King replied.

"How about we start right now?" Mya urged, wanting to call Sway.

"I'll see you in a minute."

181

"Bring a towel or a blanket." She hung up, then dialed Sway's number, but he didn't answer. *I'll get them later.* Mya ended the call.

She found a nice spot on the sand where she could see the beach house, but still enjoy the scenery. Looking up at the sky, Mya's heart cried out the tears that she couldn't.

"Ain't no sunshine when she's gone," King sang as he approached. He kissed her forehead as he sat next to her, extending his arm over her shoulder and beckoning her to relax.

"Nothing concerning you takes God by surprise," King softly said. His words were perfect. As if God himself was speaking to her!

She was so grateful her head lay against him because as she had grown accustomed to, she cried silently. He never said another word. His arms spoke for him. They talked for a few hours and headed back to the beach house. King seemed content, yet a bit solemn. Mya worrried about Sway's mental health. *He's gonna go crazy if he doesn't get some help soon.*

That Saturday morning at 5:30 a.m., Mya opened her eyes, surprised to find herself still bowed on her knees, elbows pressed against the mattress. *I must have fallen asleep again while praying,* she thought. She entertained the idea of getting straight up, but the subtle tugging in her spirit compelled her to stay. Without restraint, she worshipped the One who had brought her this far, for the grace he promised was renewed every morning. For his hedge of protection to be placed around her family and friends. She then cried her heart out, pleading with her redeemer to keep her and not allow her own emotions to deceive her. Was Sway doing drugs? Had her distance drove him to such measures, and had she blown the possibility of leading him to Christ. The entire situation exhausted her. Mya remained on her knees until her tears ceased. Today would definitely be a day that she walked by faith. After brushing her teeth and washing her face, she put on her brave face and slipped on a tank top and leggings, headed for the complimentary gym.

The chaperones would handle breakfast while she got in a workout, her daily routine.

The sun was barely peeking over the horizon, shining through the glass windows of the beach house. She could see herself starting off each day like this. As if she hadn't missed a day, she worked up a good sweat on the treadmill, and then maneuvered to the weights, moving at a decent pace.

"When I couldn't locate you in the kitchen, I knew you would be in here," Judah announced as he walked into the room. Mya smiled, relieved she had gotten at least forty-five minutes alone.

"So how's the birthday boy?" She grunted, trying to lift herself on the bar.

"You would think by now, you would realize I'm a grown man," Judah stated as he adjusted the weights.

Mya knew she had a grown man on her hands, but he was still her baby.

"You need me to show you how that's done?" Judah teased as he laid back to bench press.

"If I did, I would have asked," Mya retorted, looking on as Judah lowered the bar and pumped it up several times. "Now you might can help me do that. I'm curious as to how much I can lift."

"I don't think you're ready for this. This here is for a man." He bench pressed a couple more.

"If I wanted your opinion, I would have asked for it," she teased.

"Aunt Mya, let me ask you something." Judah set down the weights and looked her square in the eyes.

"What is it? Why do you suddenly look so serious?" She kneeled beside him and took his hand into hers. "What, baby? What's on your mind?"

"Ol' boy was here last night, wasn't he?" Judah got straight to the point.

Mya's brows furrowed, her act of obliviousness was just beginning. But she and Judah were too close for that. "Yes. Yes he was. I imagine he somehow got word about your party, maybe on Facebook, Instagram, or Twitter." Judah didn't respond. Mya couldn't deny the wave of shame that washed over her. *I need a drink*, she thought, breaking eye contact. She stood quickly and walked over to the window and stared out of it, holding herself as if she'd suddenly caught a chill. A few seconds passed, and she glanced back at Judah, who flexed his jaw as his anger began to grow.

"Well, Ju, say something. How did you know?" she asked, hoping it wouldn't ruin his day.

"Buddy is going to keep fooling around and get dealt with. You and I both know how he knew where we were. Alfred and Shon said you specifically told everyone not to post it on social media. So he had to have followed us here."

"There's no need to trip. I took care of it."

"I don't trust him, period. Aunt Mya, stay away from him."

"Judah . . ." Mya wanted him to let it go.

"Judah nothing. I saw you getting out of his car too."

Her heart stopped. Had King saw her as well? She turned to face Judah, searching his eyes for answers. King had called her after she and Sway parted.

"No. He didn't see you. I got up to answer my cell, and I just so happened to post up in the window." He knew her thoughts and it surprised her. She placed her hand on one hip, thinking about how bad last night could have turned out. In her heart she knew it wasn't a good idea to talk to Sway, but she felt he needed someone outside of his so-called mother. She and Judah were all the family he had.

"Aunt Mya, you can't save the world. Some people don't want to change, and some people only God can change. It doesn't happen on your terms."

"Good morning," King said as he walked into the room and gave Judah some dap. He then walked over to Mya, who was still standing at the window, and hugged her. "Just wanted y'all to know that breakfast is ready."

"Thank you. Let me wash my face and hands. I'll be right there," Mya replied.

"Okay." King looked from Mya to Judah, turned on his heels and made his exit.

"We'll finish this conversation later," Mya stated to Judah as they left the weight room.

In five minutes, Mya had made it to the kitchen. "Mmm, it smells good in here. Real good!" Mya said as she found a place to sit at the dining room table. Alfred's mother, Victoria was setting the table. King was taking the last batch of bacon from the skillet.

"King, you know what you doing?" Mya asked.

"Most definitely . . . This is all me," he boasted. Mya looked at the food that was arranged on the table. Pancakes stacked a mile high, fluffy scrambled eggs, home fries, sausage, grilled steaks, omelets and the bacon that King was bringing over.

"You cooked this all by yourself, huh?" Mya asked in disbelief.

"Everything but that orange juice Ms. Victoria made using freshly squeezed oranges." Ms. Victoria smiled and sat down at the table.

Mya smiled as well, happy to be able to sit down and eat a meal she hadn't had to make herself. "Oh, a sister can get used to this." Shon and Alfred also joined them at the table after greeting everyone with good morning.

"Just say the word and you can have whatever you like." King caught her off guard. Mya blushed.

"Hey now. You gotta go through us before you can have her," Shon said, addressing King.

"Really?" Judah asked, speaking to Shon from across the table.

"Yeah! You know how we feel about Aunt Mya," Alfred replied, dapping Shon beneath the table.

"Yep . . . and y'all know how I feel about you two." Judah tried not to sound menacing; his homeboys' parents were present. However, if anyone had taken the time to look in his eyes, the threat was visible behind his serious stare.

185

"I'll tell you what. It's good to know I have so many caring men in my life. Y'all make a sister feel important." Mya saw Judah's disposition slipping. "King, will you bless our meal?" She extended her arms and grabbed the hand of the person sitting on both sides. Everyone followed her lead. King's voice boomed forth, loud and confident and full of the love of God. In the distance, Mya heard her phone ringing.

Forty minutes later, only bones were left on plates, and a couple of pancakes were on the serving plate. The bacon had completely disappeared and so had the eggs and home fries. Everyone was sitting around talking and laughing, except Mya. She had excused herself from the table and headed to the bathroom. She sat on the toilet listening to the messages Sway had left on her voicemail:

5:51 a.m.

"Nothing pisses me off more than to call you and not get an answer. You do all that talking about loving me, but look at how you treat me. If you don't want to be with me just say it."

6:12 a.m.

"I can't stand liars! They make my skin crawl . . ."

6:43 a.m.

"Mya, answer this phone, baby. I need you . . . I love you."

7:00 a.m.

"Ain't nothin' different 'bout you. You just like these sluts and thots out here in these streets. I don't know what I was thinking trying to marry a thot-slut like you."

Mya bowed her head, grateful she was alone. Her hand shook and her head pounded at her temples. Fury was the only feeling she could identify. *I'm so fed up with Sway. What the heck is going on with him? Romantic during one moment and the next he's calling me all kind of names. He's like night and day.* The level of disrespect had gone too far. *I'm sick of this back and forth with him.*

Instead of going back to the table, she tiptoed to her room to pack up her things, preparing to leave. *I can't protect myself by staying on this beach. I need to get Judah and myself home.* She thought only of the shears in the

186

drawer at home. Shears were no match for Sway, the street-savvy hood dude, who at the drop of a dime could become a ravening, glock-toting beast. *Please let me find a gun at home in one of Sway's hiding spots,* she prayed, although she knew she shouldn't have.

Be not wise in your own eyes: fear the Lord, and depart from evil.

CHAPTER 24

Beach house (11:15 a.m.)

"Judah, I need your set of house keys and my extra car key," Mya said after they'd left everyone in the dining room.

"Where are your keys?" he asked, looking confused.

"I don't know. I've looked everywhere and I can't find them."

"What was the last time you saw—"

"Judah!" Mya snapped, interrupting him. "Baby, I know you mean well, but I can't do this right now. I need your keys, and I'll meet back up with you later to make sure you get them back. Stay here and enjoy yourself. I love you. If you want to contact me, just call my cell, but I can't go into details."

"Okay, but at least tell me if something is wrong," Judah said as he pulled out his keys from his pocket. She took a deep breath, wishing she could just tell him about the messages, but she didn't want him to worry.

"I got some stuff on my mind, but I got to get back into the city so I can get my hair done."

Judah searched her soul for sincerity and truth before he handed her the keys. Mya knew he wasn't buying it, but was relieved that he hadn't kept pressing her. She hugged him briefly. "I love you, baby and

189

everything is going to be all right. We just have to trust God to be what we can't and to do what we don't have the power to do." Again she hugged him, then left the room. She headed back into the dining room and encouraged the guys to get a good swim in before check out time.

Ten minutes later, Mya smiled at the sight of the guys having fun in the water. She blew Judah a kiss and told him to call her if he needed to and she would be back. King met her at the door.

"You going to hold down the fort until I get back?" Mya asked King with a smile.

"Mya, have I failed you yet?" He stopped her in her tracks on the front porch.

"To think of it, you haven't." Mya grinned slightly. She could sense King wanted to be serious, but she wasn't in the proper state of mind for that. Not right now. "If you need me, call my phone, okay?" He grabbed her hand as she tried to step away.

"Mya, I just want you to know that no distance and time can change what I feel regarding you and Judah. Your past, the present, or even the future can't deter or hinder my love for you. I'll stand on the sideline cheering you on, praying that my Heavenly Father guides you directly to my heart."

Mya stared into King's hopeful eyes. He was a good man, one any smart woman would love to have as her own, but she couldn't be that woman right now. She didn't know if she would ever be able to love anyone outside of Sway. She parted her lips to speak, but nothing came out. Closing her eyes, Mya prayed for the words to say. When she opened her eyes, nothing had changed. She was still at a loss for words. Against her better judgment, she leaned down and pecked King's lips. As she pulled away, King gently grabbed the back of her head. She did not resist, and they kissed a lot longer than she had anticipated. Finally, they broke their contact.

"Mya . . . I—" King attempted to speak.

"I have to go." She cut him off as she rushed down the stairs, knowing she shouldn't have kissed him. But how could she hurt him?

How could she tell him that she didn't know if she was capable of loving him? She pressed the unlock button on her key fob. The fob didn't sound off because the doors were already unlocked. Slowly, she pulled it open and peered inside. Nothing looked out of place. However, she turned to check her backseat and the sight almost terrified her. The word *SLUT* was carved into her cream colored leather seats. She knew exactly who had done it.

"What in the world!" King asked, taking Mya by surprise. He stood there in utter disbelief. The seats had been sliced several times in multiple places. Even her dashboard had been carved with the word *SLUT* and her keys were already in the ignition. Her anxiety made her miss the first carving.

"Mya, we need to call the police," King demanded, pulling her into his arms.

"No. Don't call them. I'm going to handle it. Sway is responsible for this." She pulled away and got in her car. "Give these to Judah." She passed King Judah's door keys.

"I think I should go with you," King pleaded.

"I'll be fine." She was fuming. "Call my cell if you need me, and whatever you do, don't tell Judah. Let me tell him myself." She started the ignition and pulled out. "I'll be fine, King." She closed the door and drove off abruptly.

Mya barely made it in the door when she heard her home phone ringing. Whoever it is will just have to leave a message. She just wanted to shower. Her temper was calming, but it wasn't enough to give Sway a pass. She decided she would miss her hair appointment and see if she could catch Sway on his turf.

During her shower, she dismissed King's words and refused to pray because she wanted to keep the momentum of her anger. She wanted to remain in the "pissed off" zone. She cut the water off and grabbed her towel and stepped out of the shower.

Her phone began ringing in the distance, but she was in no rush to answer it.

"Where's the lotion?" she said aloud as she searched the countertop for it, but couldn't locate it. She opened the drawer hoping it would possibly be in there.

The first thing that caught her attention was the shears. Immediately, images of the night her bathroom looked like a crime scene flashed before her eyes as if it was happening all over gain and not months ago. She shook her head vigorously to get the vision out of her head. She felt an ache that started in her heart and rushed to her gut just thinking about what Sway had done to her that night. Looking in the mirror, she felt blessed that there were no signs of bruising on her face. She could have cried but refused. She walked into her room and grabbed the Bath and Body Works lotion, swiftly moisturizing her skin. Afterward, she headed to her closet and decided to wear black denim and a hot pink tank top and her black leather Jordan's with hot pink trimming. She removed the jeans from the hanger and headed out of the walk-in closet, but was brought to a halt at the image before her.

"So you too good to answer the phone now?" Sway stated, more so than questioned as he stood in the closet looking deranged. He was dressed in the same clothes he'd worn the night before. Blood streaked his hand.

"How did you get in my house?" Mya questioned, contemplating getting dressed right where she stood.

"Don't answer my question with a question. You know I hate that."

"Being too good has nothing to do with it. I simply have something to do. Now answer me." Mya did her best not to seem phased by his presence. But his racing eyes told her the best thing to do was to get him to calm down, to appease his rage.

"Where you going? You going to meet that lil bitty dude?" He took a step closer.

"No. But how about you explain why you did that to my car." She spoke in the calmest voice she could muster. "Could you do me a favor?

Can you go in my drawer where I keep my underclothes and get me one of my black strapless bras?" Her main focus was to get out of the closet, so she wouldn't be cornered. But he didn't budge.

"Well, if it's like that, I'll get it myself." She attempted to walk past him, but he stepped in her way. "Sway, I don't have time for this. Unless you're trying to help me understand why you did what you did, you're wasting my time. She felt herself losing her composure.

"What you need to do is go into the bathroom and wash your hands because you're dripping blood on my carpet!"

"Woman!" he yelled. "Don't tell me what I need to do."

"I should've known you have not changed. You were this sweet guy last night, but then I listened to the type of messages you left on my phone. Then I saw what you did to my car seats . . . and now look at you . . . The same thing. Yelling at me, acting like you are about to hit me at any second."

"I have changed." He took another step closer.

"Sway, I just think it's best you leave. I don't want Judah to come home and see that you're here. Just give me some time." Cautiously, she stepped back, and he stepped forward.

"Mya, why can't you see that I love you? I don't mean to hurt you. I'm trying to get it right. I really am." Tears began to well up in his eyes.

Her insides were flipping, and her spirit yelled, "No. Don't give in!" She began to pray, but it came to a halt once Sway dropped to his knees and started crying. Pulling her closer, burying his face into her thighs. She was hesitant to hold him, knowing this was the perfect time to escape, but she reasoned that maybe this was the hand of God.

"Mya, I need you. I can't do this by myself," he said between sobs. He squeezed her tighter.

Sway, who you need is Jesus. He is the only one who can really bring you through. She wanted to say those words. She thought about what the deacon and deaconess said at church when someone was obviously bound in sin. "I'm going to pray for you."

He nodded yes as he continued to weep. "My Father in heaven, who

I have trusted since I was a girl. I ask that you forgive my sins so that this prayer is not hindered . . ." She took a deep breath. "Lord, I'm asking that you take control of Jermal's life. Come into his heart and show him the way to live, to everlasting life. To dry his tears and give him peace." Gradually, his sobs turned into soft weeping and eventually a little sniffling. Mya was convinced she had done what the Lord would have wanted her to do. She pried his arms from around her. For the first time that day he looked like himself. The very affectionate, caring man she fell for.

"Thank you," he said, fairly above a whisper.

"Don't thank me, thank the Lord. It's only through him that you feel better in the least."

"I'm sorry about your seats, getting blood everywhere and for your glass door." She looked down at her carpet and the towel she still wore. "I'll pay the repair and cleaning bill." He slowly got up and reached down in his pocket and pulled out a wad of money, then peeled off fifteen crispy one-hundred dollar bills and put them in her hand.

"Thank you. Do you mind stepping out so I can get dressed?" She knew by the look in his eyes where his mind was going. She just hoped it wouldn't lead him there.

"Huh? What did you say?" he inquired, never taking his eyes off her.

"I need you to step out of my closet. I have to get dressed and be off to my hair appointment."

"Oh, I was hoping you would let me have that towel to wrap my hand up since it's already covered in my blood." He walked closer to her, his physique towering over her.

"Give me a second, and you can have it." She felt vulnerable, even awkward with him being this close, but that wasn't as bad as the fact that she felt herself desiring him.

"I miss you, Mya Sincere Jenkins." Once again he had that look in his eyes, like no other woman could compare.

"Sway, I think you should wait for me out there." She skipped over her words.

He leaned down to kiss her, but she slightly turned her head. So he kissed her neck instead. A soft moan escaped her mouth. To her shame, his touch was arousing. She kept telling herself to stop and tell him to leave. "Sway . . ." His name seemed to be the only thing she could say as he removed her towel and exposed her nude body.

"Yes, tell me what you want," he asked as he caressed her.

"Please, don't do this. I can't sleep with you. It's just not in our favor to do this. I can't be what you want me to be; I'm trying to get things right with the Lord." He never stopped kissing or touching her as she made her plea.

"You don't have to sleep with me, but there is something I must do. I need you to know how bad I want you in my life." Immediately he got on his knees and began to do the very thing that was hard for any woman to resist. Images of the word "slut" carved into her dashboard flashed in her mind. She pulled away.

"Mya, you don't have to sleep with me to satisfy me. Just understand I need you. Please . . ."

"You should leave." She cut him off as she stepped around him and swiftly put on her underwear and jeans and snatched a shirt from her drawer and slipped it on.

"So now you don't want me to touch you?" Sway looked hurt as he got off his knees.

"Sway, I love you, but I need some time away from you."

"Mya, don't do this."

"Just leave, Sway. Please don't make this harder than what it has to be." On the inside she was shaking, but outwardly she looked sure of herself and strong.

"Mya, you think I'm about to stand around and just let some lil dude come in and take my family from me?" His tone was rising.

"Jermal, this is not about another man."

"You think I'm stupid, Mya?" He inched toward her.

"This is what this is about." She took her hand and pointed to Sway. "You losing your temper every time I don't comply with your demands.

And you keep putting your hands on me." Mya's voice rose as well. "That's what this is about!"

"I ain't tryna hear that mess you talkin'."

"I don't care, Jermal. All I want is for you to get out of my house." Mya headed toward her bedroom door. Sway grabbed her by the neck. But for some reason she didn't fold. She was sick of the roller coaster.

"Where you think you goin'?" he asked through clenched teeth as he pulled her back. She reached around and dug her nails into his hand until he let her go. "Girl, stop before I beat your a—"

"Do it!" she interrupted him. "Go ahead and do it! You'll still be the same weak, poor excuse for a man. Do it, Sway!" she screamed. "I've had enough, Jermal!"

Perplexed, he stared at her.

"As far as I'm concerned, I don't want to see you or hear from you until you get it together."

Bam!

Sway backhanded her. Mya grabbed her face as she slowly got her balance. "Are you done? Because I'm ready for you to leave."

Do not be anxious about anything, but in everything by prayer and supplication with thanksgiving let your requests be made known to God.

Philippians 4:6 (ESV)

CHAPTER 25

Monday (8:00 a.m.)

Mya paced her den, constantly praying. She couldn't help but believe God would do something in her situation. Tension invaded her home like a well-manned army. She waited until Judah returned home to show him her back door and her car. As expected, Judah flipped. She begged him not to take matters into his own hands. He was all she had and she didn't want to see him locked up for doing something foolish. She practically had to grab Judah's legs and hold on just to keep him from leaving while pleading with him. He didn't understand why she didn't want him to put Sway out of his misery. They even argued over the matter. Judah accused her of protecting Sway, but that was far from the truth. She let their disagreement rest because they had repairs to make because of the damage Sway created.

King put plywood on the window. He and Judah had nailed the three pieces down until she could get a replacement. Now she was waiting on the men to arrive to replace the entire door early this morning. King had also taken her to drop off her vehicle to get her seats and dashboard repaired.

Judah was upstairs asleep, although he should have been in school.

He made it known the night before that he would not be going; he had to be sure Sway wouldn't show his face anywhere near their home.

Mya returned home and began cleaning. Once she finished, she went down to her studio to paint, her way of unburdening herself of her problems. She didn't know how long she had been downstairs, but she decided to take a break to check on Judah. She opened the door to find him bobbing his head to some music and playing a video game. The sight made her smile, knowing his hot temper had cooled off. She decided to check the mailbox and took out several envelopes. Some was junk mail and others were legitimate bills. She was surprised to see an envelope marked DNA Diagnostics. "Oh my God! The results!" she said aloud.

It had been a few weeks since Coach Riley and Judah had given blood and saliva samples at the DNA testing center. None of them trusted the store bought tests. "I'm nervous like I'm the one who took the test," she said as she walked back into the house and closed the door. She took a deep breath. *Should I call Coach Riley? Gosh, I need a drink right now. I'll start cooking lunch, and then gather the guys.* She poured herself a glass of red wine and took out her ingredients.

Mya set the table for two and placed the envelope with the test results in front of her and waited for the aroma of the food to do its magic. In the meantime, her wine would do its magic. She chugged the remaining wine down and poured another.

"Good afternoon," Judah said.

"Good afternoon. You mind joining me for a quick lunch?" she asked. Judah pulled the chair out and sat next to her.

"Thank you," Mya stated sincerely.

"It's lunchtime. You're drinking kind of early. I thought wine was usually for dinner."

"According to whose judgment?" Mya glanced at the half-empty bottle.

"I didn't even know that you drank alcohol." Judah ignored her question.

"Usually, I don't. It's just something I've discovered I enjoy sometimes." Mya wasn't in the mood to defend herself. "This came for you today." Mya picked up the envelope and handed it to him. She watched her nephew closely. For weeks she wondered how this moment would affect their lives.

"Do you want to do this now, or would you prefer Riley be present?" Judah sat there stunned, holding the envelope and staring at it. He placed it beside his plate and picked up his fork.

"Bless the food," he instructed. Mya set her glass down, grabbed his hand and prayed over their meal.

Silently he took several bites of his parmesan chicken and twirled his fork with spaghetti. Half-way through the meal, Judah picked up his glass of fruit punch and emptied the glass.

"I'm ready," he said in a low tone and picked up the envelope.

"You sure?"

"Yes, ma'am. I just wanted to eat something first in case the results take away my appetite." He smirked a little. Mya admired his sense of humor. Judah took a deep breath and tore into the envelope. Hastily, he pulled out the paper and his eyes raced toward the print. A couple of seconds passed and he handed it to Mya. Normally she could read him, but this time she was clueless.

She looked at the paper and began to read, not realizing she had been holding her breath. Mya set the paper on the table and inhaled for four seconds and released.

"So, he is your father."

"Janell listen, I don't know what this fool wants, all I know is he keeps calling and texting me. Leaving me voicemails, begging me to come meet him." Mya practically yelled at her friend who was stretched across Mya's bed.

"Girl, if Sway keeps calling, why not just answer. It seems like the most logical thing to do."

"Because we just found out that Coach Riley is Judah's father and that's got me stressed out. I don't have the time nor the energy for Sway and his emotional rollercoaster."

"Mya, maybe you're being too hard on the man." Janelle sat up.

"Too hard on him?" Mya couldn't believe her ears. "Do you know that last time I saw him, he was still on some BS? Janelle, he put his hands on me again. All that talk about change and he did the same thing." Mya's emotions were stirring, threatening to pour out full throttle, but she pushed them back. Her days of crying over this cat were done.

Janelle took Mya's hands into hers. "Mya, I understand where you're coming from, but avoiding him isn't going to get rid of the problem. He won't let up. You have to face him. Somehow, you have to get him to understand you don't want to be with him like that anymore and you two can remain just friends."

"I know, but lately I don't know who I'm dealing with. It's like he gets a thought in his head and the rest is history. Girl, you would have to see the cold, empty glare that shows in his eyes suddenly—I mean it comes out of nowhere."

"Sounds like he's using drugs or something."

"Girl!" Mya practically jumped off the bed. "I've been wondering the same thing. It's the only thing that makes sense, but Sway is against using drugs." Her phone rang. She reached for it as it lay in her bed.

"Speaking of the devil." Mya held her phone up.

"Just answer it," Janelle said.

"No. Because I already know what he is going to say: I need to see you, or we need to talk, or can you meet me somewhere? Absolutely not!" Mya replied.

"Well, let's do it. If it will help get him out of the picture. We can go meet him somewhere together. I dare him to put his hands on you in my presence. All them uncles and cousins I got! They'd be all over him if he even think about coming at you wrong. Answer the phone and just dead this whole thing," Janelle suggested. Mya complied.

Dang I wish I was as brave as Janelle. Honestly, Mya had grown tired and just wanted to move forward. She stared at her phone and pressed the call button. Was she really ready to cut ties with Sway? That was the question. Or would he be so willing to let her go without a fight? That should have been her major concern.

Thirty minutes later, the two women were on their way to put an end to all of the relationship drama Mya had going on with Sway.

"Janelle, this doesn't make no sense. Why in the world would Sway want to meet here? Especially all the way out here in Orange Park?" Mya said as they made their ramp exit. This meet-up spot seemed weird, and she hoped he wasn't trying to set a trap for her.

"Girl, I don't know, but I got my uncle on standby," Janelle said. They both laughed.

"I can't wait to see his face when he realizes I didn't take a cab and you brought me instead."

"He'll be all right. All that—take-a-cab-and-come-way-out-here sounds like some foolishness. He's about to be in for a rude awakening." They drove for several more minutes.

"That's it right there. This is the restaurant right here. Bones," Mya said as Janelle pulled into the parking lot. "I heard a lot of corporate big wigs blow up to $6,000 on wine in here."

"This is nice!" Janelle admired the decor as someone approached the car. "I might find me a man, or a man might find me." She grinned.

A valet dressed in black slacks and a button down and bow tie approached the car with a clipboard and asked if they had reservations.

"Honestly, sir. I don't know. I'm here to meet a friend," Mya responded.

"Your friend's name is?" he asked politely.

"Jermal Edwards." The valet scanned his clipboard.

"Oh, yes. Mrs. Edwards . . . table for two," he sang, and then looked at Janelle.

"Oh, I'm alone. I don't have any reservations," Janelle said quickly, not missing a beat.

"Okay . . . well then, I will gladly take over your vehicle." He opened the door for Janelle and handed her a chip as she got out and he got in the driver's seat. Mya remained in the passenger's seat.

"Mya . . . Mya!" Janelle walked around and opened the door. "What are you doing? Let's go." Mya didn't move. "Girl, you can do this. What did you used to tell me when we were in high school, and I was trippin' over stuff going on at school or at home?"

"God got you," Mya uttered.

"Exactly! And he got you now." Janelle reached for her hand and helped her out of the car. It was apparent the valet had questions because his face was balled up, but he stayed silent. Mya stepped out and shut the door. "Enjoy your meal, ladies," he said.

The two entered the restaurant, and a cheerful face greeted them.

"Hey!" Suddenly Mya grabbed Janelle by the arm and stopped her in her tracks.

"Sis, come on. I know you're not this afraid of him." Janelle pulled her arm slightly.

"Do you still carry mace in your purse?" Mya asked.

"Yeah," Janelle huffed, openly showing her frustration. She stared at her friend, dressed in an all-black Prada pantsuit. Her hair was parted on the side with her bang hiding her eye. She was badd! And didn't have a clue. "Mya, you better boss up. Standing here dressed like you run the city, but looking scared to death." She grabbed the mace from her purse and placed it in Mya's red leather Prada clutch. She pushed the clutch toward Mya's chest.

"Now, we going in here. I'll be sitting at the bar or a table nearby."

"Okay." Mya still sounded hesitant. Janelle slightly tilted her head and sighed softly.

"Big Momma's probably turning in her grave," Janelle said.

"What you mean?" Mya snapped.

"I mean what I said! This dude been beating your behind, tearing up your stuff, and causing strife in your home and you're too much of a coward to walk in here and face this jerk! You must like it," Janelle said, folding her arms.

Mya gasped. "I don't like nothing!"

"I can't tell. Just tell him it's over. Stop acting like these vulnerable, gullible, narrow-minded women. If you want respect, carry yourself as such. Get it together, sista." Janelle left her standing there and walked up to the hostess's booth.

The dark-haired man smiled as if he hadn't heard their conversation. Mya stepped forward and gave Jermal's name. He checked his list and told her, "Right this way." She followed close behind and passed Janelle, who was seated to the left of where the guy had seated Mya.

Sway rose to his feet, looking extremely wealthy in an expensive designer suit and designer frames that made him look like an intellectual.

"Thank you for showing up," he said, looking Mya over completely as he pulled out her chair. "You look really nice."

"Orange Park?" Mya ignored his compliment. She was curious why he wanted her to take an hour and a half drive. He took a few steps over and sat down across from her.

"Mya, I'm going to get right to the point. I have done some real messed up things in my life." Sway's expression was serious.

"Hmmm," Mya muttered. His words had turned her initial fear into furious anger. Sway looked away.

"I have sabotaged everything in my life. You and Judah were the closest thing to perfect that I knew. Despite everything you have lost, you still dare to cope with the pressures of life."

"I'm saying I haven't been the man you fell in love with. I'm saying, despite everything you've sacrificed for me, I allowed my desire for more to change me. The women, the money, the respect, the reputation . . ." His tone of voice went almost to a whisper as he dropped his head.

"So you're sitting here telling me that you have cheated on me?" Mya could see herself slapping him.

"Quite a few days I woke up to women I barely knew. I couldn't dare look at the man in the mirror." He looked up, as if he searching her eyes for answers. Gradually, she sat up straight and slid her hand back into her lap. She really didn't want to make a scene in this nice restaurant.

"So you're saying you subjected me to an STD? Sleeping with women you don't even know!" Mya was trying to stay calm.

"Mya, that didn't change the fact that I loved you. In all reality, I would have told you, but I couldn't hurt you like that. So I held it in and it ate me alive. One day everything just fell apart. There was a drought in the streets. And I almost got my head blown off by a couple of wild youngins. You weren't there for me because of everything going on with Judah. I felt so low and alone, and started thinking about my childhood and being placed into the system. It felt like nobody gave a damn about me. So I snorted some coke to make the thoughts go away."

"Cocaine! Sway, are you serious? You followed in your father's steps? Using your own supply?"

"Don't throw that back in my face," he barked.

"Why not? That's exactly what you're doing. And let me guess, that's the reason you started hitting me?" Mya's words fell in silence. She tapped her foot and pressed her lips together, seething by just thinking about those brutal nights. "Answer me! I deserve that little bit, Sway."

"Mya, you got to know I would never hurt you." He reached out for her hand, but she declined.

"Well, you did. Over and over again, Sway. And I have never done you wrong." She stood.

"I'm sorry. Baby, I am. You have got to know I'm trying to fix this." He looked around, seeing that they'd drawn unwanted attention. "Please sit down, Mya. Please." She didn't oblige him.

"How, Sway? How are you trying to fix anything? Just days ago you broke into my house and put your hands on me—again! And for what reason? I was busy. I didn't answer the phone. Did it ever occur to you that I'm human just like you? That I bleed too, that I get tired too? That I get weak if I don't eat, just like you? That I get lonely, too? That I get scared? Did it? Did you ever think about what exactly you were doing to me every time you hit me? Every time you chose your lifestyle, your money, your groupies over me."

"Mya, please. Let's not do this." Sway begged, trying to get her to lower her rising voice. She was almost hysterical.

"Please, what! I can recall begging you, pleading for the very same thing—for you not to do what you did." She turned to leave. "Sway, you need help." He jumped up to block her from leaving, wrapping her in his arms. Ignoring the attention they were drawing.

"I know. That's why I had you meet me here. I'm checking into rehab today. I need you to drop me off and drive my car home. You can keep it, or park it in my garage. It doesn't matter to me. But I realize if I don't get some help, I am going to lose the only things that matters to me. You and Judah." He had never talked so fast.

"As far as I am concerned, you have already lost us." Mya looked him straight in the eyes. "Now, I'm going to ask you politely. Take your hands off of me." He didn't know the woman standing in front of him. Very hesitantly, he released her.

"Is there a problem?" the hostess asked after walking up to Sway, who reached in his pocket and peeled off two crisp hundred dollar bills and handed them to him. Then he rushed out behind Mya.

Be ye not unequally yoked together with unbelievers: for what fellowship hath righteousness with unrighteousness? and what communion hath light with darkness?

2 Corinthians 6:14 (KJV)

CHAPTER 26

Stair Steps Rehab Center (8:48 p.m.)

"Well, everything is in the bag. Toiletries, T-shirts, underclothes, calling cards, and a few jogging outfits. Can you think of anything else?" Mya asked Sway, after getting out of Janelle's vehicle. It was now 8:48 p.m. They had pulled in front of the in-patient facility that would be Sway's home for the next six months.

"Nah. Now from the looks of it, you got everything." He just sat there looking at her through the window. "Can you come sit with me for a minute?" Mya looked around the parking lot. Janelle was on the phone.

"What? What is on your mind?" She walked around to the passenger side and got in.

"Just hoping you'll still be waiting for me when this is over." He looked so sincere sitting there. No signs of rage, mere stability. Alongside that, he was very attractive. She was weak for him and he knew it. Why wouldn't she be? This was the only man she had been with. She stroked his face.

"The most important thing is that you get through this program successfully and keep this habit at bay."

209

He gently grabbed her hand and kept it on his face. Leaning closer he said, "The most important thing to me in this world is you." He stared at her with such intensity, she wasn't sure if he wanted to make love to her right then and there, or if that was some type of warning. She chose not to ponder on either. The only thing she wanted was for him to take his rehabilitation seriously.

"Come here," Sway told her. She sat there for several seconds toying with the idea.

What could it hurt? she thought as she leaned in to peck his lips. Before she could pull away, his hand cuffed the back her head and his tongue was gliding into her mouth. His breath was sweet and his touch familiar. Passionately, they kissed. She didn't even stop him when his fingers began to fondle her body. She felt herself submitting to his touch, and she questioned if she was willing to go where he was taking her. Then suddenly, King's face flashed in her mind. She tensed and subconsciously stopped kissing him. He realized it before she did.

"What just happened?" Sway asked as he sat up just enough to see her face.

"Huh?" She could barely respond, too busy trying to figure out why she suddenly felt like she was degrading herself.

"Where you at, Mya? Why did you just disconnect from me like that?" He was now sitting completely up.

"This isn't right," she managed to say, unwilling to look at him.

"What do you mean this ain't right? What's not *right* about it? You my wife!" His voice was starting to excel. He gestured between her legs. "This mine." He pointed to her mouth. "Them my lips! What's not right about what we doing?"

"Sway. I want to get something straight. If I'm going to help you through this, be your support. We can't keep doing this."

"Doing what, Mya?"

"We are not together, Sway. I'm trying to be your friend." Mya was losing her patience.

"Why can't we be together?" he snapped, looking perturbed.

210

Because we're just not on the same page! "I'm not about to sit here and fuss with you." She looked around the parking lot to see if anyone was around to possibly hear him.

"Good. Don't fuss! Just answer my question." His eyes were dancing again. She knew it wouldn't end well. Mya grabbed his small tote bag and told him, "Let's go." She exited the car, and strutted across the parking lot so fast she almost walked in front of a passing car. By the time she heard him slam the car door, she was almost to the entrance. When she got to the door, she opened it and looked back. *At least he's coming,* she thought, despite his aggressive body language. Mya stepped in and waited for him to enter. He glared at her like he could rip her apart. She was in a safe haven now, so it didn't matter. Still he searched her eyes as she began leading the way toward the receptionist's desk. At least he didn't budge; Sway just stood there seething, as if contemplating knocking the crap out of her.

"Please . . . Jermal, please," she pleaded, staring him in the eyes. He just leered at her.

"You slept with him?" he asked, barely above a whisper.

"What!" She was taken aback.

This time through clenched teeth, he repeated his question. "Have you slept with him?"

Mya almost burst out laughing. "Absolutely not! You're the only man I've been with." She could tell he heard her, but it wasn't registering. She felt eyes on them and grew uncomfortable. He didn't seem to care either way. "Is that what's wrong with you?" she said, putting the tote bag down and stroking his face, then his chest. She knew merely touching him would snap him out of his funk. She could see the resistance he was trying to maintain.

"Sway, stop trippin'. I can have friends without being active. I wasn't active before I met you." She touched his face again. "Now let's get our focus back on what's at hand." Mya smiled at him until he relaxed.

"That's what I'm talking about."

She turned to pick the bag back up, but he grabbed it instead. He handed her the car keys and intertwined his fingers in hers as he led the way to the receptionist's desk." She didn't want to admit it, but the sinking sensation in her abdomen made her feel that if he didn't make it through this program, he would only get worse. And that 'worse' might cause someone to get seriously hurt.

That someone just might be me, she thought.

"What's up?" Judah asked as he opened his front door.

"I was hoping we could talk." Coach Riley rubbed the back of his head, looking as uncomfortable as Judah felt standing there. "I noticed you didn't come to practice today."

"Yeah. I didn't feel like it. I wanted to be by myself," Judah replied, still holding the doorknob as if he was planning to close it at any given moment.

"If you got a minute, I would like to come in and speak with you." Coach Riley purposely overlooked Judah's remark. Judah stood in the doorway considering if he wanted to be rude or not.

"Judah . . ." Coach Riley sighed. "Son, I think it will do us both some good to address these results."

Judah knew he was right, but he wasn't about to admit it. He just did an about-face, and walked toward the den, left Coach Riley standing at the door. Riley wasn't moved, he was well acquainted with this house.

As he walked into the room and sat down next to him on the sofa, Judah still didn't acknowledge him.

"So how do you feel?" Coach Riley got straight to the point.

"You said you wanted to speak to me." Judah never took his eyes off the Sports Channel.

"Okay . . . Well, I'm glad you finally got your answer. I'm relieved to know, you know I'm not lying." Coach Riley looked at Judah, hoping he would reply. A few seconds of silence passed. "Now that you know, I'm hoping we can be a family. I would like the chance to be a father, your father. Not Coach Eric Riley, or the mentor I once was to you. I want to know what's on your mind, how everything makes you feel. Tell you goodnight every single day I have left on this earth, and turn my guest room into your room at my house." Judah looked at him for the first time since he had sat down. He could feel Riley's sincerity. "I love you, Judah. You got to know that."

"You know . . ." He was slow to speak. "I've waited my entire life to hear my father say that. I love you for the role you have played in my life, Coach Riley. For the times you listened when I felt I needed a man's input. But I struggle because you knew all the while I was yours and you didn't say a word for nearly two years.

"That's over seven hundred days of our lives you kept that kind of secret to yourself."

"Judah, I'm sorry I didn't handle this sooner."

"It just makes me wonder if there is anything else you're hiding from me." Coach Riley just looked at Judah. "Is there anything else you need to tell me?"

"Judah . . ." Riley interrupted him.

"Are you dying? Do I have any more siblings somewhere out there? Do you know where my mother is?" His eyes watered.

"No, son. No, I'm not dying. I don't have any more kids, and as much as I wish I did, I don't know where your mother is." He pulled Judah into his embrace. Judah didn't fight him, but he did fight back his will to cry. As he sat there cradled in his father's arms, he sensed there was something Coach Riley wanted to confess. He was keeping something from Judah and secrets had a way of manifesting themselves.

213

He who finds a wife finds a good thing and obtains favor from the Lord.

Proverbs 18:22 (ESV)

CHAPTER 27

Three months later . . .

Saturday (8:58 a.m.)

"King, what would my life be like without you?" Mya asked sincerely, sitting across from him on the patio. He'd just finished up the breakfast he had come over just to prepare for her and Judah.

"I'm not sure what yours would be like, but I know it seems the sun shines brighter since you walked into my life.

"You're so sweet." She stood and leaned in for a kiss and pecked him on his lips.

"Woman, I told you not to be putting those wanna-make-me-lose-my-religion things on me. A brother's strong, but you trying to keep me from making the finish line."

"Finish line? King, what on God's earth are you talking about?"

"The finish line! You know when I make you my wife and—"

"Your wife?" she interrupted. "You really want to marry me? Even after everything I've told you?"

It had been a little over three months since Sway had been in rehab, but she and King had been going to church regularly, and having Bible study together faithfully. One night after being in prayer together, she felt compelled to tell King everything. How he impacted her life, Sway's unexpected visits, his addiction, the phone calls they had, places they met up, even the sexual gratification. There was something in his eyes. Disappointment? Hurt? She wasn't sure and was too ashamed to ask. She felt relieved when he excused himself to the bathroom. It gave her a second to ask the Lord for strength. When he returned, he didn't raise his voice, his hand, or even look at her in disgust, like she knew without a doubt that Sway would have. She vowed in that moment to never hide anything from King again. At whatever cost.

"If you want to go right now, we can."

"What? King, what are you talking about?"

"I'm serious!" She playfully punched him, after sitting in the chair closest to him.

"Mya, I'm serious! We can go to the church right now. Get Bishop to do the ceremony and everything!"

She was laughing, but not at his words, but his animation. "Woman, yes, I'll marry you. I love you!" Her laughter came to a halt as his confession spilled from his lips. She knew he loved her. Any sincere man or woman of God loved people. But something about hearing him say it, grabbed her heart. For a while she believed she loved him too.

But in that moment looking at him, she felt the glory of God surrounding him, the consistent peace. *Oh my God, the inner peace I have just being with him.* King's greatest concern was his personal relationship with the Lord. His gratitude for the simplest things she did and the way he respected her. She sat there staring into the eyes of this confident man of God. His eyes beckoning her to come closer. Mya got up and sat in his lap. He opened his mouth to say something, but it was her turn to speak. She hushed him and began to pour out her own heart.

"At first I didn't quite understand you, and I was even a little afraid of being around you. How you've always known what to say, as if you were having a conversation with my mind. It seems when I need someone the most, you appear. I have never felt so safe with a man before like I do with you. You've been so patient with me in the midst of my struggle with my ex. For the last three months, you've spent three nights a week with me, examining and searching the scriptures with me for answers. Never once have you made me feel as if I had to do anything, or be anyone other than who I am today with you." Her eyes filled with tears, but she didn't care to look away. Not this time. She took a deep breath and continued. "It's crazy how my mother used to tell me to wait on the Lord. Because He had the man of my dreams searching for me. One that would love me more than I loved myself but loved the Lord most. And to be careful because the counterfeit would come before the genuine.

"I feel so guilty, King. Like I don't deserve you. I was almost there, but I gave in to the trick of the enemy. I know this now. What I had saved just for you, I allowed Sway to talk me out of—the promise that we were getting married." King attempted to tell her it was okay, but she refused to let him speak.

"I kept myself all these years to express to my husband just how much he meant to me. That he was worth the wait and that what I have, only he deserved. King, please forgive me.

"I've been running and running and running. God has blessed me beyond what I could ask for. But yet I've been living like what God has ain't good enough, and now I got all this baggage. All these psychological issues and soul ties to this man, contaminated by the world . . ." She took another breath. "If only I had waited and trusted the lord." She placed both of her hands on his face. "But I don't want to run anymore, King. I don't want to be double-minded. I want to be free from the fear of loving you and being loved by you. Do you understand what I'm saying?"

Now that he had the chance to speak he didn't want to. King just nodded in affirmation. Feeling like his prayers and fastings were finally manifesting the purpose of it all.

She smiled for the first time in minutes. "I want God's will to be done in my life, our lives, Judah included. And I want you to know that I'm in love with you as well, and I see you. I see everything you so effortlessly, without hesitation, do for me and my nephew. I love you, and this day I promise to uphold you as my man. That is, if you still want to be with me."

"Woman, don't play with me. I've trusted God since I began to mature as a man that He knew the plans He had for my life. And since the day I met you, I knew he had ordained you to be mine. I'm not about to turn my back on you because you were lost and human. I understand you need to be loved and wanted, and I promise by the grace of God you'll never have to look to another ever again."

Mya didn't have anything else to say. She wished they had already tied the knot because she wanted to make love to him right there. But she respected what God was doing in and through him. So she leaned forward and kissed him passionately. Making sure he knew she meant every word. She felt herself getting lost in the scent of his skin and hair, the taste of his mouth, warmth of his body. It almost scared her when he jumped up.

"What's wrong?" she questioned, balancing herself.

"No, ma'am . . . No, ma'am!"

"King, what? Did I bite you or something?"

"Mya, you will not be kissing me like that! I'm still a man." She looked toward his crotch. She knew it was wrong but thanked God if she did marry him that he would be capable of pleasing her. Then she felt embarrassed.

"I'm sorry, King," she said as she attempted to approach him. He jumped back.

"No, ma'am! Just stay over there." He used his head to emphasize the space between them. She couldn't keep from laughing.

"King, you're exaggerating." She put both hands on her hips.

"Think whatever you want to think, but I call it being wise." She laughed for a few more minutes as his sense of humor came out. She loved how he made her laugh. Finally gathering her composure, she asked if he wanted to sit back down and finish talking.

"Absolutely not! I'm not crazy. Mya, I'm not fooling with you!

Besides, we've got to head out. Remember, Judah and I are going shopping for our trip next month, and you have to go see about your man," King said sarcastically.

Judah had received several scholarship offers and invitations to visit several college campuses, and they would began their tour the first of next month.

"He's not my man, thank you! And I had honestly forgotten about him."

"Well, believe me, he hasn't forgotten about you. Dude ain't seen you in a minute either." Mya thought about the last time she'd seen Sway. The day she dropped him off at rehab. She drove his car to his house and locked it in his garage. At first they talked at least once a day, but when King encouraged her to get more involved in church activities, she wasn't always in a position to talk to him. There were times when she and King would be chilling, or out eating and Sway's inconsiderate attitude was the last of her concerns.

"Are you going to come upstairs and help me pick out something to wear?" Mya loved the way it felt being so open with him. Plus, the fact that he was so vulnerable to her. It was adorable.

"As if that's what you want, but I'm comfortable with whatever you decide. I know you're mine." Her heart felt so light. This wasn't some insecure, unstable child in a male's body. This was a grown man! Very confident and in touch with life. It wasn't her heart but spirit that confirmed her belief that this brother was God sent. Why wouldn't she choose King over Sway? He reached out for her.

"But I do want to pray with you before we go." Gladly, they joined hands and bowed their heads. She listened attentively as he petitioned the Lord to protect his woman and grant her the words to encourage Sway to move forward in life and to help him understand she was only in his life as a friend. She gently squeezed his hand tighter as an expression of her gratitude.

At this moment in her life, Mya felt blessed. She was blessed, and had never felt so much freedom. Freedom like this only came by being in right standing with God. Not implying she was perfect and without sin, but merely having a heart that sought to do that which pleased Him, to do things the way He wanted them done.

She knew, whether Sway wanted to accept her friendship or not, she wasn't going to remain a part of his life, pacifying him with any hope that they would ever be anything more, any longer. It hadn't been that long since she'd come to realize this, but she was more than absolutely certain her future was destined for King. She sighed deeply as she checked her phone. Mya had missed over 100 of Sway's phone calls in a twenty-four hour period. *I'll have to take his call eventually*, she thought, knowing his reaction would not be a good one.

O taste and see that the LORD is good; How blessed is the man who takes refuge in Him!

Psalm 34:8 (NASB)

CHAPTER 28

One months later . . .

Thursday (9:00 a.m.)

"Ju, so everything is in place. Our flight leaves tonight at 8:30. Once we land in Texas, someone from the university will be waiting. We'll be escorted to our hotel. We should have some time to get cleaned up and see the city a little before we get some rest and head over to Texas A&M tomorrow morning," Mya informed him.

"And transportation?" Judah asked.

"King has already arranged for us to get a rental delivered to the hotel," she responded. "Now let me finish, please." She looked up to a very excited teenager, as she sat in front of her laptop in her room. And she understood why. He had come so far, and in her opinion, he's all the man he is because of the grace of God. He deserved to have every college in the nation competing for him.

"Once we're there, we'll get a tour of the athletic department, the workout area, and the campus, of course! If you want, we can swing by Texas University, but I think you've already decided A&M."

"All I can say is God is good. I told you one day I would take you all over the world."

"You did."

"And I haven't even went pro yet. We're going to five states alone this month, and it has not cost you a thing." He smiled, sure of himself.

"That is, if you don't count me getting up early to feed you and King."

"Aunt Mya, stop trippin'. These folks are going to be serving us."

"Says who? Ain't nobody going to be cooking for my men." They both burst out laughing.

"So you love him for real, huh?" Judah suddenly got serious.

"Judah, you know I have always tried to include you in my relationships. Your opinion means the world to me. So I'll admit, I do love him. It took me years to see what I thought I had with Sway could never be blessed, and the day he lost sight of my self-respect we had to come to our end. That relationship was not love. It was fear, control, co-dependency, obligation. With King, everything seems so natural. And he adores me, he adores you."

"Yeah, he's a cool dude."

"I went to go see Sway."

"What! Aunt Mya, why are you still dealing with that dude?" His frustration was apparent.

"Wait a minute before you trip. I visited him a couple times last month. He's in rehab, and I honestly have been trying to give him moral support, but I'm getting to the point where I just don't think that I'm the one to help him. I mean, I'm not trying to turn my back on him, but he's . . . still too much. He hasn't really learned to let go of the past."

"I know you're not surprised. He's a leech, all they do is suck you dry. Always taking and never giving."

"He got upset because he called while I was at the movies with King, and I said I couldn't talk. He was also so upset because I didn't visit him on Saturday; someone from the rehab terminated our call because he was out of control."

"Wasn't King and I shooting ball Saturday?"

"Yes. And I was getting my hair and nails done. Shoot! The month has been hectic. Excuse me if I don't run down there to see him every visitation. And Tuesday I was handling all our dry cleaning and making sure there was someone to look after King's dogs while we were gone. I have a life too. A new life, if I may say so myself, and it is not all about Sway."

"You know I'm not upset; you don't owe him anything. You should feel lucky I pray for him because sometimes I want to kill him."

"Judah!"

"Aunt Mya, don't act like this is something new from me. I'm still me. Seeking God and all, I struggle not to hate him."

"I understand, baby. It's going to be all right. Just give it time."

"Can we change the subject?" Judah didn't want to think about Sway anymore.

"Of course. So do you have everything packed up?"

"Yeah, but you probably want to—"

"Check and make sure you don't forget something." She finished his reply.

"Exactly." He laughed a little. "But that's not what I want to talk about." Mya looked at him, giving him her undivided attention, wondering what he could possibly want to talk about.

"What? You got somebody pregnant?" Mya stood up and walked up in Judah's face as he sat on her bed.

"Judah, I told you not to be fooling around with these hot behind lil—"

"Aunt Mya, chill!" He held out his left hand, palm facing downward to signal her to tone down. "Go on somewhere with all that. I just wanted to tell you he asked for your hand in marriage."

It took Mya all of these seconds to register what Judah had just said. Her face went from confused, to excited, to nervous.

"Stop *playing!* When! What did you say?" She was on the edge of the sofa now, and he was laughing.

"Fall back, thirsty," he said calmly.

"Fall back? Fall back where? Like this." She leaned back into her egg-shaped chair. "Is this what you're talking about? Why? Why do I need to sit like this? What does this have to do with what I asked you?" She was spitting her questions out all so fast it seemed she didn't pause to take a breath. Judah was cramped up laughing at her so hard. Sitting there looking goofy.

"Sit up, Aunt Mya. That's a slang term we use. But I gave him my approval. I just warned him if he ever hurt you, I will hunt him down and torture him—no lies." Mya knew he was serious and didn't want to press the issue. In her heart she knew King would never intentionally hurt her. Before she had a chance to respond, her cell phone rang. She grabbed it off the table.

"Speaking of my angel." She beamed as she picked it up and walked out of her room, and into the hall to get some privacy.

"Good morning, my King! I was just talking about you." She peeked over her shoulder at Judah who told her, "Shhh!" She knew he was telling her not to repeat what he had just told her. She gave him a thumbs up, just as she heard her doorbell ring.

"I'll get it," Judah told Mya. She wondered who it might be and descended a couple stairs from the top of her stairwell so she could get a visual of who was at the front door.

"I'm missing you," King confessed on the opposite end of the phone.

"Yeah. I bet not as much as I miss you," she teased, and the two lovebirds went back and forth.

"Who is it?" Judah asked, approaching the front door.

"Riley." The voice came from the opposite side of the door. Gladly, Judah opened the door and they embraced.

"What's up, man?" Coach Riley asked as he walked into the foyer. Mya saw that it was Riley and walked back into her room.

The two walked into the living room. "Did you get my text telling you I'll meet you in Mississippi?" Riley asked as he made himself comfortable on the sofa.

"I did. It's no pressure because I got my aunt." Judah sat not far from him. "So, were you able to find out anything about my mother? I been coming up short. I don't understand. If her body was never found, then how is it a closed investigation?" He stared at Riley, hoping he could offer more information.

"Nah, son. I don't know what to tell you in regards to Honesty." He took his hat off and shifted in his seat.

"You sure about that?" Judah knew he wasn't being honest. He could discern his turmoil.

"Is your aunt here?" Riley asked, changing the subject.

"Yeah, upstairs making sure all our reservations and stuff are secured." Judah watched him like a hawk.

"Judah . . . um . . . I . . ." He struggled to speak his mind. "I hate to come over here on such an exciting day with this, but I haven't been completely honest with you about something." Riley finally got it out.

Judah's heart pounded, anticipating Riley's next words, but his disposition showed no signs of such. "So what you lie about?" Judah asked, hoping it was in relation to his mother.

"Judah, it's not so much that I lied about something. I just didn't want—"

"Come on already." Judah cut him off. "Man up and spit it—" The doorbell rang. Judah stopped mid-sentence. He looked in the direction of the door, and then at Riley. He wasn't expecting any more company.

"Aunt Mya!" he yelled toward the stairwell as he got up to open the door. She popped out of her room. "You expecting somebody?"

"No. King won't be here until sometime after lunch."

"Who is it?" Judah asked as he slightly slid the curtain back and looked out the window that was next to the door.

"It's some Caucasian lady." He looked back at Mya, who was now standing at the bottom of the stairwell.

"It's Megan!" the woman said from the opposite side.

"Just open it, Judah, but I don't know a Megan," Mya stated. He opened the door to a beautiful brunette. She took one look at him and was at a loss for words. Tears welled up in her eyes.

"May I help you?" Judah asked, discerning the sight of him somehow broke her heart.

"I just can't believe this . . ." she kept repeating, using the threshold to hold herself up.

"Ma'am, are you all right? Do you want us to call the paramedics?" Mya asked, stepping in front of Judah. The lady gasped but never closed her mouth, as if someone had taken breath out of her body.

"He said you were dead! I am not believing this! He said you were dead!" she yelled as elephant tears poured down her face. Mya didn't know who this woman was, but she wanted Judah out of harm's way.

"Baby, go get my phone. Just in case I have to call the police," she instructed Judah, but he didn't move. "Ma'am, are you sure you've got the right residence?" Mya further inquired.

"Call the police for what?" Coach Riley asked as he stepped into the foyer. "Megan?" he address the upset woman by name. She looked up and locked eyes with him.

"Was I not enough, Eric Riley?" I was willing to give you children, but you wanted me to remain on the pill!" She was almost hysterical. Mya stood on her porch watching the drama unfold, and Judah stood in the foyer in shock.

"Megan, it's not what you're thinking," Coach Riley said in his defense.

"It's not what I'm thinking?" She began to close some of the space between the two of them. "This boy looks just like you, and that's the woman on the picture in your shoebox in your closet! The one you said was dead! I have given you the last eight years of my life, and this is how you repay me by sneaking around."

"Megan, you really need to calm down because you've got this all wrong."

"I got it wrong!" She slung her purse on the porch.

"I left my family in Wisconsin and came to Florida with you because you asked me to." Riley was getting impatient.

"Megan, be quiet for a minute and allow me to explain!" He stuffed his hands in his pockets like Judah did when he was trying to keep his composure.

"Is our marriage even official?" Megan asked as she walked up on him, now standing in Mya's foyer.

"You're married?" Judah asked, clearly remembering him saying he wasn't.

"Eric Riley, is that your son Judah?" Megan asked "Is it?" She pointed her finger in his face.

"Yes, to both questions, but I would appreciate it if we could all sit down so I can explain."

"I can't *believe* you lied about being married?" Judah spat as he walked toward the stairwell.

"Eric Judah Riley! I don't want to hear nothing you've got to say. I've seen enough!" She turned to walk out the house. Mya stood in her doorway.

"Uhhh, excuse me. But I'm not the woman in the picture. She's my sister. I think we should sit down so we can talk."

"Baby, are you at the house yet?" Mya asked King as she sat behind the steering wheel of her car, looking ahead trying to see why the traffic on the expressway had come to a stop.

"I'm getting off the expressway now. I take it you're not there?"

"I'm not, and you're not going to believe where I am." Mya made no effort to hide her frustration. She gave him a quick dialogue of how Deaconess Price called asking her to pick her up from her doctor's appointment because she didn't trust herself to drive home after having minor surgery. Mya compiled this with the fact that Deaconess Price hadn't even told her she was having surgery. She immediately left the house, and now she was stuck in traffic.

"I just can't believe today of all days this is happening."

"I understand your frustration, but I think it's best you calm down." King tried to comfort her. "Being that the plane leaves in a little over three hours from now, Judah and I will put all the luggage in the car, load up everything, and when you get here we can just leave."

"Baby, I'm stuck on I-95 still, and it'll take you every bit of thirty minutes to get to the airport."

"So, just meet us at the airport then." King was sure he had solved the problem. "Regardless of the traffic jam, it won't take you an hour to get through."

"Only problem with that is, I don't want to catch the flight with what I have on. I was just working around the house. Making sure everything was ready for our departure," she whined and really wanted him to rescue her. "Plus, I don't want to leave my vehicle at the airport. You know people breaking in folks' cars and doing anything for money these days." King sat silent for a moment. She could hear him entering her house and greeting Judah.

"This is what we are going to do. Judah and I are going to take care of everything here. Load up everything. I wish you would just tell me what to pick out for you to wear, and you could change at the airport, but I know how you women are. So, I'm going to make a few phone calls. One will be to arrange someone from my lot to come get you and drive you to the airport. Then I'm going to find out what time the next flight leaves because you can meet us at the airport. But we're not leaving without you. So, put on some praise and worship music, relax, and call me when you get moving. Or do you want me to stay on the phone with you?"

As much as she would rather just talk to him, being that he always seemed to know how to soothe her, she knew he had to handle their business.

"I'll let you go and call you back in a minute."

"That's right, baby. It'll only be a minute. Declare it by faith."

"I love you," she sang in the phone.

"I'm in love with you, and I can't wait to hold you again." She was all smiles now. He had to know what he was doing! She found herself telling the Lord thank you for this man.

The minute turned out to be twenty, and as Mya raced to get home she convinced them to go ahead and leave her. She would meet up with them. She rushed into the house, hoping to make it through the security check point in time. She called King to inform him the car wasn't waiting when she arrived, and she would just have to drive herself if it didn't hurry. Mya decided to wait until they were on the plane to tell him about the drama and outcome of Eric Judah Riley and his wife Megan Riley.

Let the words of my mouth, and the meditation of my heart, be acceptable in thy sight, O LORD, my strength, and my redeemer.

Psalm 19:14 (KJV)

CHAPTER 29

Jacksonville International Airport (6:35 p.m.)

King and Judah sat inside the airport wondering if Mya would make their flight on time.

"Baby, that's not even a problem. By the time you get dressed, the car will be there. Okay, I love you." King hung up.

"That's Aunt Mya?" Judah asked, finishing up his double cheeseburger.

"Yeah, she just pulled up. Haven't even made it into the house yet," King responded as he sat at the departure gate eating a burger also.

"She's a nervous wreck, huh?"

"Was it my conversation that gave it away?"

"Actually, it wasn't. I can feel her." Judah sat back satisfied.

"Word?"

"Always have. For as long as I have been able to remember. She said when my moms was pregnant with me she used to stay up all night long talking to me. Telling me about her day, her hopes and dreams, wishing I'd hurry up and come so she could spoil me." Judah laughed like he could see it. "Always placing her hands on my mom's belly, praying for me." King grinned. "It's just crazy to me how close we are; she's like

233

my twin sister more so than my aunt. I can only imagine how my mom and I would have been." Judah had a look of longing in his eyes.

"Well, let me ask you something. Is Mya the only person you can feel, or do you tend to feel others as well?"

"My connection to her is the strongest. Like it doesn't matter what her mood is, I pretty much can sense it. With other people, not everybody, but sometimes I can feel when something's wrong. Like I knew when my grandma died before we got the call. And that night at the beach house, you didn't get much sleep. You were heartbroken, and as a result you questioned the Lord about Mya."

King looked taken aback, but he knew enough to know only the Lord could have revealed this to Judah. He thought back to that night, how he had excused himself minutes after Mya stepped outside. Initially he followed her, in an attempt to get her to take a walk on the beach with him. He was going to ask her to be his lady. But her phone rang, so he took a few steps back toward the house to give her some privacy. After what seemed like a few minutes, he didn't hear anything sounding like her having a conversation.

King turned up his swag, walking to where her vehicle was parked. Trying to prepare himself to face her with his confusion. But his hopes were quickly diminished when he made his way to the rear of her car. He saw her getting into Sway's car on the passenger side. His breath was being sucked from his body. He couldn't move if he wanted to. Dumbfounded, he stood there watching the woman he had finally admitted he was falling for, the same woman he heard the voice of the living God tell him, "This is your wife. The woman I have chosen for you. You are to yield yourself to me that I may love her through you," lock lips with a man who had caused her much turmoil and pain! King had turned on his heels and headed back toward the house, then changed his mind and went to the patio. With uncertainty, he headed for a walk along the beach. Just somewhere, where he could meditate and God could strengthen him.

"Yo, man, that was the night I actually considered God deserved more credit than I was giving him. Because I witnessed with my own eyes His ability to carry a man in his pain," Judah continued.

"Straight up?" King asked, sincerely trying to shake how that might make him feel. The struggle he had with making the decision if he was going to commit to loving this woman until she discovered the love and plans Jesus had for her life.

"Yes!" Judah said, nodding his head. "It was crazy because I felt your pain and sort of heard your heart's cry. Then I saw you struggling, but the next morning you were the Mr. King I was growing to know."

"Judah, it's crazy, but God is good. It still amazes me—the peace he'll give you once you wholeheartedly decide to give him a situation, or when we truly invite him to carry us through the hardships of our lives. It's like there's a secret place in him that he hides you, where the energy can't penetrate your mind, or oppress you with the stress of weariness that naturally comes when faced with disappointment, mishaps, or heartaches of this life."

"It is crazy, but I'm so grateful he still loved me even when I hated him."

"Judah, God knows we're fragile, and we will trigger ourselves to do things we'll regret. Therefore, he already knew exactly what you would do when your Big Momma died. He understands man, and the thing I love the most is that none of that stops the purpose he has for us. We have to do more than just be mad at him for a few years to prevent him from fulfilling your destiny." King was loving the direction their conversation had gone. He loved the hope that had become the twinkle in Judah's eyes over the last few months. He wasn't sure just how much longer Mya would be away, but he was enjoying this time with his soon-to-be nephew. His next goal would be to help Judah recognize that his feelings were actually called discernment, and it was a gift from God.

"Don't mean to change the subject, but Mya told me you been trying to find your mom, because you believe she's still alive," King stated.

"Yeah! It just doesn't make sense that she disappeared into thin air and nobody knows anything. No body, no clothes, a trail . . . nothing."

"That is crazy." King shook his head.

"I feel like this . . . God has been in my life for this long. This whole thing with my dad . . . why not trust Him concerning my mother? And truthfully, I feel she is alive, just living under a different name or something."

"Well, I think we should hire a private investigator and see what they come up with."

"Word! I never thought of that," Judah confessed, looking hopeful.

"Honesty could be staying across town and we might not even know it."

In my distress I called upon the Lord; to my God I cried for help. From his temple he heard my voice, and my cry to him reached his ears.

Psalm 18:6 (ESV)

CHAPTER 30

Mya's residence (7:05 p.m.)

Mya flew into the house pulling off her top as soon as the door was shut. The day wasn't completely dark; the setting sun shined a little light through the blinds. She looked around the room, her heart filling with pride as she observed that they had cut off all the lights. She dashed up the stairs and burst into her bedroom. She was halfway to her closet, still undecided on what exactly she wanted to wear when the sight of Sway crying and sitting in the corner next to her closet took her breath away. Turn around and run, she thought. But for some reason her feet wouldn't move. She couldn't! The sight of the glock resting on her plush carpet next to him almost made her knees buckle. Is he about to commit suicide right here in my bedroom? Or is he planning on shooting me? Lord God, I don't know what all I'm about to encounter, but please protect me. Please Lord, don't let this turn into a crime scene.

As quietly as she could, she took a step back. Not sure what her plans were, but it definitely involved getting out of the range of a bullet.

"So . . . you just going to run up in here, and then leave without saying a single word to me?" Sway spoke in a tone that was foreign to

239

her. Call it tripping, but it didn't even sound like he had been crying either. She took another step backward. "Take one more step, and I'm going to blow your brains out and mine too." Sway stood to his feet, robotically. He finally made eye contact. Chills swept down her back. He didn't look the same. His eyes had that cold emptiness it did on those nights when he beat or violated her. Suddenly, Mya realized she had removed her shirt. She began putting it back on.

"Oh, so now you want to cover yourself? Let me guess . . . you wouldn't want your boyfriend to walk through the door and think you are being the slut that you are!" His voice was more menacing than it was elevating. She was scared, but she also felt herself getting pissed. He had no right to address her as anything other than her name.

"You know what, Sway? You're full of it." She answered him as if he had asked her to. "I've been honest with you the entire time, and now you're up in my house disrespecting me. Get out!" She folded her arms across her chest. "I've been nothing short of a friend to you, and now look at what you're doing! Threatening to kill me. Why, Sway?" For some absurd reason she took a step toward him instead of backward. "Why? Because I don't want to be with someone who beats me every time he doesn't get his way? Because he rapes me like some predator. I mean, let's be real here. What are you even doing? You're supposed to be at rehab for heaven's sake! You probably left before your time was up."

"Shut up!" he finally yelled. "You think you know everything! Like you got it all figured out. I see through you. You think I'm just going to let you walk out of my life just like that? You're the only reason I even went to rehab." He was walking toward her, but she wasn't about to allow him to close the space between them.

In the distance, her phone began to ring. She hated that she set it down when she first walked in.

"Who's that? Your lil boyfriend?"

"Why don't we go downstairs and get it so we can see?" She didn't know exactly why she said it, but the look in his eyes quickly let her know they wouldn't be going to fetch it.

"Get on the bed," he ordered.

"Jermal Edwards, I will not. You are not taking me through this anymore. Enough is enough!"

Pow!

Sway shot a bullet toward the ceiling.

Mya dropped to the floor covering her head, praying to the God whom she had begun to serve wholeheartedly.

"You think I'm playing with you? I'm not! You want to be a slut? I'm going to treat you like one. Get on the bed and take your clothes off." Sway was pacing the floor; Mya was sure he had lost his mind. She looked in the direction of her bed, then glanced at the door. It was open enough for her to make a break. She slowly walked toward her bed until she had a clear view of her exit and stopped.

"You know, Sway. . ." She was careful with her words. "You always have liked when I put on something sexy. Why don't you look in the drawer and pick me out something to wear." She did her best to sound as if she actually wanted to be intimate with him. It was obvious he was considering what she said but was still leery at the same time.

"Noooo, you come over here and get it." That wasn't exactly what she wanted to hear. She walked past him and over to her dresser drawers. She opened one and stood there, hands resting on the wood as she felt the hard, cold metal against her head. She could feel his physique towering over her.

"What are you waiting for?" he questioned, nudging her in the head with the pistol.

"I'm trying to figure out when we got to this point." She dropped her head and all of the emotions began to surface. Fear of losing her life and leaving Judah all alone. The agony of all the violence Sway had ever done to her. The disappointment she felt for ever being back into his schemes, but most of all regret. The regret she felt for putting herself in this position. There were so many signs that this wasn't the man God had for her. Mainly the one that pressured her into being intimate with him out of wedlock. If I had only waited on the Lord. Maybe this is the consequences of my actions. Lord, I only ask that if you allow him to take my life tonight that Judah will become a mighty man of God. King will find someone to love and adore him. And some young, naive girls will learn from my mistakes. She didn't stop her tears that flowed. Silently, she wept. But I have to at least try to get out of this.

Slowly she turned to face a deranged Sway. The pistol that was in the back of her head was now in the center of her forehead.

"Where did I go wrong with you? I loved you more than life itself. To me, you placed the sun and the moon in the sky. Nothing you wanted was too much of you to ask me. Home cooked meals three times a day. Breakfast at three and four in the morning. Never giving you any heat about the inconsistency of the time you left home and when you returned. Only doing the things you wanted to do, going to the places you wanted to be, and socializing with the people you approved of."

"I did you a favor. Them so-called friends you had wanted your man," he retorted, in attempt to defend himself. Still pointing the gun at her.

"And rumor has it that one of those so-called *friends did* have my man." He looked a little surprised. "But I never treated you any different. Why? Because I loved you." She used her shirt to wipe her face. "I changed who I was for you, Jermal. I was just fine being single and having great friendships. I was painting and caring for Judah and going to church faithfully. My life was full. Back then I was much more focused on my event planning business. I lost sight of myself the moment I laid with you. In a way I died mentally and emotionally and gave all that I am to you. Almost died spiritually too, as if you were my god . . . I can't believe I did that to myself. That I allowed you to do that to me." Mya shook her head as the tears came pouring down.

"I knew you were mine. I knew I had your heart."

"At first we were good and I thought we'd eventually fuse our goals and dreams and become one. But now . . . for the past year, I've gotten absolutely nothing in return from you. But by the grace of God . . ."

"Shut up, Mya. I don't want to hear anymore," Sway said.

"If you really love me like you claim you do, then why did you do this to us?" She took her index finger and wiped the powder substance from his nose and showed it to him. For the first time that night he looked human. Sway looked away in shame. She slowly took her left hand and guided his glock away from her head and down by his side. He just looked at her. She wrapped her arms around him and buried her face in his chest.

"Jermal, it doesn't have to be this way. It's not too late to get some help." She felt his body relaxing, and knew she was getting to him. Her cell phone rang again in the distance and just like that he tensed up again.

"Or, I could just kill us both, and then neither one of us has to suffer as a result of my failures." She didn't let go, but his chest was heaving again. "And since your lil bitty dude keep interrupting us, I might as well get back to what we started." He took his left hand and caressed her backside. Pushing himself into her, causing her to back into the dresser as he used the same hand to outline her back and fondle one of her breasts. It was dark in the room, but she could still see the glock by his side. She felt his crotch harden against her stomach. As his hand traveled beyond her breast and up her arm, she knew he was about to grab the back of her neck to position it for a kiss. The thought made her nauseous. She closed her eyes to brace herself. Sway interpreted the gesture as something else.

"I *knew* you still wanted me," he said, before he began ripping the buttons off her shirt. He pressed his manhood against her firmly as he fumbled with her shirt. "I got to get this." He forced his hand inside her pants and panties. She braced herself to be hit once he discovered she wasn't aroused, but the blow never came. Instead he set the gun on the dresser and used the other hand to sit her on the dresser. He began tormenting her down beneath, very roughly stabbing inside her.

"Jermal, not here," she spoke only once, almost pleading. At first she thought he didn't hear her because he seemed to be in a world induced

243

by his sexual desire. She was about to speak again when he instructed her to undress and get on the bed. He took a few steps back to allow her to get up. Mya glanced at the gun. Sliding off the dresser, she walked toward the bed, pulling on the rest of her shirt buttons as if she were about to take it off. She didn't wait to see what he was doing, but dashed out the door and ran up the hall passing several doors. Sway screamed out threats and obscenities at her. She contemplated running downstairs, but that would give him the opportunity to shoot her. She ended up in Judah's room. Quietly, she closed and locked the door, hearing his steps in the hall while looking for her. Although she was a nervous wreck, she searched the room for something to protect herself with. She grabbed one of Judah's trophies, then considered opening the door. She took the chair from his study area and propped it against the doorknob. *I have to get out of here.* There was no way she was staying in this house. It took some effort, but she finally got Judah's window to budge. She looked out and knew there was no chance in jumping. Not from the second story. A pair of tail lights flashed in front of her residence. Judah's room window was positioned on the side of the house, so she couldn't see the vehicle. It had to be someone from King's rental place coming to get her. Hope pierced her heart. She thought about screaming, but that would be a dead give-away to Sway. Whatever she was going to do, she had better do it quickly. She could still hear her phone ringing in the distance.

Mya snatched everything off Judah's bed and threw it outside to the ground. It landed hard against the concrete; it was not enough. She went in his closet like she did at the end of every winter. Most of the stuff he didn't wear again the following year, she would donate it to a family less fortunate, or he'd give them to his boys. She tossed five heavy bags out the window, and hoped they would provide some support in case she fell. Sway, taunting her, was right outside the door. The doorknob slowly turned to the right as she now sat on the ledge and steadied herself to turn around so she could climb out.

"I know you're in there!" he yelled with everything in him. Her heart raced, but now was no time to be afraid, or even think for that matter. Slowly, she eased down on the siding, trying to find sure footing, only holding on by the ledge.

Pow!

Mya flinched after hearing the gunshot. She looked up and didn't see anyone. She could hear him slamming all his weight against the door. "I'm going to kill you! You hear me, you little black slut!" he threatened from the hallway.

Mya still held on to the ledge, unsure for how much longer. *Lord, if you get me out of this, I promise you I'll serve you the rest of my life and marry King.* She looked down and panicked. Going back up wasn't an option, and the ground was too far to jump.

Bam!

Judah's door was crumbling beneath something.

Oh my God! He's coming! Tears welled up in her eyes; his voice sounded so near. She was trying to stay calm, but the reality of it all just mounted her shoulders at once, and her nerves gave out. It seemed the world began moving in slow motion as she lost her balance and fell to the pile she previously made. She hadn't even realized she had been screaming until she felt pain in her back and backside, but nothing to the degree that would make her lie there. She could hear her neighbor's dogs barking in the distance. As she sat up, frantically touching herself, she heard Sway before she saw him.

"Oh, I got you now, lil slut! Think you can get away from me?" he yelled from the window she had just made her exit out of. She was barely on her feet when she heard another shot. Mya wasn't quite sure exactly where it landed, but she heard it mostly in her left ear. She ran the opposite way toward the back of the house to dodge the other rounds of his glock she knew were coming. She had a mind to jump over her wooden picket fence and make a break to the neighbor's yard. But the faster she ran toward the fence, the more ferocious their pit bull became. She needed to get somewhere out of sight before Sway made it out the house.

Put on the whole armour of God, that ye may be able to stand against the wiles of the devil. For we wrestle not against flesh and blood, but against principalities, against powers, against the rulers of the darkness of this world, against spiritual wickedness in high places.

Ephesians 6:11-12 (KJV)

CHAPTER 31

Mya's residence (8:11 p.m.)

King knew something wasn't right. "I can't get her to answer. We probably shouldn't have waited this long," King told Judah, hanging up his cell. People were already boarding their plane. Suddenly he felt compelled to pray.

"I'm telling you, man!" Judah stood from the table. "Something just ain't right. She's scared, and I bet that punk got something to do with it." Judah headed toward the exit with King in tow.

Judah couldn't think of enough ways he would make Sway suffer if he did something to his aunt. He could see the exit up ahead once he bypassed the security point and then the check-in desk, but the fear that gripped his heart brought him to his knees. Everything and everyone around him seemed to blur. Sweat beaded up on his forehead and slid down his face. The sound of gunshots rang in his ears. He grabbed his head in an attempt to make it stop. Unbeknownst to him, his mind made pleas to the Lord that he couldn't fathom, as words spilled from his lips in the form of intercession through the Holy Spirit. The busy airport had become the altar to the throne room, in which Judah sought the only One who could intervene in the situation he'd just discerned was life-threatening. King looked around and wasn't surprised to find that all eyes were on Judah. *Really, Father . . . right now? You want to do this here?* King prayed. Seconds later, he saw Homeland security officers and two EMTs pushing through the crowd.

"Please, sir . . . please, just let him be," King pleaded with the first EMT who was kneeling before Judah. Dude was buff, and King likened him to a WWF wrestler. He wouldn't dare attempt to push him away.

"What's your name, sir?" the handsome, ebony-skinned EMT asked, checking Judah's pulse.

"King Lee. I'm a minister at New and Living Way Church under Pastor Anthony Sprint. I know what this looks like, and I'm sorry for the disturbance, but he is not hurt in any way, nor does he pose a threat to anyone else." The EMT checked Judah's breathing.

"What is the issue?" he asked King, but never took his eyes off Judah.

"We are having a family crisis right now. He is overwhelmed and felt compelled by God to pray for the only woman left in his life." King knew unless the guard had a relationship with God, what he just explained would seem foolish. The guard didn't look moved.

"Sir, I can't permit him to cause this type of . . ." He looked as if he was at a loss for words. "This type of . . . disturbance! We need to get him to medical right away."

"Please, sir. It's not what you think." King began praying for God to intervene. He didn't have the energy to deal with this man. He was doing his best not to lose his composure just thinking about them not getting to Mya in time.

King just didn't believe Jesus would allow Satan to prevail and take another person away from this hurting child like that—take his future wife away from him just like that! There was no way. He had spent too many hours laboring in prayer for her, sacrificed too many meals for the sake of her being free from the bondage of her sins. True enough, she had abandoned her covenant with God and turned back to the ways of the world, but would it cost her, her life, their lives together? The spirit of God that helped and aided, refused to guide him in fear. Jesus had made him a promise regarding this woman, this family. He would not be moved.

"How long do you think he'll keep this up?" the Homeland officer blurted.

"Sir, honestly . . . I can't say," King replied and watched as the officer sent the additional EMT away once they acknowledged that Judah's vitals were stable. He then set his focus back on Judah. The other EMT stayed at Judah's side, waiting for him to wake up out of whatever trance he was in.

Swiftly, King called his car rental company who informed him that he had a driver sent to Mya's residence and would get them to contact him ASAP. At first, the way God was dealing with Judah made him uneasy. Solely because they were in an airport, but the more he thought about it, his God had a tendency to do what he wanted whenever and wherever he wanted to. He wished the Holy Spirit would have endowed Judah in the car. As the minutes passed, King asked God was there something else Judah needed to do? He wanted to get Judah to the car for some privacy and get back on the road to rescue his soon-to-be wife, but he didn't want to touch Judah and interrupt God.

King's vibrating phone made his body tense. *Lord, give me the strength,* he prayed, before acknowledging the familiar number. "Yo, Chris, man. Tell me what's up?" King answered as dread filled his heart.

"I'm not so sure. I'm outside Ms. Jenkins' residence, but she's not answering her phone; it doesn't appear as if there's any lights on inside."

"Did you try knocking on the door?" King knew he had a new policy, but this was personal.

"No sir, I haven't. But if you want me to I will."

"Yes, if her vehicle is in the driveway." King subconsciously paced the floor. Making a circle around Judah, he could hear Chris exiting the vehicle. "Chris . . . Man, something's not right. My baby is in danger. I'm starting to feel it."

"Sir, if I don't know anything else about you, I know that you're a God-fearing man and a man of faith. So whatever it is, I believe your God will come through.

"I believe that too."

"Her hood is hot, so I'm headed to the door," Chris stated. A few seconds of silence passed. Suddenly a gunshot rang out.

"What the—" Chris blurted out.

"Yo, Chris! My man, you good? What's that noise?" King's questions forced their way out as he gripped the phone tight. He prayed within as he listened attentively. And there was another ring of gunshots.

Pow! Pow! Pow!

The shots rang out before Chris had a chance to respond.

"Yo! Somebody's shooting! And it sounds like it's coming from her house!" Chris stated, making a clear dash back to the security of his car.

"Chris, call the police! Man, call the police and don't leave. Back away from the house if you have to, but please don't leave my baby out there alone."

"I got you, Mr. King. I'll call you right back."

They disconnected. King called the police as well, giving them his suspicions about Sway's likelihood to be behind all this. His description, vehicle, and whatever else information he could extend. After hanging up, he looked over at Judah. *God, there has to be something else I can do! I need to get to my lady.*

King looked in the direction of the guard, who was pacing back and forth around Judah. Wondering if he could get the police to Mya's house quicker than a local caller. He made eye contact with King, and for the first time in almost ten minutes he looked sympathetic.

A creamy, caramel-complexioned woman dressed in a white dress approached him. But he hadn't noticed her until she was holding his hand. His natural reaction was to snatch away, but her soft touch and soothing voice humbled him.

"Son?" the small-framed woman spoke in a low tone, yet her single word seemed louder than the voices and sirens in his head.

King turned to face her and looked into a set of intense eyes that seemed to wrap him in compassion. Oddly, he felt his tears mounting in his throat. Still nodding, she spoke again.

"Listen." She released his hand with her right hand and touched the top part of his stomach, as if to impart something supernatural, or stir his spiritual man.

"Listen to what God is saying to you." Then she gently blew toward his face. King suddenly felt the presence of God so tangible. His knees buckled, but he remained upright. She released him, and he had to catch his breath. Kneeling down, he was within arm's reach of Judah. He wanted to worship. He wanted to exalt his God and praise his name.

"I have given you authority!" the voice of God calmly thundered through him. Instantly, he knew what he was to do; it was as if he had been revived with tears of adoration flowing from his eyes. In a tone of voice unknown to him, he spoke aloud. "Satan, by the power that is invested in me through the spirit of the living God. I declare unto you no weapon formed against Mya Sincere Jenkins shall prosper! I take authority over every satanic strategy you have devised against her life. She is covered in the blood of Jesus!" Then he leaned closer to Judah and spoke in a hushed voice in his ear.

"By the authority that has been invested in me, I command your spirit to be at peace. Receive the peace of the Lord!"

It is of the Lord's mercies that we are not consumed, because his compassions fail not. They are new every morning: great is thy faithfulness.

Lamentations 3:22-23 (KJV)

CHAPTER 32

Mya knew now wasn't the time to think about anything other than running for her life, but as she hid behind her toolshed, she felt it was the perfect hiding place until she could figure out her next move. From her vantage point she would be able to see if Sway exited the back of her home. Her heart broke as she wondered, *How could this be? Why am I dodging bullets from the man I had given my all to?* She had sought beyond her own strength to meet his needs and wholeheartedly devoted herself to him. Even compromised her relationship with the Lord in the name of love. Over and over again she forgave him and put up with his nonsense, hoping he would realize that love was right in front of him.

But did it really have to come to this? Was she so wrong for wanting a stable life? To be adored, appreciated, treated like a lady, but most of all respected? She gave Sway the best of her, and he took her for granted.

Instead, Jesus gave her King, and she couldn't deny the love she felt in her heart for him. *But maybe . . . maybe I should have just stayed by myself. Then Sway wouldn't be so devastated,* she reasoned with herself as she slumped down to her beautifully landscaped backyard, considering

253

giving up. *This is all my fault! I'm always doing stupid stuff.* Suddenly, she felt compelled to pray. The urge stronger than her need to flee. Barricaded by her pain, she spoke barely above a whisper as her tears washed her face.

"Father, I've really gone and done it now. I know you're merciful, but my stupidity has landed me in a situation that's more than I can handle. I know you can deliver me, but I don't feel I deserve it. Maybe this is a due penalty for turning my back on you, and not putting what you wanted before Sway's expectations.

"But a part of me still wants to live. I want to see Judah reach his highest potential in life. I still want to serve you. I want a life with King, Lord. To know what it's like to be loved, even when I make mistakes instead of being beaten. To speak my opinion and not worry about the repercussions. I want a chance for my life to bring you glory. So, if you can overlook my reckless mistakes and make something out of the mess I call a life, I'm asking you to remember you are my Father, and before I made things complicated, you promised to take full responsibility over me. If you don't help me, I'm going to die."

Be strong and courageous. Do not fear or be in dread of them, for it is the Lord your God who goes with you. He will not leave you or forsake you.

Deuteronomy 31:6 (ESV)

CHAPTER 33

Jacksonville International Airport (8:25 p.m.)

Judah came to with the sound of a male's voice in his ear praying for his strength and ability to trust Jesus beyond what he felt, or what a thing appeared to be. Slowly he looked around and saw a small crowd of people standing around. He looked in the direction of the man who was praying for him and at first he didn't recognize him. His face had such a glow about it; he had to blink several times to focus. Finally, he recognized King, who was now smiling at him and helping him to his feet. King pulled him into his embrace, and Judah saw an elderly woman walking away. She turned and locked eyes with him. He felt her presence, as if she was the one hugging him. "Do not fear! God is our refuge and strength and ever present help in trouble."

As he listened to this woman speak what had to be life into him, he now felt fully clothed in courage. The part that amazed him most was that although she was a few feet away from him, he heard her voice as clear as the day. He wasn't sure of all the details, but something supernatural must have taken place since the time he picked up on Mya until now.

257

"Let's get out of here, man," King instructed Judah as he released him from his embrace.

"So have you heard anything? It's hard to explain, but I heard gunshots!" Judah told King as they rushed to the parking lot.

"I heard them too," King admitted, making a mental note to trust God no matter what.

"You did? Judah was shocked.

"I was on the phone with Chris. He was there to pick her up, and I heard shots in the background," King explained as they got in the car.

"I'm going to kill Sway! I put that on God," Judah yelled, punching his fist. King didn't say a word, knowing now wasn't the time to reprimand him. Instead he prayed. After a few seconds of silence, Judah spoke.

"My phone!" King looked over at him. "I left my phone in my luggage."

"We left our luggage at the airport," King said. "Hopefully, we'll get it in lost and found."

"I need to see your phone." Judah got King's phone and called Coach Riley.

"Judah, I am so glad you called. I really want to apol—" Eric Riley started to say.

"Dad, listen," Judah interrupted him. "I really, really need you."

"Judah, I'm sorry that I have done nothing but disappoint you." Coach Riley was determined to make peace.

"Okay, I hear what you're saying. We can talk about that later."

"It's just that I didn't know I would ever have you in my life, and when I got with Megan . . ." Riley took a deep breath.

"Dad, shut up and listen!" Judah yelled. "We don't have time for that right now. Aunt Mya's life is in danger. I need you! She needs you!"

Greater love hath no man than this, that a man lay down his life for his friends.

John 15:13 (ASV)

CHAPTER 34

Mya's residence

A cool wind danced across Mya's wet face. She raised her eyes to the sky, believing it would open up and receive her, or she would see angels descending a ladder to save her. She squeezed her eyes shut once seeing a beautiful night sky. I will live and not die to declare the works of the Lord. Those words rang out in her spirit. The scripture was a familiar passage for her. Oftentimes she would hear believers at church saying it when they battled some form of sickness or infirmity. As she opened her eyes, she felt a peace wash over her. She found herself speaking it aloud.

"I will live and not die to declare the works of the Lord."

In the distance she could hear glass shattering. Immediately, she sprang to her feet. Staying low and as close to the toolshed as possible, she made her way around the side of it. What the huge oak tree didn't block of the street, her wooden picket fence did. She thought about jumping the fence and running across her front lawn and into the street. But Sway could be looking out the front door, or even waiting on the porch to open fire. Just as she was about to take a step, she spotted a pair of headlights turning the corner.

"Oh my God! King. Judah!" She panicked. "What if it's them?" She felt she didn't have a choice; she had to do something and do it quickly.

Especially, before the neighbor's dog gave her location away with all its barking. She took a chance and ran across her backyard to the right side of the house and heard a car door slam. Mya looked toward the front yard, listening for the direction of the footsteps. The gravel on her driveway crunched beneath her careful steps. What if this man realizes someone else is out here?

She looked down on the ground and picked up the biggest rock she could find. Running to the back of the house, she threw the rock through her kitchen window, hoping to redirect Sway's focus. Then she ran back around to jump the fence. She struggled, but she managed to get atop of the fence. With fear pumping her adrenaline, she looked to the left and could see straight into her dining room and locked eyes with Sway.

Pow!

Sway shot at the window.

"Jesus!" Mya screamed as she fell forward and tried to brace her fall, as she hit the gravel.

"I got you now!" Sway yelled from the inside as a couple more rounds sounded off. But it all sounded like a loud muffled sound to Mya, as she jumped up, ignoring the pain in her body and the ringing in her ear as she raced toward safety. There was no time for anything, not even thinking. She walked toward the figure that was now slouching behind her car, gun drawn. Her sudden appearance was greeted by the barrel of his gun.

"Don't shoot! I'm not armed," she pleaded with the police officer who appeared to be even more relieved than she was. He motioned her to take cover.

"Sir, we have to get out of here! My ex is in there with a gun. Trying to kill me. We have to go!" Mya demanded, apparently spooking him.

"Ma'am, I need you to calm down. I'm calling for backup!"

"Sir, we have to stay out of view of the door and windows." Mya buried her face in her hands as the officer called for backup.

"Ma'am, I asked where are you shot at?"

"I—" She raised her head to look at him. It sounded as if he was mumbling something. She knew she had to stay alert. He repeated himself. Mya saw his lips moving and his dead set gaze, but his voice sounded as if they were having bad reception over a cell phone, alongside the ringing in her ear.

Mya pressed her hands on each side of her head to stop the ringing. Feeling slightly light-headed, she wasn't prepared for what she saw when she reached for the bumper of her car to maintain her balance.

"Oh my God!" she stated, as she examined blood all over her right hand. She trailed her face with her bloody hand. It only took seconds for her to find the wound. It felt like her ear was set ablaze as her fingers fondled it. The intensity from her touch seemed to spark every nerve in her body. She almost freaked out as she realized part of her ear was missing.

"The SOB shot my ear off!!" she shrieked. Despite the pain she felt every time her fingers touched the raw wound, she couldn't restrain her fingers from touching it. "This jerk shot me!" she repeated as realization set in. Rage began to resurrect within her. She forgot all about fearing for her life, and the officer calling for backup. She'd lost her ability to rationalize in a matter of seconds as she reflected on everything she had sacrificed for this man! Her feelings were beyond hurt; Mya was scorned, and Sway needed to feel her pain!

Despite feeling dizzy and the muscles in her right upper body aching, she jumped to her feet and began calling for Sway by his biological name. Mya stepped from around the car and approached the house.

"Jermal Swayze Edwards!"

"Ma'am, you need to stay down!" the officer yelled, trying to maintain his cover.

"Jermal Swayze Edwards! Put the gun down and come out and face me!" Mya screamed toward the house.

"Ma'am, get down!" the officer demanded. "I'm instructing you to get down!" He pulled at her arm.

"All of your foolishness that I put up with! And you gon' shoot me!

You ain't no man! You're a coward! A poor excuse for a man! Too afraid to man up and get the help you need instead of beating me until I could barely get out of bed." She continued to rant as tears poured from her eyes. She didn't notice her neighbors peeking out their windows and front doors. Nor did she observe King's car approaching, or the two police cars.

All the screaming was making her more lightheaded on top of the fact she was losing too much blood. But that wasn't enough to make her stop yelling.

"Jermal! Come out here and face me!" When she didn't see him come out or answer, it made her more upset.

"What? You man enough to beat me behind closed doors, but your punk behind can't come out in the open!"

The front door swung open, and the police officer encouraged Mya to take cover. She could hear someone screaming, but her need to understand why Sway sought her harm over-ruled her logic.

"Do you love him, Mya?" Sway yelled, still remaining out of sight.

King and Judah jumped out the car as Riley ran up to them. One of the officers who'd just arrived on the scene pleaded with them to remain out of range. Judah yelled for his aunt, but she couldn't hear him.

"Tell me in the presence of your all-knowing God, do you love this lil bitty ass dude?" Sway now stood on the porch with his pistol pointed to his head staring at Mya.

Just seeing him with a pistol pointed to his head alarmed her. She couldn't hear a word he spoke; her ear was still ringing.

"Don't do it, Jermal! Don't do it," she pleaded.

"Answer me! Do you love him?" He swung his gun in the direction of where King stood, and then pointed it back to his head. "Or me?"

"Sir, drop your gun. I'm ordering you to put your pistol down," one of the officers addressed Sway.

"Shut up! Don't nobody tell me nothin'! Unless you telling this whore to answer my question!" he ranted, losing his temper.

"Sway! Sway! Jermal, Look at me!" Mya took another step.

The officer reached out for her, but she pulled away. "Ma'am, you are going to leave me with no choice but to use force if you take another step," the cop yelled, trying not to put his own life in danger.

"Look at me." She tried to get Sway's attention. "Hey! I'm over here!" She waved her hands until he focused on her. The look of death had manifested in his eyes. She swallowed hard and began to pray for him. "Sway . . . Jermal. You don't have to do this. Now is the time to prove this ain't you."

"Mya, are you still in love with me?" She couldn't hear him, but she read his lips. Clearly. She considered his question. Was it love that she felt for Sway, or was it lust or even codependency? The need to be needed, wanted, desired. Up until her relationship with King, she was convinced it was love. She looked up at Sway, and tears filled her eyes because she knew without a shadow of a doubt that she was not in love with him. Mya was unapologetically and happily in love with King Lee. She suddenly had a deep longing to just be with her family. With Judah and King. For the first time she looked around and behind her. Police surrounded both sides of the street. Judah and King stood at the guard line. King looked as if he was praying, and Judah paced back and forth while saying something.

"Lord, please let me get through this," Mya prayed. She turned back, feeling extremely light-headed. She bent over to steady herself. After a few seconds she stood upright, but tottered as if she would lose her balance.

"Jesus," she said as she turned and walked back to her car.

"Mya!" Sway called after her when she turned her back to him. "Whore, you don't hear me calling you?" She really didn't.

"Just a few more steps, Lord!" she prayed, trying not to pass out.

"Mya, this is your fault!" Sway pointed his gun at Mya and pulled the trigger. Mya hit the ground, and then Sway put the pistol back to his head. The bullet ripped through his brain first, but before his body slumped to the porch floor, several bullets from the police officers assaulted his body.

Judah broke past the police and ran to Mya where he jerked her body up from the ground and cradled her in his arms. "Somebody come help her!" he screamed. "Somebody come help her!" he yelled at the paramedics.

And he said unto them, Go ye into all the world, and preach the gospel to every creature.

Mark 16:15

CHAPTER 35

Hospital chapel (10:32 p.m.)

Judah Jenkins knelt on the altar. He had been in this same position since they arrived at the hospital about an hour prior.

"God, I know you are not going to do this to me. I know you are not that hateful!" Judah had, had his share of losses, and he just couldn't escape the idea that he was about to lose his aunt as well. "If you don't do nothing else for me, you've got to do this!" he pleaded.

King sat in the pew praying for the young man and Mya. Judah had been so upset and protective of Mya, that no one was even able to see where she got shot. True enough, his faith was wavering slightly because the doctors had not come and given her condition. He couldn't just absolutely worry about her pulling through; God had already told him his purpose in Mya's life. He trusted he would be the vessel that God used.

"Mr. Jenkins . . . Mr. Lee?" a male voice snatched them both from their thoughts.

"Yes, sir!" Judah jumped to his feet. His clothes were covered in Mya's blood. He rushed to meet the doctor who stood by the chapel's door, along with Coach Riley who was standing in the hall.

"Ms. Jenkins is fine!" the doctor said.

Judah exhaled as if he had been holding his breath.

"Based on the scene that the officers described, her passing out from having lost so much blood saved her life. Other than part of her ear being shot off, her only other injuries are some scratches and bruises. She's very weak, but she's a fighter. We trust she'll be fine."

Judah could barely keep himself together. He hugged the doctor and King and then raced back to the altar, shouting!

"My Heavenly Father, you have been so merciful! You heard my cries. You delivered and you protected her. I promise from this day forward I'll trust you! I'll walk close with you! In Jesus' name. Amen!"

"I came as soon as I heard it on the news! Is Mya okay?" Janelle asked as soon as she burst through the chapel doors before observing her surroundings. Mascara streaked her face, clearly displaying that she had been crying.

"God is good, Janelle! God is good!" Judah exclaimed as he pulled her into his embrace.

"So you ready to see her?" the doctor asked.

"Most definitely!" Judah responded. Looking over at King made him emotional.

"Unc," he called out for the first time. King wasn't sure if he should acknowledge Judah. "I just want to say thank you." They hugged. "Thank you for showing her something different, something real. And thank you for being with me through this." Judah released his embrace, sincerely grateful to have King in their lives.

"The pleasure is all mine, nephew!" He smiled back. "Now, let's go check on my wife-to-be so we can see how long it will be before we can catch that flight and you can use your platform to tell the world what God has carried you through."

"I will do just that!" Judah smiled back just thinking about how bright his future was.

The End

Author's Bio

Falicia Blakely is a native of Jacksonville, Florida, but relocated to Atlanta, Georgia, where she experienced a rough upbringing as a child. This resulted in her committing various crimes as a teen and her inevitable imprisonment.

Since 2005, she has been an active member of The Children's Center, an organization which allows her to visit and interact regularly with her only child while she is imprisoned. As a victim of Domestic Violence and Human Trafficking, Falicia has dedicated her life to raising awareness about these social ills by writing books, skits (plays), and performing interpretive dances. Also, she has joined thousands in the fight against HIV/AIDS transmission after receiving a HIV-positive status in 2003.

In 2012, she devoted her life to becoming a mentor and now facilitates faith-based, self-help groups that focus on breaking the cycle of being victimized and wholeheartedly making peace with the past. She has obtained her GED and some technical college education and is now a licensed Master Cosmetologist/Barber, where she strives to uplift the self-esteem of other female inmates. Her mission is to live each day on purpose and speak out about her past in hopes of preventing someone else from making the same grave mistakes as she has. Today, Falicia trusts in Yahweh, her Savior, for His plans with her life.

Currently, Falicia is incarcerated in a North Georgia maximum security women's facility, serving a life sentence without the possibility of parole.

7 Figure Publications Titles

Traces of My Blood

Life of a Star

A Treacherous Hustle

The Falicia Blakely Letters: From a Pimp

Diary of a Black Rose

Beautifully Ruthless

Murder Breeds Mayhem

Golden State Heavyweights

Facebook: @7figurepublications

Instagram: @7figurepublication

Sign up for our mailing list by visiting us at:

http://7figurepublications.com

Write to us at:

7 Figure Publications
PO Box 9334
Augusta, GA 30916

7 Figure Publications Titles

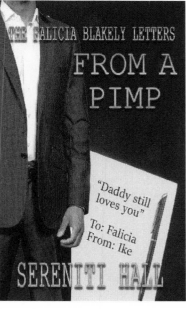

7 Figure Publications Titles

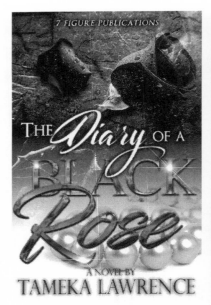

92301297R00171

Made in the USA
Columbia, SC
30 March 2018